DARK DEEDS ON A WHITE CHRISTMAS

A RETIRED SLEUTH AND HIS DOG HISTORICAL COZY MYSTERY

ONE MAN AND HIS DOG COZY MYSTERIES

P. C. JAMES

Copyright © 2024 by P. C. James

All rights reserved.

No part of this book may be reproduced in any form or by any electronic or mechanical means, including information storage and retrieval systems, without written permission from the author, except for the use of brief quotations in a book review.

Important Notes:

1. While the **places** named in this book are **REAL**, the **people and events** are **NOT**.

2. This is a work of **fiction** and any **resemblance to real people** then or now is **entirely coincidental**.

❀ Created with Vellum

1

NORTH RIDING OF YORKSHIRE, ENGLAND, NOVEMBER 1964

RETIRED INSPECTOR RAMSAY and his dog, Bracken, were once again staying at Dunroamin, Mrs. Golightly's guest house in Robin Hood's Bay. Ramsay had become a regular guest for he'd visited on two occasions since helping to solve the smuggling mystery in the village only a month before. It wasn't just the village he visited. It was more his young assistant on the smuggling mystery, Eliza, and, of course, her parents Doris and Colin Danesdale. Ramsay knew he shouldn't keep visiting. Eliza was too young to be a romantic partner, he was fifty-five and she only nineteen, and he didn't really need a sleuthing assistant because he didn't intend to investigate any more mysteries, but he couldn't help himself. Her energy, enthusiasm, and zest for life drew him back week after week.

Ramsay had driven down from his home in Newcastle-upon-Tyne, rather than travel by train as he did when he'd become embroiled in the recent murder and smuggling mystery. Having a car meant being able to take Bracken and all three Danesdales on jaunts around the north Yorkshire moors and dales, the shallow valleys where streams and rivers had, over centuries, cut their way through the higher ground. On one of the first tours, the five companions noticed a sign for a Christmas Break at Harkness Manor Hotel.

"I've been considering what to do for Christmas," Ramsay said to Eliza, sitting in the front passenger seat, leaving her parents cramped in the back of his old Ford Popular. "This may be the ideal spot."

On returning home after solving the smuggling mystery, he'd considered maybe visiting his extended family in Scotland. Only, it'd been twenty years since he'd last spoken to them and neither side had been in touch. Eliza and her family now made up his only circle of friends so here he was.

"Can you afford it?" Eliza asked. "It looks expensive."

"Since I met you, I've grown accustomed to spending more than I'm comfortable with," Ramsay replied, chuckling.

Eliza bristled. "I'm not an expensive girlfriend. You just like to show off."

Ramsay laughed. "I'm pleased you said that because I thought a nice old-fashioned pub dinner would suit us all this evening."

"I'll second that, Tom," Colin Danesdale said, leaning forward from the back seat. "A simple pie and pint will suit me down to the ground."

"What about you, Mam?" Eliza asked. "A pie and pint as well?"

"Well..." Doris Danesdale began.

"We'll find somewhere with a menu suitable for ladies too," Ramsay interjected. "We've seen some nice country pubs along the way."

Ramsay did wonder if the Christmas Break suggestion

would find favor with Eliza's parents. That day, they hadn't responded with a suggestion either way. After all, this year of nineteen-sixty-four could be a difficult time for parents. Once upon a time, they could, and would, have absolutely refused to have their daughter go off to a hotel alone with a man, even one as mature as Ramsay. But in nineteen sixty-four and 'the times they were a-changing' someone called Bob Dylan had just sung, parents couldn't be quite so protective of their daughters. Maybe he'd learn more over dinner.

Ramsay didn't learn more that day, the subject never came up over dinner, but then, during his next visit on the following weekend, Eliza's parents asked tentatively if they might join Ramsay and Eliza for the Christmas Break.

"We haven't had a holiday since we had Elizabeth," Colin, said. "And now she's managing for herself, we think it's time for us to take some time for ourselves."

"You would be very welcome," Ramsay replied, relieved. He wasn't sure he wanted to spend a week away, alone with Eliza. "You deserve a break, I'm sure. You both work so hard." He glanced at Eliza sitting next to him in the front passenger seat; they were once again driving out in the dales and moors. She looked a lot less pleased.

"What about you, Bracken?" Ramsay asked his Border Collie, sitting between the front seats, snuggled against the gear stick, watching the world go by.

Bracken grinned and panted as he looked at his favorite two people in the world. 'Of course, I'm happy with this plan. You and I will go for walks, and Eliza and her family will continue to feed me handsomely. It's perfect.'

"Then," said Ramsay, "I suggest we include Harkness Manor in today's trip and make reservations. The weather is too cold and wet for going outdoors much."

"I hope they still have space for four at the event," Eliza mused. "It's only a month away. These things often sell out quickly."

"They still have posters up," Doris remarked. "I spotted one in Scarborough just the other day."

Harkness Manor had two rooms available for the event and they took dogs, Ramsay's principal concern. They booked both rooms, one with beds for three and one single for Ramsay and Bracken.

* * *

ALONE, later that afternoon back at the Danesdale's house in Robin Hood's Bay, Eliza grumbled, "It would've been better with just we three." She stroked Bracken's head to confirm who she meant.

Ramsay said, "You and I will have plenty of time to get to know each other better because your parents will want to do different things."

"No, they won't," Eliza replied. "They'll be watching you like hawks in case you get frisky."

Ramsay laughed. "I'm too old for frisky. I'm sure they know that."

"You don't have to tell me," Eliza snapped. "You need to tell them."

Ramsay felt himself redden. He avoided all of Eliza's attempts to inveigle him into an amorous clinch. In his mind, it wouldn't be fair to her. Eliza would grow out of this infatuation soon and be glad of his forbearance.

They walked along the clifftop path where Ramsay, only weeks before, had gazed out over the bay, wondering how anyone could smuggle anything into the tiny fishing village.

It lay between vertiginous cliffs and a winding, narrow lane that led up to the higher ground and the wider world.

Ramsay said, "I promised to drop in on Len Pritchard on this visit."

Bracken, as before, darted to and fro, chasing rabbits, real and imagined, while his two humans wandered toward Ness Point with its view out across the North Sea, where wind-whipped waves foamed white against the dark water. Another wild day on the coast.

"I'll come with you," Eliza suggested. "I haven't seen him since he tried to have us imprisoned for blackmail."

Ramsay laughed. "To be fair, we tried to have him imprisoned for smuggling and murder."

"We tried giving him the opportunity to prove his innocence, not prove us guilty," Eliza cried.

"Len didn't understand that," Ramsay said, smiling. "No matter, I'm going to visit him. You can come, if," he paused, before continuing, "you promise to behave."

"Oh. I'll be as good as gold," Eliza almost purred, tucking her hand under his arm and snuggling in against the wind.

"I wish you'd say that more convincingly."

Eliza laughed. "I promise. Now, how are we going to turn our detecting partnership into full-time jobs?" This was a theme she returned to whenever they were alone. Eliza had already brought several local people with possible criminal puzzles to meet Ramsay, and he'd turned them all away.

"We aren't," Ramsay replied, "as I keep telling you. Major crimes don't happen often enough to make a living at it. And I refuse to investigate divorce cases or anything sordid like that."

Eliza continued, as if he'd never spoken, "Maybe we'll

have a murder at the Manor over Christmas. Wouldn't that be something?"

Ramsay groaned. "I spent every Christmas for the past thirty years in my office working on crimes of every sort, including murders. This one, I hope, will be different."

Eliza sighed. *Older people can be tedious at times. Even nice ones like Ramsay. I wonder, if we don't have a murder, could I create a mystery?*

2

A CHRISTMAS BREAK, WEDNESDAY DECEMBER 23

As RAMSAY's old Ford Popular climbed out of Robin Hood's Bay and up to the high road over the moors, its springs groaned under the weight of four adults, one dog, and all the baggage needed to keep them looking their best for the whole ten days of their Christmas break. Worse, when they reached the high road over the moors, it was icy and already snow-covered in places. Ramsay lived near the coast, where snow rarely lay for more than a few minutes, and he wasn't familiar with these conditions. He drove slowly the whole way, making it a long drive for car and passengers. When they pulled into Harkness Manor's driveway and parked, the short winter daylight had almost gone. Outside the car, an icy wind whipped at their coats and nipped their noses.

"One of those dark days before Christmas indeed," Colin Danesdale grumbled, as he struggled with two large suitcases across the dark parking area to the front door, where welcoming lights blazed out across the icy ground. The snow they met on their journey hadn't yet made its way down into Harkness Dale, the local name for the valley, but the low dark clouds scudding overhead told them it would soon be here.

They, with their bags, stepped inside the doors and at once the fears of the drive slipped away, as they gazed on the tall colorfully decorated tree and the green and red garlands around the room. Bunches of holly graced shelves or pillars with strategically placed mistletoe hanging from the ceiling. A roaring log fire filled one wall, with over-sized stockings hanging from the mantelpiece above. After the dark and anxious drive, the hall made a welcome sight.

"Welcome," the middle-aged, gray-haired woman at the reception desk said, as Ramsay deposited his bag on the floor before straightening to greet her.

"Thank you," Ramsay said. "We're glad to be inside. The weather is growing nasty out there. I'm Tom Ramsay, and this is Bracken."

Bracken reached up and placed his paws against the wooden frame of the counter.

"Welcome to you too, Bracken," the woman said. "We have some Labradors you'll find very friendly. They can show you all the best spots for rabbits."

Bracken grinned. 'Finally, someone who understands the important things in life.'

"Colin Danesdale," Eliza's father said, arriving at the counter alongside Ramsay. "We're all together."

"I see that on your reservations," the woman replied, smiling. "However, our larger rooms, where you are, are not as close to the smaller ones as you may have wanted, but I hope you'll find they aren't so very far apart."

"So long as we don't have to go outside to meet," Colin said, chuckling, "I'm sure they will be fine."

Ramsay finished filling out the guest book and took his key.

"Your room is on the ground floor, Mr. Ramsay," the woman said. "I should have introduced myself earlier. I'm Mrs. Price-Ridley. My husband and I own and manage the Manor. If there's anything you need, let me know."

"I'm sure everything will be fine, Mrs. Price-Ridley," Ramsay said, thinking this would be a mouthful to say every time he spoke to her.

"Please, call me, Joyce," she said. "Everyone does."

Ramsay thanked her and waited while the Danesdales signed in and took their key. They were on the floor above, but in the same wing of the building.

"There are stairs at each end of the corridors," Joyce told them. "You'll soon find which is closest for you."

They parted at the foot of the grand staircase and agreed to meet in thirty minutes in the bar.

Ramsay and Bracken found their room and Ramsay unpacked while Bracken examined every inch of the room. A sleeping basket beside the radiator took a lot of Bracken's attention. Though the cushion inside looked spotlessly clean, the wicker frame obviously held the scent of the many dogs that had stayed here before.

With his clothes packed away, Ramsay and Bracken made their way back to the lobby where he hoped to learn the layout of the building before meeting his travel companions. He felt sure with two women in the Danesdale party, there'd be time to explore before they were dressed. However, Ramsay had only walked the length of the west wing and returned before he glimpsed them crossing the hall among a throng of arriving guests.

"Well met," he called, as they appeared to be unaware of him. Eliza, waving in reply, tugged at her parents' arms to bring them to Ramsay.

"What a crush," Doris Danesdale said, looking back at

the crowd and their assorted bags milling in front of the reception desk where Mrs. Price-Ridley was signing them in.

"She needs Mr. Price-Ridley to come and assist," Ramsay commented as they turned toward the glass doors that separated the bar and dance floor from the hall.

"Men," Eliza said, "never around when you want them."

Her mother laughed. "You can't be so cynical at nineteen. You need to have some more experience to pull that off."

They entered the bar with Eliza, her arm linked with Ramsay's, amiably disputing with her mother her right to complain.

They took a table set in a bay window, through which they saw snowflakes swirling down in the darkness. A waiter took their order.

"We got here just in time," Colin said. "The forecast for snow turned out to be right."

"It's my experience they're right whenever they forecast bad weather," Ramsay said. "It's good weather they're a bit shaky on."

The others laughed.

"Snow isn't bad weather," Eliza protested. "At least not when we're indoors, warm, dry, and going to be well-fed for the next ten days. 'Let it snow, let it snow, let it snow', I say. Our holiday photos will be all the better for it."

The older members of the party seemed about to rebut Eliza's youthful bravado when three people burst through the doors into the bar. An angry older man that Ramsay judged to be in his sixties, a middle-aged woman, perhaps late forties, and a younger man, their son, Ramsay guessed. The young man might be mid-twenties, but his expression of sullen resentment made him look like a teenager. One of those kinds of youngsters he'd often had the misfortune to interview as a police officer.

"No," the older man snarled, in response to something the woman had said as they entered.

"Leave it, Mum," the younger man growled, confirming Ramsay's guess. "I'm no more interested in being his son than he is in being my father."

His mother hushed him and appealed again to his father, "Paul, it's Christmas. Can't we bury the past and look to the future? That's what the Christmas and New Year season is about, isn't it?"

"If he wants to live off my money," the man shouted, "he can come and work in the business. Until then, he'll stay lost to me."

Eliza's mother whispered, "I do hope they won't be seated next to us in the dining room." Doris had already examined the dining room, determined its size, and ordered her husband to be up first thing each morning so they might have some privacy while they ate breakfast.

"They're likely just tired from the journey, Doris," Colin Danesdale replied. "They'll be better after a good night's sleep."

Ramsay, examining the warring family, found himself agreeing more with Doris than Colin.

Eliza did too. "Oh, Dad. You're a real 'Pollyanna' at times. They aren't tired. They just don't like each other, and that woman is an idiot for bringing their son along to a Christmas event. 'Softly, softly, catchee monkey', is what my old schoolteacher would have advised."

Ramsay laughed. "I fear you're right, Eliza. Short visits to home on quiet weekends would have been more successful than a week or more in a crowded hotel of partygoers."

"But that's where her strategy might pay off," Doris

cried. "With so many people and so many amusements, they won't have time to fight. Sitting looking at each other over a cup of tea in the family living room would've soon brought out the worst in those two."

"You may be right," Ramsay agreed, still smiling. "Anyway, we're stuck with them for the duration unless one or the other storms out in a rage."

The doors flew open again. Ramsay wondered if they'd still be on their hinges by the time this Christmas period ended. A loud party of six twenty-something year-olds pushed in, all chattering together and listening to no one.

Eliza grinned and asked, "Well, Mam, would they be better seated next to us at dinner?"

Her mother grimaced. "No, they wouldn't. At least we won't be bothered with them at breakfast." She tut-tutted. "Just look at the hemlines on those dresses."

Ramsay felt tempted to say he couldn't actually see a hemline on one of the dresses but knew this wouldn't be conducive to the evening or even the holiday.

"At least they'll provide noise and merriment," he said. "Christmas should have some good cheer, after all." He couldn't help noticing even Eliza stared at the girls in disapproval. *This trip might be a terrible mistake. Sometimes, country mice can be too shocked by town mice*, he thought, remembering a book he'd read to his children.

"Well, these two won't give any offence," Colin said, nodding at the two middle-aged women who'd entered the room behind the rowdy group.

"They won't contribute much to the good cheer either," Eliza said, glancing at the older ladies before returning her gaze to the three young couples. *Rather wistfully*, Ramsay thought.

"At least I might have someone sensible to talk to," Doris said, crossly, "while you folks are doing silly things."

"You have to do silly things too," Ramsay told her. "It's part of the revelry, I'm afraid."

Doris looked about to argue but instead replied, "They've done a wonderful job on the decorations, haven't they?" She pointed to the garlands and streamers hanging down from the ceiling.

Eliza nodded. "Much better than my feeble efforts with colored paper and glue?"

"I didn't mean that at all, my dear," her mother said. "Only it's nice to see places decorated for Christmas. It's such a dark, depressing time of the year, otherwise."

"It's like midnight outside now," Colin agreed, pointing to the window, "and the snow is getting worse. I think anyone who hasn't arrived will struggle to get here by tomorrow morning." Outside, large white flakes swirled in the light from the window. Already, an inch of snow lay on the windowsill.

"I expect they're used to it up here in the dales," Ramsay said. "I'm sure they'll have the road cleared by noon."

They stared into the darkness for a few minutes, sipping their drinks, and shutting out the noise of the young people.

"At least with those couples in the party," Doris said, as if sensing everyone's thoughts, "we won't hear that awful family, who are still snapping at each other."

As Doris spoke, their attention fixed on the mother still trying to reconcile the two men, only the men would have none of it. What they said, however, remained a mystery because the boisterous three couples on barstools sat between the warring family and them.

"What do you think the old dears are making of this?" Eliza said, nodding toward the two elderly ladies.

"Hey," Doris cried, "less of the 'old dears'. They're likely the same age as your dad and me."

Eliza laughed. "It isn't their actual years. It's their chosen years. They're dressed and behaving like retired schoolmistresses."

Ramsay smiled. He understood Doris's protest. He'd also thought the two women were mid-fifties, like himself, but understood Eliza's point. They did appear ten years older. He feared they would be the censorious, complaining sort and would depress everyone for the next ten days.

Ramsay's attention became immediately taken by the doors opening again, this time in a less energetic manner. A smartly dressed professional couple entered, looked at the assembled crowd, and chose a table near Ramsay and the Danesdales.

As the couple ordered from the attentive waiter, Eliza said, "They look out of place. It's as if they've arrived for a business event."

Ramsay also thought something similar. The man, thirtyish and handsome in a predatory way, his gleaming hair, slick with oil, looked reptilian, in Ramsay's mind. A lawyer, he decided, one of those theatrical ones that were invariably unsuccessful but won clients over with their misplaced confidence.

"They probably traveled straight from work," Doris said. "Once they're settled in, they won't look so out of place."

Ramsay hoped Doris was right because he was beginning to get uncomfortable feelings inside – and his hunches came true too often for him to easily dismiss them.

3

THE HOST

THE DOOR OPENED AGAIN, and a tall, elegant man entered. He took up a station near the center of the room and asked for a moment to speak. When silence descended, he began, "Welcome everyone, I'm Frederick Price-Ridley and your host for this Christmas holiday. I'm sorry I wasn't able to greet you on your arrival, the weather delayed my return from Scarborough as I'm sure it must have delayed some of you."

A murmur of agreement rippled through the room at this, and he waited for possible comments. When none came, he continued, "We're booked up for our Christmas season, and you'll find more guests arriving maybe later tonight or more likely tomorrow morning, if this snow continues. I'm assured by the Council they have enough snow removal equipment so we shouldn't be isolated here for long, if we are at all."

"So long as you have enough booze," one of the young men called, "we don't care if we're cut off until spring." His two male companions guffawed; the three girls giggled.

Ramsay's heart sank. He feared there would be a lot of guffawing and giggling over the next ten days. He'd shut himself away in his work for so long after the death of his family, and he knew he needed to get out more, but rejoining the wider world was painful at times like this.

The host continued speaking, outlining all the events planned, the hypnotist, the Lord of Misrule, as listed in the advertising, but added, "If this snow lies, we have toboggans, a sleigh, cross-country skis, and if it grows cold enough, skates for the pond. Don't worry about going through the ice, the pond is only waist-high at its very deepest."

"How many skis and skates?" one of the young men asked.

"We have a dozen skates of all the usual sizes," the host replied. "I'm sure you'll find some to fit most of you. And the skis attach to your own shoes or boots, so you should have no trouble finding a pair that fits you."

"What pulls the sleigh?" asked one of the young women.

"A nearby stable provides a horse when we need one," Frederick replied. "And I hope we will need one during your stay."

"Where does the sleigh go?" the young woman continued.

"Wherever the snow lies deeply enough, really," the host replied. "There's often snow here in the grounds, but if it's deep enough outside the grounds, we can make our way to the village or along the fields of the valley floor."

"Are the toboggans suitable for adults?" one of the young men asked.

"Absolutely," Frederick replied. "Most of our guests are adults, except in the summer when we have more families staying."

The irate father, tired of defending himself against his wife's pleading, suddenly asked, "This Lord of Misrule, you mentioned, what is that?"

The host laughed, rather nervously Ramsay thought. "A medieval custom we decided to revive for this occasion. Someone is given the power of a ruler and issues commands that must be obeyed. Of course, I will see that those commands are not unpleasant, nothing more than harmless, silly nonsense. If it goes well, we will repeat it in the future."

The irate father didn't look as if the explanation pleased him, and Ramsay understood why. Older people were the most likely victims of the 'ruler's jokes'. In truth, Ramsay didn't much care for the sound of it either.

"Fancy not knowing about the Lord of Misrule," Colin whispered. "Where did he go to school?"

Where indeed? Ramsay nodded.

"Oh, Dad. Not everyone cares what people were doing five hundred years ago," Eliza said, shaking her head. "And it certainly wasn't in the history lessons I remember."

"Do you remember *any* lessons, Elizabeth?" her mother asked, smiling mischievously.

Eliza giggled. "Touché, Mother, but I would have remembered something as fun as a Lord of Misrule. Right after old Freddy there stops speaking, I'm going to apply for the position and you three can expect the worst."

"Old Freddy, as you call him, is younger than I am," Ramsay pointed out.

Eliza sighed. "Which means he may be interested in a young Lady of Misrule. Not so stuck in the mud as you three."

The combined protests of her parents and Ramsay were hushed by the host speaking again, "Your bags will be in your rooms by now and your cars in our covered parking. Enjoy your relaxation and pick up your keys at the desk whenever you're ready. Dinner is served at seven tonight, and I'm sure you'll all want time to prepare for that. During the meal, we have musicians playing and later the full band for dancing. Tonight is very relaxed to let you find your way about the Manor. You're free to wander anywhere and find your bearings." He left the room and for a moment the room was quiet, but then the young couples began noisily chatting, one young man imitating their host in a manner Ramsay found most unpleasant. His concern for their short vacation grew more pressing.

Eliza jumped to her feet, saying, "I'll be back."

"Elizabeth," her mother called to Eliza, already at the door.

"Oh, dear," Doris said. "I do hope Mr. Price-Ridley won't be foolish enough to let her be Lady of Misrule."

Ramsay shook his head. "I'm sure someone's already in the job, and they'll have been well-primed not to do anything to upset the guests."

The Danesdales didn't look convinced. "Eliza can be very persuasive," Colin said.

Ramsay, however, noticed glances being exchanged between the irate father and a man Ramsay felt sure was a lawyer. He witnessed the man jerk his head, ordering the 'lawyer' to come to the table where the man and his family were seated. The 'lawyer' spoke to his wife, and they crossed the floor.

Introductions were made. Ramsay deduced the two men knew each other but not the women. The couple joined the three at their table and, Ramsay noted, the bickering stopped as the two groups got to know each other.

Eliza returned to her chair, a broad smile on her face

"Eliza, you didn't," her mother said.

"Didn't what, Mother?" Eliza asked, her smile becoming broader. "Really, it isn't a conversation for public ears."

Dark Deeds on a White Christmas

"Ask to be Lady of Misrule."

"Oh, that," Eliza responded. "I forgot about that. No, I just went to the loo. I thought it odd, you asking what I did or didn't do."

"Eliza!" her father exclaimed, scandalized.

Eliza laughed. "You are so easily duped; it's hardly sporting to do it."

"Then maybe you shouldn't, Eliza," Ramsay said, frowning.

Eliza flushed pink. "You are all aware the world has moved on, aren't you? People don't buy into your old taboos and polite conventions anymore. We're free of all that."

"Some of us aren't quite ready to join your new world, Elizabeth," her father said. "You'll have to bear with us until we are."

Ramsay's unease grew with each passing minute. *It does illustrate my concern about Eliza's infatuation,* he thought. *I'm too old for her, and I need to make her see that as kindly as I can. My inclinations are the same as those of her parents.*

"If we aren't going to be late for dinner," Doris said, rather too quickly, "we should go and unpack."

Ramsay rose to his feet as Doris and Colin did, only to find Eliza remained seated, toying with her glass and staring mutinously out of the window.

Ramsay followed her gaze, noting how deep the snow now lay on the windowsill. "I hope you've brought plenty of warm clothes," he said.

It was Doris who replied. "I shan't be doing any skiing or skating. I may go on the sleigh if they have plenty of blankets to wrap me in. Otherwise, I'll be indoors enjoying the library with the occasional short trip out to the bonfire he mentioned. Are you coming, Elizabeth?"

"I'll be up soon," Eliza said, before sipping her drink.

Her parents left and Ramsay sat down. "We have to get along, Eliza, or the Christmas break will be spoiled."

"Don't you start," Eliza responded. "Why ever did you let them come?"

"We need to get to know each other better," Ramsay replied. "After all, they don't like the idea of you being a partner in a crime fighting agency, and I don't blame them. If they don't trust me, they'll make things difficult for us both."

"I'll leave home then they can't," Eliza snapped.

"You're their only child," Ramsay reminded her. "You're all they have. Work with me to re-assure them and before they know it, they won't mind you being a private detective. You'll see."

"If Mother won't leave *inside* the Manor all week," Eliza said, suddenly grinning, "then I plan to be *outside* all week, and you are going to be with me."

Ramsay laughed. "I'll certainly be with you, if only to stop you breaking your neck on a toboggan."

"You'll be on the toboggan too – and the skis and skates," Eliza said, taking his hand. "No wriggling out of it. Maybe the shooting as well."

Ramsay frowned. "We don't have shotguns, so I'm pleased to say we'll have to forgo that pleasure. I didn't realize they did shooting parties too."

"Those young men," Eliza nodded in the direction of the noise at the bar, "they're here for that."

"I noticed," Ramsay replied. "The good thing is, they'll all be out most of the day on the moor killing harmless birds. We'll see less of them than I feared we would."

"Do you think the hotel has guns to borrow?" Eliza asked.

"I hope not," Ramsay said. "Why do you want to go on a shoot?"

"I've never fired a gun before," Eliza replied. "It would be interesting to try it."

"You'll have to ask one of the Hooray Henrys over there." He nodded to the young men. "They might let you fire a cartridge or two."

Eliza nodded. "I might just do that."

"We should be going to change," Ramsay said. "I don't want to be late for dinner."

They left the bar and crossed the lobby, where the outside door was being held open by a porter, letting in a blast of icy air, while another struggled through with two large cases and what looked like a hat box.

"There's a foot of snow out there," Ramsay said, peering out as the door slammed shut. "The local council workers will be hard pressed to clear all the roads tomorrow."

Eliza slid her hand inside his arm. "Why do we care. We're on holiday. More snow means more fun."

They parted at the foot of the grand staircase. Eliza climbed the stairs to her room on the upper floor. Ramsay, waving to her, prepared to saunter off to his room on the ground floor with Bracken when he heard the man with the hat box at the desk, complaining about the snow as he signed the register. The man's agitation caught Ramsay's attention. Another unhappy man was all they needed at a party.

As Ramsay watched, the angry husband crossed the lobby on his way to the bar. Ramsay also witnessed the new guest's shock on seeing the angry husband, who seemed not to notice the newcomer.

"Who is that, please?" the new guest asked, turning to face Joyce.

"Mr. Paul Chambers," Joyce said. "Why? Do you think you know him?"

"I thought so and, yes, I do know him," the newcomer replied grimly. He paused as if trying to decide what to say next, then continued, "We are not friends, but I needn't have anything to do with him here. You will make sure we're not seated together, please."

His expression as he said this made Joyce stammer as she replied, "I-I'll make sure the staff are informed. I'm sorry this has happened."

The man shrugged. "It isn't your fault. It isn't anyone's fault. It's just one of those horrible coincidences that happen, but with everyone's good efforts, it will be fine, I suppose." He signaled to the porter who had his bags and they set off up the grand staircase and the opposite wing from Ramsay.

"Who is the new guest?" Ramsay asked Joyce whose eyes followed the man climbing the stairs.

Joyce shook herself and answered, "A Mr. Ernest Wright of Leeds. I do hope this isn't going to lead to trouble. He looked ready for murder when he saw Mr. Chambers. If the taxi hadn't already left, he might have turned around and gone home."

Ramsay nodded. "It must be quite a quarrel. A business rivalry, perhaps."

"Mr. Wright describes himself as a manager," Joyce said. "But it may be a long-standing disagreement, I suppose. Oh, dear. I must go and warn Freddie. This will complicate a lot of the events that are planned, you can be sure."

Ramsay made his way to his room in deep thought and the worst of them was, Eliza's wish may yet come true. *If Mrs. Chambers or young Master Chambers don't kill Paul Chambers on this vacation, Mr. Ernest Wright may do it for them.*

4
___

RAMSAY PATROLS THE PERIMETER

From his room window, Ramsay could see the courtyard behind the house, brilliantly lit by lamps reflecting from the now deep snow and the flakes still falling. Beyond the courtyard was total darkness, though he knew from his recent drives around the area that the village of Harkness lay farther up the dale. Trees and a fold in the side of the valley hid the houses and their lamps. Beech tree branches, winter bare but lit by the courtyard lamps, swayed ominously in the wind, while fir tree branches moved with every gust, shaking off the snow accumulating on them. A wild night. It was a pleasure to look out on the view from a safe spot.

"It's lucky I brought boots, Bracken," Ramsay said to his companion, standing with his front paws against the windowsill, watching the snow fall, "or you'd be walking on your own tonight." He laughed.

Bracken gave him a severe frown. 'My walk isn't something to be joked about,' he clearly said.

"You're quite right," Ramsay said, penitently. "You must go out and I must go with you. I don't know what came over me."

Realizing he'd been too severe, Bracken dropped down to the ground and nuzzled his friend's knees to show him he was forgiven.

Ramsay checked his watch. "We'll go now, Bracken. In case it gets worse." He put on his boots and coat before clipping a leash to Bracken's collar and heading out.

Stepping outside the hotel front door shocked them both. After the warm rooms and gentle indoor lamps, the harsh blast of wind and the blueish glare of the outdoor lights looked and felt like a nightmare. Heads down to save their eyes, Ramsay and Bracken set off.

"We'll circumnavigate the building," Ramsay called, trying to be heard above the wind howling around the Manor's tall chimneys. They walked alongside the west wing of the building, the lighted windows shrouded by curtains while everyone inside changed. During a long walk into the wind, Ramsay counted twelve windows before they turned the corner and made their way alongside the gable end of the building. Here the light was less bright and there was some shelter from the wind.

"This is better, Bracken," Ramsay remarked, as he saw Bracken too had his head up and was looking around curiously at their new surroundings. The wall they walked alongside showed four more lighted windows and then a blank stone wall running off into the darkness.

"From our window," Ramsay told Bracken, "we see this west side of the courtyard and it's where the cars are stored. The garages are the old stables, I imagine."

They reached the end of the wall and turned right again. After a short walk, they came upon the entrance to the courtyard and the bright lights he'd seen from his room. Ramsay led Bracken into the empty space. Sheltered from the wind by the old stables, he heard his boots crunching the snow. Reaching the center, Ramsay stopped and looked around. Ahead of him the bulk of the building loomed, where the entrance hall and offices were situated, and at either side lay the East and West Wings with the guest rooms. Examining lower floor windows, Ramsay found his room, and then, on the upper floor, what he thought was Eliza's.

"That's us, Bracken," he said, pointing. "I left the curtains apart, so I could be sure to find it. I rather wish we were in our room right now, if I must be honest." His teeth chattered as the cold seeped through his thick woolen clothes like thin icy fingers finding the warmest spots.

The range of buildings running along the eastern side of the courtyard looked like storerooms, no doubt for the seasonal equipment. Ramsay examined each large door and then the doors and windows of the ground floor that overlooked the courtyard. Again, the guest room windows were shaded but not the kitchen, where bustling staff prepared his evening meal.

"Come on, Bracken," he said at last when the cold became too much. "We'll circle the East Wing and go back in before my toes fall off."

They left the courtyard and returned into the shadow of the courtyard's outer wall. The East Wing was, as far as Ramsay could tell, the same as the West Wing. The same number of guest room windows and an exit at the farthest end of the wing, no doubt for a fire escape.

By the time they'd reached the main entrance, both man and dog were shivering uncontrollably.

"Best we don't go so far at bedtime, Bracken," Ramsay said, dusting the snow from his coat and stamping it off his boots. Bracken shook himself free of the snow on his coat and they headed back to their room under the stony gaze of

Mrs. Price-Ridley. Ramsay understood her feelings. They were leaving small puddles everywhere their feet touched the floor.

"We must come back in summer, Bracken," Ramsay said, as they made their way to their room. "The shrubs and landscaping look as if they'd be very beautiful then."

Bracken nodded. 'There'll be rabbits and maybe squirrels.'

As he walked the corridor to his room, Ramsay looked down the corridor to the fire escape he'd seen while outside.

Unlocking his room door, Ramsay and Bracken entered. "What struck you about the Manor, Bracken?" Ramsay asked, as he unclipped Bracken's leash.

Bracken shuddered. 'What was he supposed to see? He'd noticed the cold, the deep snow blanketing all the scents, except the kitchen, that smelled good, and the snow lay undisturbed. No one had come out of the rear door since the snow began.'

"I'll tell you what struck me," Ramsay continued, as took off his coat and boots. "There's a not very secure covered walkway from the storerooms to the kitchen area and the fire escape doors at each end of the building are also not secure. We'll examine the one on our wing more closely when we go to dinner."

Ramsay took a towel from the bathroom and patted Bracken dry while sitting in front of the room's electric fire. "You stay here and keep warm," Ramsay said, spreading the towel on the floor for Bracken to sit on, "while I go and bathe for dinner."

* * *

RAMSAY AND BRACKEN looked their polished best as they left their room for the evening meal.

"First, we'll go and inspect that fire escape door, Bracken," Ramsay said, leading the way to the end of the corridor.

A door opened and two elderly women emerged.

"Good evening," Ramsay greeted them. "We appear to be neighbors."

The two women stared at him. He couldn't decide if their expressions showed fear or just slow thinking.

"I'm Tom Ramsay," he said, holding out his hand to the nearest woman, "and this is Bracken."

The woman took his hand slowly, as though still not sure if she should trust him. "Miss Agatha Forsythe," she said, and shook his hand firmly enough. "And my friend is Adelaide Dove."

Ramsay shook the second woman's hand. Their handshakes told him who was the dominant one of the two.

"You're going the wrong way for the dining room, Mr. Ramsay," Forsythe said. "That way is the fire escape."

Ramsay agreed, adding, "I like to check out the emergency exits of places I stay. My training, you see."

"Are you in the fire brigade?" Forsythe asked.

"The Police Force," Ramsay replied. "We're just as obsessive about entrances and exits, I promise you."

"Then I expect we'll see you soon in the dining room," Forsythe replied, and she and her companion left.

Ramsay and Bracken made their way to the stairwell. It was much colder than the corridor and Ramsay soon saw why. Snow blowing under the fire escape door from the outside, formed a small drift on the mat. He examined the door, and it confirmed his earlier observation. It may have an alarm, it said so, but anyone could enter or leave by this means any time they wanted. The manager, like many in the countryside, relied on their remoteness and the general goodwill of their neighbors for security.

"Time for dinner, Bracken," Ramsay said, opening the door that took them back into the warmth of the ground floor corridor. "I'm relying on you to keep me safe in my bed for the next ten nights."

Bracken yawned. He'd been thinking much the same thing himself, only in his mind the roles were reversed.

Entering the dining hall, Ramsay was impressed by the elegance of the company and the décor. At last, it felt like a vacation. Eliza waved at him, and he crossed the floor to join her.

"You're late," Eliza said, crossly. "I had to change the seating arrangements to sit you here next to me."

Ramsay kissed her cheek. "How odd," he said, "that they should seat us apart."

"It's so we get to know everyone," Eliza explained. "Mam and Dad are over there with the new man and the two old biddies."

"The Misses Forsythe and Dove," Ramsay said, and explained about meeting them on his way down.

"They've been here hours," Eliza complained. "Where have you been?"

"They haven't been here more than a few minutes," Ramsay retorted, "and I've been investigating the fire escape."

"What on earth for?" Eliza cried. "Are you expecting a fire?"

"No one expects a fire," Ramsay said. "Except an arsonist, I suppose," he added as an aside. "No, I just thought I should know how to get out should there be one."

Eliza shook her head in dismay and Ramsay could see 'old people are mad' in her expression. It hurt him a little, but he knew his answer was for the best. She had to come out of this infatuation as gently as she'd entered it and knowing how dotty old people could be would only help.

"The angry family members are still furious," Eliza said. She nodded toward the next table so Ramsay could see who she meant.

Ramsay didn't need her help. They were the first people he'd seen on entering the room because of their sullen, angry expressions. It telegraphed their unhappiness in a way the rowdy table of youngsters couldn't quite overcome.

"I hope a good meal and sleep will repair their Christmas cheer," Ramsay said. "The father looks like he could kill his wife and son."

"That's no good," Eliza exclaimed. "There'd be nothing for us to investigate. We need a murder among the Hooray Henrys over there, or that sexually repressed couple who look as if they've tasted something off." She nodded to the couple that Ramsay had decided were a lawyer and his wife. They'd been placed at the same table with Eliza's parents and looked disgusted to be in such inferior company.

Ramsay smiled. "And if there is a murder among any of them, who would you, my financial expert, suggest we should bill for our investigative services?" he reminded Eliza. She'd boasted they could make a living as detectives because she would always find someone willing to pay them to investigate.

Eliza's expression became thoughtful. "With the Hooray Henrys it will be easy. One of them is sure to be arrested for the murder or one of the others will be under suspicion. People like them will always leave clues behind, even when they're innocent. And they have money. They or their parents will pay."

"And the two professional-looking people?" Ramsay asked.

"Whichever one of them that isn't arrested. Again, they have money, and they'll stick together to keep it," Eliza said. "Unless there's a will, of course. Then we might have to find the victim's family or the one on trial. Either way, there's money somewhere."

Before Ramsay could reply, they were joined by the two elderly women Ramsay had spoken to.

"Excuse us," Miss Forsythe said. "We can't stay near those people." Their table with Eliza's parents was between the youngsters and the warring family. "I hope you won't mind if we move here." She didn't wait for an answer. Lifting the as-yet-unclaimed place card, she pushed Miss Dove into the seat and marched off to put the place card where she'd been seated. She returned a moment later, to peals of feminine laughter from the young couples.

"We're happy to have you join us," Ramsay replied, smiling at them as Forsythe sat down. Eliza smiled as well, though not warmly.

"Thank you," Forsythe said. She introduced herself and Miss Dove to Eliza who nodded across the table but didn't offer her hand. "If we'd known the kind of people who'd be here, we would never have come but it looked such a nice place. We've driven past many times in summer and always wished we could stay."

"I'm sure everyone will settle down," Ramsay said. "It's the first day excitement for the younger people and a horrible drive here for the drivers, so they're probably on edge. Tomorrow, they'll be more themselves, I'm sure."

Miss Forsythe looked at him with a steady, appraising gaze. "I'm sure that *is* themselves, and I suspect you are sure too. We're none of us fools, Mr. Ramsay."

Rather taken aback at this frank exchange in so young an acquaintanceship, Ramsay replied, "I believe in giving people the benefit of doubt before passing judgment. I find it's generally best."

Miss Forsythe's emphatic, "Humph!" in response said she didn't agree.

"The weather was awful wasn't it," Miss Dove said, gently. "Coming here, I mean."

"I thought it exciting," Eliza interjected, before Ramsay could reply. Forsythe's aggressive speech to Ramsay had raised her ire.

"As the driver," Ramsay said, smiling at Miss Dove who timidly smiled back, "I too thought it awful." She was a small, plump woman in her mid-fifties who appeared lost just sitting at a table. Ramsay couldn't quite explain what he meant by that. The word just came into his mind.

"If you can drive well," Miss Forsythe said, "it was fine. Go slowly and snow and ice are just another obstacle to overcome. It's men, who speed all the time, that find it dangerous."

As Ramsay hadn't exceeded thirty miles an hour throughout the whole drive, he could have taken exception to this. However, he said, "I expect you're right. Now, we should listen to our host who's trying to catch our attention."

The host waited, for the young couples were still making jokes about Miss Forsythe's rejection of a place near them. The young women, in particular, seemed to be enjoying themselves.

Eliza, though she sympathized with the young people's merriment, whispered to Ramsay, "Is the female of a Hooray Henry, a Hooray Henrietta, do you think?"

"I imagine so," he replied. He too had grown tired of waiting.

"It isn't just the noise or the crude jokes," Miss Forsythe added. "Only one of those women is wearing a wedding ring. The other two are only engaged."

"It's a new world," Ramsay agreed.

"No, Mr. Ramsay, it's a very old world. There's nothing 'new' about it." Miss Forsythe's hard expression, her eyes flinty with outraged disapproval, spoke of deep anger.

Ramsay's heart sank. Miss Forsythe may yet be the match that lit the explosive mix of passions he felt swirling around them all.

5

GROWING UNEASE

Fortunately for Ramsay, he wasn't obliged to respond because the host finally had the silence he needed to begin. He spoke about how some of the dance band and the serving staff couldn't be here tonight because of the snow and hoped everyone would be understanding to those who had been able to arrive. Service may be slower than they would like, and the band may not be able to play every tune they would like but there would be service and live music. He re-iterated the local council's confidence in clearing the snow overnight and the following day.

When he finished speaking, orders were taken and soon servers began with the first course.

Ramsay was thankful for the break because it prevented Miss Forsythe speaking. Eliza was a sensible young woman, but she wouldn't sit quietly while the frosty old lady made autocratic remarks about Ramsay, or their fellow guests, and Ramsay could sympathize. He also found this kind of absolute certainty of rightness troublesome. His years in the police had taught him to expect pleasant surprises from the least likely people.

"I'm guessing you'll want to listen to the band from the bar," Eliza asked Ramsay, breaking into his thoughts.

"If you mean, I don't want to dance, you're right," Ramsay said. "The last time I danced, the Charleston was all the rage."

"You must have seen the Twist somewhere," Eliza persisted. "No one can have missed that."

Ramsay laughed. "I don't have a television, and I stopped going to the cinema twenty years ago, so I haven't seen the Twist."

"You need to be taken in hand," Eliza retorted, "before you really become a fossil."

Ramsay shrugged. "If it isn't too hard, you can show me how."

"It isn't hard at all," Eliza told him, her attention caught by the minor flare-up of tempers at the table where the angry family sat. "Tomorrow night, we must insist on having a table with Mam and Dad."

Ramsay nodded. "I agree. Mixing us all up to break the ice would work if we were all much of a muchness, but we're not."

Eliza's parents rose from their chairs and moved quickly to an empty table near Ramsay and Eliza, carrying their soup dishes with them. This left the lawyer and his wife and the new man sitting alone. The man not following the Danesdales rather puzzled Ramsay. He'd said he disliked the angry man and yet he remained sitting near enough to hear every word the family snapped at each other. The family appeared not to have noticed their neighbors, so intense was their anger.

"I bet he kills his wife before the night is out," Eliza whispered, as they watched and listened in horror. "And to be fair, I think he'll be justified."

"How can you say that?" Forsythe cried. "Blessed are the peacemakers, remember?"

"But she isn't making peace is she," Eliza retorted. "She's brought a small-scale war into our lives. She must have been mad to imagine this a good idea. I've never seen two people so opposed to one another as her husband and son."

Ramsay prepared to rise and attempt to calm the two men, when the host arrived and asked them to remember their manners or settle this outside. The two stared into each other's eyes, each hoping the other would accept the offer, but the moment passed, and the father sat down, mumbling something that might have been an apology to the host. The mother and son also returned to their seats and began eating in silence.

Ramsay's interest was caught by the professional man, the one he thought a lawyer, staring at the warring family and particularly at the father. There's a connection there and not one the 'lawyer' likes.

"Chambers does bring out the worst in all of us," Ramsay said. "None of us like him."

"She does," Eliza replied, gesturing toward the lawyer's wife.

Ramsay couldn't help but agree. Mrs. Phillipson was staring at Chambers with approval.

"She likes aggressive men," Ramsay said, laughing. "Some do."

"Mam," Eliza said, turning to address her mother, "do you know that man Chambers?"

Replying for his wife, Colin said, "Many years ago, he had a food service company and we bought from him. Doris didn't like his manners, that's all."

"You're the second person I know of here who has a connection to him," Ramsay mused. "Mr. Ernest Wright," he pointed to the table where the man sat alone, "knew him from the past as well. I heard him tell Joyce that."

"It's a small world," Doris replied, "and the North Riding of Yorkshire isn't such a big place in it, so it isn't too much of a coincidence."

Is her explanation, while true, too ready and too convenient? Ramsay became uneasy again. A lot of the drama he was watching unfold felt like it had something going on underneath.

A commotion across the room drew all their attention. Chambers, back on his feet and roughly grabbing at Wright, who was rising to his feet angrily and pushing back, shouted obscenities. Wright's arm went out toward Chambers' chest. Chambers had the advantage of height and his blow landed square on Wright's mouth. Wright fell back momentarily before thrusting upward for revenge but two of the young men intervened. For a moment, the older men looked ready to continue, then Chambers turned away and stormed out of the room.

"Good riddance," Doris said, as Mrs. and Master Chambers followed him.

Wright wiped his hand across his face and stared at his bloody hand. Then, he too left the room.

"I hope he isn't going to continue the fight," Colin said, anxiously.

"We've booked into a madhouse," Ramsay replied.

"I told you we'd have our next case here at Christmas," Eliza gloated, buzzing with excitement.

"Don't say these things, Elizabeth," her mother said. "You're making it worse. I'd be happy to leave right now, if I could."

"You haven't said if you'll take my bet," Eliza said to Ramsay, when the room had almost returned to normal.

"I'm not betting on the death of anyone," Ramsay replied.

"Quite right, Mr. Ramsay," Forsythe interjected. "It would be most unseemly."

"Nobody asked your opinion," Eliza replied. She glared at the woman whose steadfast expression didn't flinch.

"Eliza and I were having a private conversation, Miss Forsythe," Ramsay said. "Perhaps you and Miss Dove could do the same. We can't have another table that needs the host's peacemaking tonight."

Forsythe nodded and didn't reply though she wasn't in the least put out by Ramsay or Eliza's replies. Ramsay rather admired that but wished she'd go and raise the moral tone of another table.

Eliza was about to speak, but Ramsay's frown shushed her. She took three very obvious deep breaths before asking, "What will we do tomorrow?"

"What would you like to do? Ski?"

"I'd like to join the shooting party, if it's still on," Eliza said. "I expect you'd like to curl up in front of a fire with a whisky and a book."

Ramsay laughed. "After dinner, we can ask if the hotel has guns to rent. I don't approve of guns, but we trained with them every year. I'll be happy to shoot with you, so long as you don't expect me to kill any birds."

"Well, if *I* do, *you* won't be invited to share them when they're cooked up for dinner," Eliza retorted.

"If they don't have guns to rent, what then?"

"I've never skied before," Eliza said, "but how hard can it be. We'll do that."

"I was afraid you'd say that," Ramsay replied. "I rather liked the thought of the sleigh ride."

"When I'm in my dotage, and you're completely gaga,

we'll do a sleigh ride. Until then, we're going to do things living people do," Eliza replied. "By the way, there aren't any real hills here. What will we be skiing down?"

"I imagine it will be on the flat ground," Ramsay replied. "I don't know. I've never skied either."

"We can ask about that when we ask about renting guns," Eliza said, and began eating her second course with all her usual youthful heartiness.

* * *

THE HOTEL DIDN'T RENT guns and didn't know anywhere local that might. Mrs. Price-Ridley did explain about the skis. They were cross-country skis and meant for skiing on the level ground or very gentle hills, which she advised against until they were strong enough skiers to manage the skis on a hill.

"That doesn't sound exciting," Eliza grumbled as they made their way to the ballroom. "On the movies, skiers race down steep hills without any effort. Walking for miles with two planks on my feet isn't anything like that."

"Maybe it's like skating," Ramsay said, as they joined Eliza's parents at a small table on the side of the dance floor. "Can you skate?"

Eliza shook her head. "There's no ice rink near us."

"What's this?" Doris asked.

"I thought cross-country skiing might be like skating," Ramsay said. "Skaters move pretty darn quickly; it seems to me. I thought that once we got the hang of skiing, we'd be speeding all over the valley, which would be exciting enough for Eliza."

Eliza snorted in disbelief but was distracted from further comment by the band beginning to play *The Locomotion* and the young couples forming a conga line with added train-like arm movements. She grabbed Ramsay's hand and dragged him onto the floor. "You know what a steam train looks like, I know you do" she said, attaching herself to the back of the conga-line with one hand and holding Ramsay's hand with the other.

Beating down his rising embarrassment, Ramsay joined in. He not only could remember steam trains, having traveled on one a month or so ago, but he could also remember doing the conga a long time ago with his wife. The memory caused a brief stabbing pain in his heart that soon passed. It was replaced a moment later by a different feeling as he watched Eliza's back sinuously moving to the beat. Once again, he thought, *I must be careful not to let her see or hope he felt this way about her.*

Ramsay was relieved when Eliza's parents joined the line, with Doris holding his waist. He became even happier to see the lawyer and his wife joining the back of the line and staying there until the music stopped. The dancers applauded the musicians who took a bow and began organizing their next number. The excited dancers, however, began talking and then introducing themselves. Ramsay learned that the professional couple were Quentin and Julia Phillipson and, yes, a lawyer in London. They were here because of the angry family, the Chambers, and because her family lived in the area.

The young people were harder for Ramsay to remember because they talked so quickly and over each other. He grasped there were three couples, Mr. and Mrs. Pugachev, Nicholas and Muriel, Oliver Trubshaw and his fiancée, Celina Daventry, and Marcus Partington and his fiancée, Sarah Onslow.

The much-depleted band had decided modern music

was required for this audience and announced *The Twist*. Ramsay groaned as Eliza grabbed his hand and began demonstrating what he should do with his legs.

"What about my knees?" Ramsay cried.

"They need the exercise," Eliza told him and demanded he show he'd understood her instructions. The band began playing and the young people began cavorting all around him before he could. *Thank heavens there's nobody watching this,* Ramsay thought as he continued twisting, gingerly lowering himself on gyrating knees until they complained, and he stood back up and stayed that way until the music stopped.

"Hey, you're doing okay for an old man," Eliza said. "Maybe you're younger than you think."

Ramsay's cutting reply disappeared into the music when the band began playing again. This time a tune he remembered and memories of dances in Newcastle with his wife came flooding back. He felt tears prickling his eyelids and quickly blinked them away.

"You must know the *Tennessee Waltz*," Eliza said, taking hold of his hand.

"I can vaguely remember it," Ramsay agreed and, placing his arm around her waist, they began to dance. Slowly, Eliza's head rested on his shoulder as they moved quietly around the floor and Ramsay's heart ached for what was lost and what could never be.

6

BRACKEN FINDS FRIENDS

It was dawn when Ramsay and Bracken set out for their morning walk. The snow had stopped, though low dark clouds above suggested it wasn't stopped for long.

"At least it isn't too cold, Bracken," Ramsay said, as Bracken sniffed apprehensively at the blanket of white that reached his body.

'It isn't your belly rubbing along it,' Bracken's angry glance said in reply.

"We'll be back inside in no time," Ramsay said, bracingly, "and think how warm that will feel."

Bracken declined to answer this in the way he wanted. His friend was generally sensible but sometimes not so much and he just had to accept that.

They crossed the unmarked snow to the bushes that bordered the drive where rustling sounds made Bracken's ears perk up. 'Rabbits!' He began tugging at the leash while Ramsay pulled him back. "We're not chasing them, Bracken. We're here to make you comfortable and nothing else."

They returned to the hotel and were preparing to return to their room when Mrs. Price-Ridley appeared behind the reception desk. "Good morning, Mr. Ramsay and Bracken. Would you and Bracken like to come through and meet our golden Labs?"

As Ramsay felt sure there were times when Bracken would prefer to be among friends instead of being stuck watching humans do boring things, he agreed they would.

They were led through a Staff Only door and into a passageway Ramsay realized was the one he'd seen while in the courtyard on the previous evening.

"This first door," Joyce said, "is our Cold Room. Our dogs have the last of the old rooms along the corridor for their home. They have lots of room, things to do, and a flap to go outside whenever they wish." She stopped at an arched opening, which had a wooden fence and gate across the lower half and was open above waist height.

Three golden Labradors ran to greet her. They stood up on the fence rail to lick her face.

"I haven't come to feed you," she told them, when she could speak. "I've brought a new friend for you to meet."

They dropped down on all four paws and examined Bracken through the fence. Ramsay feared Bracken would be nervous about the attention, but he appeared unconcerned and trotted to greet them in return. When sufficient time had passed and all seemed well, Joyce opened the gate and the four dogs huddled briefly before a Lab led them off and up a ramp to a higher elevation.

"They won't push Bracken off there, will they?" Ramsay asked.

Joyce laughed. "It wouldn't matter if they did. You can't see from here but there's thick straw mats down below. They can jump or fall from there quite safely. We can leave them to get to know each other, if you wish."

"I'll stay for a while," Ramsay replied. "Just to be sure.

Dark Deeds on a White Christmas   43

Bracken is still very young and may do something impetuous."

Joyce laughed again. "Larry will keep him right. He's the oldest and wisest. He keeps Harry and Barry in order all the time."

"Interesting names," Ramsay said, smiling.

"Our children's idea," Joyce told him. "We got Larry first for our eldest, Jennifer, and she thought Larry the Labrador sounded funny. When our younger children got dogs, they added the rhyming names. The children have flown the nest, and we have the dogs to serve as a daily reminder."

"Do they live far away?"

Joyce shook her head. "Oh no, but you know how it is. They have busy lives, and we have a hotel to run so we don't see each other as often as we would wish."

As they were talking, one of the Labs ran down the ramp and out of a flap in the wall at the back of the room. The others, and Bracken, followed.

"Should we follow?" Ramsay asked.

Joyce shook her head. "They're quite safe. Their area back there is fenced off. They can't get on the road or out into the grounds. I expect they'll be back soon enough once they've run off some energy."

"I'll wait," Ramsay said, still a little unsure of the wisdom of all this. "If you need to get back to reception, I can find my way home."

"I will leave you because we have a guest arriving this morning. He waited in Scarborough overnight because the taxi service wouldn't come into the dale. Now the snow has stopped, and the roads are being cleared, he'll arrive soon, I expect."

Waiting alone felt surprisingly eerie, Ramsay decided. The corridor, lit only with a stark, pale light, had strange furtive noises echoing along it. The scratching sounds of rats or mice, he thought, accounted for some noises and others the walls and roof adjusting to the cold, the snow and the warming morning sun. Still, explaining the sounds didn't stop them, and they made the silence feel lonelier. Shouldn't he be able to hear the kitchen staff? Ramsay wasn't a particularly sensitive man, but he was pleased when the flap suddenly opened and a golden Lab popped through, followed by Bracken and the two other Labs. He watched them shake themselves dry and realized how rarely he'd seen happy dogs.

It soon became clear Bracken didn't need him and Ramsay made his way back to the lobby. *My trusty companion's deserting me when I need all the help I can get. Something feels wrong. Or was it just Eliza's constant doom-laden pronouncements playing on his nerves?*

7
SLEDDING AND SLEIGHING

Ramsay and Eliza had agreed the night before to meet for breakfast and she was waiting alone at a table when he entered the room. Eliza yawned dramatically and studied her wristwatch as he crossed the floor.

"Good afternoon," Eliza said. "How nice of you to join me for High Tea."

He kissed her cheek and wished her good morning before sitting across the table from her.

"What have you done with Bracken?" Eliza asked. "Has he taken himself for a walk this morning?"

"Bracken and I have been out already and now he's spending time with some new friends, Larry, Harry, and Barry."

"You're making that up," Eliza answered. "There are no such people."

"They're the owners' golden Labs," Ramsay explained. "Have you ordered?"

"You left a puppy like Bracken in the clutches of three sinister sounding dogs?"

"They're having fun," Ramsay replied, as a server

brought Eliza her bacon, eggs, sausage, and baked beans on toast. He told the server, "I'll have the kippers, please."

Eliza swallowed a mouthful before saying, "Look over there." She gestured with her knife toward a table where Chambers and Mrs. Phillipson huddled in earnest discussion. "They've been like that since I arrived. They must know their partners aren't coming to breakfast, I think, or they wouldn't be so cozy."

"It is very public," Ramsay replied, "but that must mean they are just friends. No one would be mad enough to conduct an affair quite so openly and with their partners only a few steps away."

"Well, I'm now certain we're going to get our murder before the week is out," Eliza said, smiling. "Our second case. We'll have the pick of the mysteries when this is over. I can see the headlines now, 'Danesdale and Ramsay Crack the Case', 'Police Baffled, Danesdale and Ramsay Solve the Mystery'..."

"Who are these 'Danesdale and Ramsay' people?"

"It's the name of our detective agency. I went with the alphabetical arrangement, you see," Eliza said, grinning.

"You don't think the senior partner, and most well-known partner, should come first?"

This discussion lasted throughout breakfast and was still going on when they left the room.

"I'm going to rescue Bracken and take him for a walk," Ramsay said, heading toward the reception desk where Joyce was talking to Miss Forsythe. Miss Dove looked on so anxiously that Ramsay knew this wasn't a happy chat.

"We should wait," he said quietly to Eliza, who had also seen the difficulty.

"But we should move closer so we can hear what she's saying."

Ramsay didn't have to guess who Eliza meant, and they slowly approached the desk, ears alert to catch the conversation.

"You won't be so blasé about this when I tell the police you're running a bawdyhouse here," Miss Forsythe replied, in response to a comment from Joyce they didn't hear.

"There's no question of such a thing, Miss Forsythe," Joyce said. "You're imagining things. Mr. and Mrs. Pugachev are married and have one room. Their friends have two separate rooms, one for the ladies and one for the gentlemen."

"Ladies," snorted Miss Forsythe. "I tell you I heard them wandering the corridors at all hours last night and worse."

"They're young people, Miss Forsythe," Joyce said, soothingly. "I'm sure nothing more happened than visiting their friends and socializing. We can ask them, if you wish. Here they are coming down the stairs."

Miss Forsythe's eyes shot daggers at the group making its way downstairs and walked away, saying, "Come along, Dove. We can't associate with these houris."

Before Ramsay and Eliza could step forward to speak to Joyce, the young people were at the desk demanding toboggans.

Joyce rang a bell and, when a manservant came out of the nearby door, said, "Follow Alfred, he'll get you kitted out with all you need."

She turned to Ramsay apologetically, saying, "Sorry about that. What can I do for you?"

"I wanted to collect Bracken," Ramsay replied. "Maybe Alfred could help us too?"

"Go through," Joyce said. "Tell Alfred I sent you."

The corridor was as cold as Ramsay remembered it. He wished he'd gone back to his room for a coat by the time they reached the second storeroom where Alfred waited patiently for the three couples to choose toboggans. As all the sleds looked the same to Ramsay, he couldn't quite understand the difficulty.

Ramsay explained and Alfred took them to the room where the dogs now lay panting in the straw. He unlocked the gate and Bracken trotted out to greet his friends. As Alfred re-locked the gate, Eliza said, "We'd like a toboggan too, please, Alfred."

As the three couples left, Alfred, Ramsay, and Eliza arrived at the seasonal equipment storeroom. Eliza examined the remaining toboggans before picking a blue one. "It will remind you of your days driving a police car," she said, as Ramsay lifted it onto his back.

Mr. Price-Ridley had assured them the toboggans were sturdily built, which Ramsay now discovered meant heavy. He imagined himself falling off and being run over by one. "Are you sure you wouldn't prefer the sleigh ride?" he asked Eliza, who was fussing over Bracken, having discovered his cold, wet coat.

"No, I wouldn't," she said. "I've never been on a sled as fancy as these ones and I want to see how fast they go."

They arrived at the desk as Joyce told the young couples where to find the hill and Eliza asked her, "Can we leave our sled here while we go and dress for tobogganing?"

Joyce nodded. "If you're quick. We have another guest arriving this morning."

Wrapped in coats, hats, scarves, gloves, and boots, Ramsay, Bracken, and Eliza returned for the sled. Joyce said, laughing, "I'm relying on your good sense to keep these younger people in line, Mr. Ramsay. We can't have them injured on the first day."

"I fear I'm the most likely to be injured," Ramsay replied, ruefully. "But I'll do my best."

He carried the sled outside and laid it on the snowy lawn that sloped down to the lake. "This might be a good place to test it before we reach the hill," he said, waiting for Eliza to jump on.

"You're coming too," Eliza said. "Don't think you aren't. You get on the back; I'll sit at the front and Bracken can sit on my legs."

Groaning, Ramsay obeyed, spreading his legs either side of the sled. Eliza sat between them, much too closely, and Bracken hopped up onto her lap.

"Let's go," Eliza commanded, and Ramsay, digging his gloves into the snow, pushed them off the level ground and down the slope. The sled ran smoothly, and in Ramsay's opinion, mercifully slowly, until they neared the icy water of the lake where he dug in his heels and brought them all to a halt.

"Very pleasant," Ramsay said, climbing off.

"I thought it disappointing," Eliza complained, preparing to rise.

"You sit still," Ramsay said. "I may be able to pull it over the snow." He tugged and, after some initial stickiness, the sled began to follow him across the lawn to the hill at the farther end of the lake.

He could have found the hill with his eyes closed, Ramsay thought as they neared noise of men yelling and girls shrieking, while they raced down the hill before towing their sleds back up to the top. From a distance, it all looked very tame. When Ramsay reached the bottom of the hill and the Pugachevs raced by at high speed, he changed his mind. Eliza jumped off and together they tugged the toboggan up with Bracken running ahead.

At the top, they made their way across the hill beyond the place where another toboggan had just set off, before turning theirs to face the hill.

"I'll steer," Ramsay said, as they watched the sled that just left swerve across the hill and tip, sending its two riders sprawling into the snow.

"She meant to do that," Eliza said. "It wasn't bad driving."

"Our first run will be slow and steady," Ramsay pronounced, firmly. "I won't bounce the way you folks do."

"It must be awful being old," Eliza said, climbing onto the sled.

Ramsay sat behind her and pushed off with Bracken running excitedly beside them. For a moment, Ramsay felt happy with the speed but then the sled moved into a higher gear. His hat lifted and before he could grab it, it flew off. Looking back, he spotted Bracken catching it with ease as he scampered down the hill after them.

The sled ran on over the wide lawn, slowing on the level ground until it finally stopped. Bracken arrived and gave Ramsay his hat.

"Much better," Eliza cried, her eyes shining, as she clambered off the sled and offered Ramsay a hand to help him rise.

He took it and got to his feet, folding his hat and pushing it in a pocket.

"If it goes this far each time, we'll be well exercised by lunch time," Ramsay grumbled before hauling the sled back toward the hill.

They stopped their second run at the bottom of the hill, so they didn't have to walk so far and by the third, they were as excited as the others. Eliza screaming for the joy of it, Bracken riding on her lap, barking wildly, while Ramsay laughed until his sides ached. As they climbed up after a run, they heard the younger crowd calling, "The horse is here."

Looking back to the Manor, they perceived a dappled gray horse being led around to the courtyard, presumably to be hitched to the sleigh.

"We should be first on it," one of the girls said and, after some excited discussion, the three couples jumped on their toboggans and shot off down the hill, leaving Ramsay, Bracken, and Eliza watching them.

"There isn't room for us as well," Ramsay said.

"Who wants to go in an old sleigh anyway," Eliza answered and sat on the toboggan. They set off and while the sled ran as fast as before, and the wind nipped their noses as before, without the excited noise of the others, it all felt rather flat.

As they pulled the sled back to the top, Eliza said, "You know, I can't decide which group of guests will provide the murder."

Ramsay laughed. "They're just squabbling. It's normal, especially when they're thrown together like this."

Eliza shook her head. "We learned at school, 'By the pricking of my thumbs. Something wicked this way comes.' I thought that rubbish, until now."

8

LAST GUEST ARRIVES

"We'll take the next turn in the sleigh," Eliza said, when they slowed to a halt. Ramsay climbed off and began pulling the sled while Eliza and Bracken rode on it like royalty.

As they approached the place where the sleigh was leaving, loaded with all three couples, two of the girls sitting on their fiancés' knees, Ramsay saw the Phillipsons approaching the spot in a heated discussion.

"He must have seen her talking with that old man, Chambers," Eliza said. "I knew it would end in tears."

"He does look upset," Ramsay agreed. "Maybe it will be Mrs. Phillipson who is our murder victim and not one of the Chambers."

"Hmm, that's no good," Eliza said. "We won't have a case to investigate or anyone to pay our fee if there is."

"Maybe his parents will pay for us to soften the evidence?" Ramsay suggested.

"I don't believe anyone would care either way if he's hanged," Eliza replied. "Now if his guilt isn't obvious, her parents may pay us to prove it was him."

"You don't feel making money off the deaths of people

isn't a little mercenary or at least morbid?" Ramsay asked, smiling.

"If someone kills someone, they need to be punished," Eliza replied. "You can help the victims get justice. I don't see that as anything but a public service. Did you think this way when you worked in the police? After all, they paid you to solve crimes and bring people to justice. There's no difference."

"Perhaps you're right," Ramsay agreed, to end the discussion for, now, they'd joined the Phillipsons standing at the sleigh ride start.

"Good morning," Ramsay greeted them. "You're going on the sleigh ride too?"

"Yes," Mrs. Phillipson said, a little too loudly and a little too cheerfully. "It's so nice now and it's supposed to snow later."

Ramsay glanced at the sky. "I'd say sooner rather than later." He pointed at the heavy, low cloud moving across the western sky.

Silence fell again. Eliza ignored the Phillipsons and fussed over Bracken. Mr. Phillipson glowered at the sky as if daring it to snow. Mrs. Phillipson fiddled with her scarf to settle it better over her ears, and Ramsay watched them all in amused delight. He hoped the driver insisted they all get in together so this small drama could continue longer.

The sleigh, with bells ringing and the young people singing sleighing songs, returned to its turning spot and slid softly to a halt. The still excited couples jumped down and ran to the toboggans they'd abandoned.

Ramsay, Bracken, and Eliza climbed aboard and invited the Phillipsons to join them. "We only need two seats," Ramsay said. "Bracken can sit on our knees."

Mrs. Phillipson thanked them and climbed up into the

sleigh. Her husband followed, still glowering at the world in general.

After the ride, which they all agreed as the best thing they'd ever experienced, the Phillipsons returned to the Manor.

"She'll be the victim," Eliza said. "I must ask her where her parents live. We're going to need to know that."

"How will you work that into a conversation?" Ramsay asked. "It isn't a natural thing to say?"

"People like to talk about their families," Eliza replied. "It'll be easy."

"Your mam and dad are coming to take a sleigh ride," Ramsay said, nodding to the Manor where Eliza's parents were just stepping out. "We should go again with them."

"I want to question Mrs. Phillipson," Eliza grumbled. "He might murder her before I've got our clients lined up."

"You're very keen on this, aren't you?" Ramsay said, chuckling.

"As the financial brains of the agency, I must have these things prepared. You'd never think of it yourself."

"That's true. But if he kills her before you've spoken to her, there won't be a case," Ramsay said. "It will be too open and shut. What you want is something devious where he has an unbreakable alibi and he's shifted the suspicion to someone else."

"I suppose so," Eliza reluctantly agreed. "Then we can go with Mam and Dad."

When the Danesdales arrived at the sleigh, Doris asked, "Have you three been on the sleigh ride?"

"We went with the Phillipsons," Ramsay replied. "Then we saw you coming out and we waited to go with you."

Colin grimaced. "We meant to come earlier but we met the Phillipsons in the lobby. They were having a furious row, you could tell, even though it was a quiet one. We waited so we didn't have to share the sleigh with them."

"You did right," Eliza said, laughing. "Mrs. Phillipson tried to pretend everything was normal, but he never said a word. If looks could kill, Tom and I would have our next case already."

Doris shuddered. "Don't talk like that. This is supposed to be the season of goodwill to all men, and, I imagine, also women like Mrs. Phillipson. Did you see her draped over that Chambers fellow this morning at breakfast?"

"We did," Eliza said, as they settled themselves in the sleigh. "They must know each other from before. I shouldn't be surprised if Chambers only employs Phillipson as a lawyer so he can be close to Mrs. Phillipson."

"Well, if that's the case," Doris replied, "Mr. Phillipson must have decided he doesn't like it and is beginning to object."

"Maybe he's only just realized," Eliza said, as the sleigh moved off. "Maybe it wasn't so obvious until this holiday together."

"Maybe," Ramsay interjected, "it's a complete misunderstanding and you're reading too much into it." He was afraid the sleigh driver may overhear this conversation and it would soon be all over the hotel.

Eliza sensed his concern. She laughed. "You're probably right. We shouldn't gossip. We've been tobogganing, Mam. You and Dad should join us after lunch."

"I think we're too old for that nonsense, dear," Doris said. "We thought of walking into the village. We've never been here, you know."

"We've driven through it many times," Eliza scoffed. "You blinked and missed it every time."

"Nevertheless," Colin said, "we're too old for tobogganing. You younger people can enjoy it better without worrying about us hurting ourselves."

"Very wise," Ramsay said, glancing at Eliza. "I already ache from my morning of sledding. This sleigh ride is perfect for my middle-aged bones. I'm sure you feel the same."

The ride ended and they returned to the Manor for lunch. Eliza let her parents go ahead of her to their room and said, "I'm glad you persuaded them to avoid tobogganing. I only offered to be polite. We don't need any gooseberries spoiling our time together."

Ramsay smiled. "They're only five years or so older than I am, Eliza."

Eliza laughed. "Five years and a lifetime older. You still look and sound young. They don't."

"*What a difference a day makes*, isn't that how the song goes?"

"In some people, yes," Eliza said. "Though I don't think my parents were ever young. Not really what we mean by young. Do you understand me?"

Ramsay nodded. "It's like that with some people. Old heads on young shoulders. Old people think that's a good thing but I'm not so sure."

"If you *were* an old person, you would be sure," Eliza said. "I want to ski this afternoon."

"Very well, but we start learning on the flat lawn," Ramsay replied, immediately showing his age.

Eliza laughed. "All right, Grandad. It will be as you wish."

As she spoke, the hotel door opened and an elderly man, stooped and tired, entered followed by a porter with his bags. He crossed the floor slowly, adding to the idea forming in Ramsay's mind that the man was seriously ill.

Joyce, at her usual station, greeted the man with a broad smile. "Mr. Redhill, I presume? Your journey didn't go well, I fear."

The man replied so quietly, they couldn't hear him.

"Never mind," Joyce said, "you're here now and we have all you need to enjoy your stay." She handed him his key and told the porter to show Mr. Redhill to his room, which Ramsay noted as being farther along his corridor.

Ramsay approached the desk and said, "We'd like skis, please, Joyce," rather proud at his humorous rhyming.

Joyce smiled and rang the bell before replying, "Tobogganing wasn't exciting enough, I see."

"A nice gentle start to the day but now we need the real thing," Eliza said.

"By which Eliza means a broken leg," Ramsay interjected.

"I hope not," Joyce said. "The snow is coming down heavily again now."

Ramsay turned to look out of the window and groaned. The only way to get his possible broken leg to a hospital may be by sleigh.

The ever-patient Alfred emerged from the staff area and led them down the corridor to the equipment room. Bracken, bored by all this activity that meant nothing to him, trotted on down to join his friends Larry, Harry, and Barry who greeted him enthusiastically. Taking a short run-up, Bracken leapt over the railing and into their room.

Ramsay and Eliza decided to leave him there while they chose skis and ate lunch. "We left our toboggan outside, Alfred," Ramsay said. "We didn't like to carry it through the hall."

"I'll tidy it away," Alfred replied, as he finished adjusting the bindings for Ramsay's skis.

With their skis and shoes, they returned to their rooms to change for lunch.

Lunch was a quiet affair. The young couples were still on the hill and the Chambers nowhere in sight.

"Maybe he's already murdered her," Eliza whispered, "and he's disposing of the body."

"Then where is the son?" Ramsay countered. "No, I think the wife and son have finally murdered him and *they* are disposing of the body."

Eliza nodded. "That would fit the facts better, I agree. Still, I think our case revolves around them somehow."

"Mr. Wright isn't here either," Ramsay said, before adding in a breathless whisper. "Maybe he's in on it too, or he's murdered the whole family."

"Now you're just being silly," Eliza replied.

"We do have our new guest though," Ramsay said, quietly. He nodded to where Mr. Redhill sat alone at the far side of the room.

"I wouldn't have thought him strong enough to walk all the way over there," Eliza said. "Poor man. He looks very frail."

Changing the subject, which he was beginning to find morbid, Ramsay asked, "Are we skiing if this snow continues?" He pointed outside the window.

"Why not?" Eliza said. "We could hardly get colder or wetter than we did this morning."

"We won't be able to see where we're going," Ramsay responded.

"Fortunately," Eliza said, "I know you aren't the drip you pretend to be. Otherwise, I'd disown you. We're going!"

"If we end up at the bottom of that lake, you'll wish you'd listened to me," Ramsay replied, before starting on his just-delivered lunch.

Eliza had already started so it took her a moment to reply, "Wouldn't that be romantic? Locked in each other's arms for all eternity."

Ramsay declined to follow that train of thought and, when they'd finished lunch, they changed and began learning to ski.

"It's not so hard, if you have a sense of balance," Eliza told Ramsay, as he picked himself out of yet another snowdrift.

Ramsay dusted down his coat, before replying, "And if you don't?"

"It will just take more practise," Eliza said, smiling sweetly, pleased to find something she could do better than him.

"It may not be one of the other guests that gets murdered," Ramsay muttered darkly, as they set off once again across the wide expanse of snow covering the lawn.

Eliza laughed. "That would certainly be a different story to the one I see being acted out before us."

9

CHRISTMAS EVE – LORD OF MISRULE BEGINS

Bracken, happy with his new friends, declined Ramsay's invitation to a late afternoon walk when Ramsay and Eliza returned to the Manor. The snow, intermittent throughout the afternoon, now blew large, wet flakes in the face of anyone foolish enough to be outside. By three-thirty, the snow had driven Eliza and Ramsay indoors from their skiing. Consequently, Ramsay, Eliza, Doris, and Colin could meet in the bar early for the beginning of the evening events.

"And how did you enjoy skiing?" Colin asked Ramsay, as they waited for their drinks.

"It's harder than it looks," Ramsay replied, ruefully.

"It never looked easy to me," Doris said.

"Well, it's much harder than that," Ramsay replied, grinning. "I ache all over and will be as stiff as a board by morning."

"You should have gone into the sauna," Colin said. "That's what Scandinavians do, I believe."

"One new experience a day, is my motto," Ramsay said.

"Sauna will be tomorrow." He gazed around the room and added, "I think everyone who's coming is here now."

Colin nodded. "It must be very disappointing for the owners. This snow can't have come at a worse time for them. They'll have to reimburse so many people, even though they will have brought in and paid for so much ahead of time."

"Spoken like a true accountant, my dear," Doris said. "And I think you're right, Tom, because here's our host."

Mr. Price-Ridley pinged a knife on a glass to announce his presence and call for quiet. "Ladies and gentlemen, honored guests," he began. "The snow has seriously reduced the number of people here, but I'm sure we'll find there are enough to create a pleasant party atmosphere. Our Christmas Eve dinner will begin shortly with Carolers from our local church choir, and, after, we'll have a hypnotist to amaze you and, of course, our band will provide music for dancing. Later, the Lord of Misrule will help us all get to know each other better with some party games I'm sure you'll enjoy."

When he'd finished speaking, Eliza whispered, "Did you see Miss Forsythe's face during that speech? I don't think she plans to enjoy any party games or the promised pleasure of the Hypnotist or Lord of Misrule."

"I suspect the latter is against her principles," Doris said. "I'm not sure I like the idea either. There's probably a good reason why that died out with the Middle Ages."

"The Chambers seem happier tonight," Colin said. "The Phillipsons, on the other hand, look unhappier."

Ramsay followed his gaze to a table where the five were seated. Colin's observation seemed right. Even the sullen son, Gregory, Ramsay had learned his name, appeared more relaxed, almost happy.

"Then our host may get his wish and we will all have a pleasant party," he suggested.

"How disappointing," Eliza said. "By the way, did you know the Hooray Henrys went shooting this afternoon up on the moors?"

"I'm amazed they could see birds to shoot," Doris replied.

"They didn't have a good day. Alfred told us when we returned our skis," Ramsay added. "They came back early because of the weather up on the tops."

"One of them got injured," Eliza continued excitedly, "by a careless shot."

"How awful," Doris cried. "I wish people wouldn't play with guns." She paused, looking at the three couples in puzzlement, before adding, "But they're all there."

"Oh, it wasn't much of an injury," Eliza said. "A pellet penetrated the sleeve of the one called Marcus's coat. Just a scratch is what Alfred said. And 'a lot of fuss about nothing'."

"All the same," Ramsay said, seriously, "that shouldn't happen. Not with experienced shooters and a knowledgeable keeper."

"Which one shot him?" Colin asked, looking at the couples without seeing any resentment on any of their faces.

"It wasn't clear any of them shot him," Eliza said. "Today's shoot included other people from other hotels. Still, it makes me wonder."

"Wonder what, dear?" her mother asked.

"Well, Miss Forsythe keeps complaining about the wanderings between the bedrooms each night, and I wonder if one of the men thought that Marcus may have been getting himself accidentally-on-purpose, lost in the dark."

Ramsay laughed. "You're like a new policeman, Eliza. You think everyone you see has just committed, or is about to commit, a crime. We solved one mystery and now you're looking at every incident as a possible new one."

Eliza blushed. "I am not. I'm just saying, it makes me wonder."

Her mother smiled. "Well, none of *us* wondered, Elizabeth."

Eliza glared at them saying, "You may laugh now but when the murder happens, I'll have the last laugh."

"I'm glad our hosts decided not to mingle the guests again," Colin said, changing the conversation. "It wasn't a success last night, I fear."

"My point exactly, Dad," Eliza cried. "There's trouble brewing, and they can sense it."

Their food arrived and they turned to the meal as a safe diversion. The band began playing soothing songs to aid digestion and harmony settled on the room.

With the tables cleared and coffee and port to keep them from starving, the host introduced the hypnotist, *The Mesmerizing Marvel,* who, despite the fine title and dinner suit, looked like he'd been performing for summer crowds on Scarborough pier.

The hypnotist asked for volunteers and at once got three, the young men of the couples. Ramsay grinned. *This is where young people really shine by keeping us wiser heads away from stage performances.*

Under the direction of the Marvel's mesmerizing spell, the young men acted out some foolish antics and the audience laughed heartily. While the applause drowned out her voice, Eliza whispered, "You know, he could…"

"No, he couldn't," Ramsay interjected, chuckling.

"You don't know what I was going to say," Eliza cried.

"We do," her companions replied, as one. "That he could hypnotize someone in the audience to murder someone over the coming days."

Eliza, though taken aback, gamely responded, "Well, he could."

The Marvel called for more volunteers and one of the young women volunteered. Ramsay felt his whole body go tense, hoping the hypnotist wouldn't ask her to do anything remotely risqué. He could almost feel Miss Forsythe bristling before the girl made it onto the stage.

True to the host's promise, however, the hypnotist kept the show at a level that Miss Forsythe seemed to accept for she applauded politely as the hypnotist finished his act and left the stage.

Their host returned and announced dramatically, with a wide sweep of his arms, "The Lord of Misrule."

Dressed in vivid red and black clothes and cloak, a giant of a man leapt onto the stage. He stood well over six feet tall and towered over Frederick Price-Ridley in a lordly fashion. On his head he wore a golden crown with red-tipped spikes and short but effective-looking red horns protruding from each side of his head. A lurid red mask covered the upper half of his face, like a hideous burn, and the lower part, a red beard and moustache that obscured his lips and chin.

"He really looks the part," Eliza said, approvingly. Her eyes shone, reflecting the reddish light that now illuminated the stage.

"A little too much for the Misses Forsythe and Dove," Ramsay said, nodding in the direction where they could see the two women scurrying from the room to a loud chorus of cheers and laughter from the young couples.

"How rude," Doris said.

"Well, those two are sanctimonious prigs, Mam. You must admit," Eliza responded.

"They just prefer older ideas, my dear," her father said.

Eliza rolled her eyes and returned to watching the Lord of Misrule make himself comfortable on an ornate throne that had been pushed onto the stage by a demonic minion who they saw, underneath his costume and mask, to be Alfred, the general 'workhorse' of the Manor.

"Silence!" The lord's voice boomed across the room. Instant silence!

It may only be a show, Ramsay thought, but the man has a presence that everyone in the audience feels. He'd startled even the boisterous young men into attention. *Maybe, the 'lord' was a Sergeant-Major in the army in his younger life.* His voice suggested exactly that.

The 'lord' told them that from this night on, until Twelfth Night, the rules would be what he said they were, and not those of mere mortals. Those who society placed high would be low, and those that society placed low would be raised high. Everything would be opposite of what the world thought right, and they would obey him or feel his wrath.

As the 'lord' continued speaking, Ramsay scanned the room, noting the rapt expressions on the faces of everyone, even of hardened old businessmen like Chambers. Ramsay shivered. It concerned him how easily, after drink, people could fall into this kind of trance-like obedience, first the hypnotist and now this nightmarish old character from the darker pages of history.

The 'lord' drew out from his clothes a small package and offered it to whoever would be first to kneel before him in worship. The room became silent until the young women whispered to their partners, and one rose to his feet and stumbled toward the stage.

"On your knees," the 'lord' commanded, and the young man shuffled forward to genuflect at the lord's feet.

"That's what too many cocktails before dinner and three or four bottles of wine between them at dinner, does to your brain," Colin whispered.

"Not to mention the brandies they've been knocking back since," Ramsay added. "I hope this doesn't get any worse."

"Pooh," Eliza said. "The Forsythe woman is gone. Everyone else can take a joke."

"Elizabeth," her mother said, anxiously.

The young man walked from the stage and handed the package to his fiancée who tore open the wrapper. As the young women guessed, the gift was a bottle of perfume and not a cheap one.

The 'lord' commanded everyone to rise. Ramsay didn't like to obey, but everyone else did, even frail old Mr. Redhill, so he joined them. There was no point spoiling the performance for everyone.

"Approach the stage," the 'lord' commanded.

They stood at the stage, a low dais not more than a foot high, intended only to stop dancers crashing into the band during dances, awaiting his next command.

"Bow to your 'lord'!"

For a moment, everyone froze, unsure, but slowly, one by one, they obeyed.

"You have accepted my rule openly and before the company. You will accept my punishment if you fail to obey." He paused, waiting for a reply.

One by one, once again, the company bowed in agreement and Ramsay found himself following their lead, though it disturbed him. The others may have drunk too much, but Ramsay knew he hadn't. He followed the order relying solely on their host's assurance of it just being a party game. He'd dismissed Eliza's theory the hypnotist might cause someone to murder. Ramsay feared this man actually could.

10

CHRISTMAS EVE BECOMES SINISTER

As they returned to their seats, the 'lord' commanded, "You! Stop!"

Everyone turned to look who he meant. Ramsay's heart sank. He was pointing at one of the young women, a tall slender girl in a dress that molded itself to her body when she moved. *If her fiancé objects, this could get ugly.*

"You want to be a model," the 'lord' said, his voice deep, threatening. "Then model for us, here, on the stage."

"She is a model," Eliza whispered. "I heard them talking earlier and the other one is an air hostess."

This made Ramsay feel a little better about the command, but he remained nervous until he watched the woman stalk across the stage without a shred of embarrassment or displeasure. Her fiancé, the same Marcus who'd been injured, watched with rapt attention. *'Smitten'* Ramsay thought. *I never knew what it really meant until now.*

Suddenly, Marcus came out of his trance, spun around, and spoke to Chambers. The older man grinned. It wasn't a pleasant expression. Marcus stepped forward before his companions restrained him.

"Enough!" roared the 'lord', his grotesque masked face pointing at Chambers and Marcus. "And you, young lady, be gone," he said to the model, waving her from the stage.

"Music," the 'lord' cried, and the band returned to the stage behind him. When they began playing, he swept off the stage in a flourish of cloak and smoke.

Ramsay and the Danesdales seated themselves.

"That could have been a nasty moment," Doris said. "Chambers really is a horrible man."

Something in the way Doris spoke disturbed Ramsay and he glanced at her. She stared at Chambers with an expression of total disgust.

"He is indeed," Ramsay agreed. "A coarse bully, I've no doubt. I'm only pleased we didn't hear what he said."

Couples began to dance, and the tension in the room slowly ebbed away. When they began playing a waltz, Ramsay invited Eliza to dance while he kept Chambers under observation. The man seemed to be tipsy; he'd never shown so much animation or willingness to speak to anyone as he did now. *There'll be tears before bedtime.*

"He keeps looking at my mam," Eliza said, when she observed Ramsay glancing at Chambers yet again.

"Does he?" Ramsay asked, puzzled. They turned in the dance and he looked again.

"Not tonight so far," Eliza replied. "But I've seen him looking when we've been moving around in the hotel."

"Maybe he just admires her," Ramsay said. "Your mother is an attractive woman."

"Mam doesn't like him," Eliza protested. "She stiffens whenever he's nearby. She hasn't said anything, but I notice it."

They turned again and Ramsay, for a moment, saw Doris

and Colin dancing some distance away. He also saw Doris observing Chambers with a hostile gaze.

Eliza continued, "This morning, Joyce had a devil of a job persuading the old biddies to stay until after Christmas."

"They're still upset about the nighttime antics of the young people?" Ramsay asked.

Eliza nodded, her eyes shining. "You should have heard Miss Forsythe. She is furious. It's all jealousy, of course. Can't stand other people enjoying themselves."

"Elizabeth..." her mother, who'd danced near enough to hear, began.

"What?" Eliza cried. "We have one or two of their kind in the village. You don't like them any more than I do."

"Here's our host," Ramsay interrupted before a new fight began.

Frederick Price-Ridley, looking distraught, asked for quiet and then said, "Ladies and gentlemen, I've just spoken to Mr. Chambers, Mr. Wright, and now Mr. Partington. They've all shaken hands on a promise of peace during this season of goodwill. I hope you'll all help them to keep that promise." He paused. If he expected rousing affirmation, he was disappointed.

"It's Chambers you need to persuade," Nick Pugachev told him. "He insulted almost everyone at our tables. Wright and Marcus only gave him back what he was dishing out and he didn't like it."

"Well," the host said, "that's all explained, and I'm assured it won't happen again. For tomorrow, Christmas Day, we'll have a bonfire outside where there'll be marshmallows to toast and hot mulled beer and wine to drink. The sleigh will begin taking passengers at ten, and with all this snow, the toboggans and skis I'm sure will be in great demand so get there early." He continued elaborating the

Dark Deeds on a White Christmas 71

events of the day leading up to the dinner in the evening before saying, "For tonight, the band will continue as long as you wish. Please forget the early unpleasantness and enjoy your evening in the true Christmas spirit."

When he'd gone, Colin asked, "Are we all staying?" The band began playing a medley of Beatles tunes and the young couples began rather self-consciously dancing.

"I must take Bracken out soon," Ramsay said. "I'll stay until then."

"I'll come too," Eliza said.

"You'll have to change," Ramsay retorted. Her evening gown, one of those gowns which so surprised him back in the autumn when they'd solved the smuggling mystery, had been what made him uneasy when the Lord of Misrule asked the model to parade before them. He knew Eliza would have been ordered to do the same, if the game continued.

"I'll go and change," Eliza said. "I'm guessing you won't want to be doing any dancing right now." She hurried away leaving Ramsay with her parents.

"Tom," Doris said, pleadingly, "you will look after Elizabeth, won't you?"

Unsure if she meant on this holiday or for the rest of his life, Ramsay said, "Eliza doesn't need me to look after her. She can look after herself."

Doris shook her head, unhappily. "It's herself she needs saving from."

"She's like most young people," Ramsay replied, reassuringly. "Certain they know everything and everyone older knows nothing. We didn't have a name for it when I was young, now we do – *teenager*."

Colin said, "Our concern is she wants to be a detective and she's too young to understand not everyone has patience with young people. She could be killed before she's grown wise enough for this line of work."

Ramsay understood their concern; he often felt like boxing Eliza's ears. "I will always do my best by Eliza, Doris. I promise."

Doris gave him an unconvincing smile. "We should go too, dear," she told her husband. "There's been enough excitement for one night."

* * *

Serious time passed before Eliza returned, dressed in thick winter clothes and a hooded duffel coat.

"Sorry it took so long," she said. "Mother wanted to lecture me about life. I think she's afraid I might have one."

"She's just worried you might fall into danger," Ramsay replied. "I'll get my coat and gloves, and we'll find Bracken."

Outside, a bright almost full moon tried to lighten the snow through thick rolling clouds. Giant flakes landed on them, splatting into shards of light.

"This is good snowman-making snow," Ramsay observed. "Wet enough to stick together."

"And snowballs," Eliza agreed, scooping up a handful from the lawn and throwing it at him.

He responded with a soft clump of snow, and they played happily for a minute or two until Bracken told them to stop. He didn't like his two best friends fighting.

Ramsay laughed as he re-assured Bracken all was well. Eliza wrapped an arm around Ramsay's waist and the three made their way over the lawn, leaving a trail in the unmarked snow.

"Something will happen, you know," Eliza said, snuggling closer as the cold seeped in through her clothes.

"It certainly looks like it might," Ramsay agreed, hugging her. "Only it won't affect us."

"We have to solve the murder when it happens," Eliza replied. "We're here on the spot. The police will need us because they can't get here. It's like a play or a film."

"Which is why you're imagining it," Ramsay said, depressingly. "In real life, everyone goes home grumbling about their holiday and that's the end of it." He spoke confidently and hoped what he said was true.

Eliza reached up on her tiptoes and kissed him. "You're so predictable. Lucky for you, I like that in a man."

For a moment, Ramsay wanted to tell her this must stop. The moment passed when Bracken sank out of sight into deeper snow.

"We must rescue Bracken," he said, letting go of Eliza and pushing his way into the snow. "Stay back," he told Eliza. "There's a dip in the ground here, and it's filled up."

When the snow reached his waist, he finally found the struggling Bracken, whose frantically wriggling paws scratched at Ramsay's knees. Ramsay bent forward, stretching down with his hands until he slid them under Bracken's wriggling body. "Out you come, Bracken, my lad," he said, lifting his friend out of the snow and placing him on his shoulder. Ramsay slowly pushed his way back to where Eliza waited and handed Bracken over.

Eliza took Bracken in her arms. "You're wet and cold, poor thing."

Ramsay recited, "And what will the robin do then, poor thing."

Eliza laughed, picking up the children's rhyme. "Yes, 'the north wind doth blow and we shall have snow'. And boy, have we got snow."

They returned to the Manor as the snowstorm grew

stronger. "We're definitely having a white Christmas this year," Ramsay said. "More snow than most of us would wish for."

Eliza laughed. "More fun for us, is how I'd put it." She paused, thought, and then continued, "And more pressure on the emotions of our already boiling fellow guests."

11

EARLY ON CHRISTMAS DAY

After their Christmas Breakfast, where Father Christmas, who looked a lot like the Lord of Misrule to Ramsay's eye, handed every guest a gift, Ramsay and the Danesdales returned to the Danesdale's room and exchanged gifts.

"I assume Father Christmas is someone local," Colin suggested. "Though he'll have had a cold walk here this morning. Have you seen how deep the snow is?"

Ramsay laughed. "I had a struggle persuading Bracken to go out at all this morning. He didn't like it either."

"The snow is taller than he is," Colin replied, "so it isn't surprising. Did you go down to the road?"

Ramsay nodded. "No one is coming from outside the dale today, you can be sure of that. We're on our own in a madhouse."

Doris shuddered. "You're as bad as Elizabeth, Tom. Stop it."

"Tom is only teasing, love," Colin said. "The bonfire was well lit when we left the breakfast room. Who's for toasted marshmallows?"

"Too early for me," Ramsay replied. "I never imbibe before midday."

"We're going skiing, Tom," Eliza said. "We'll have the hot mulled wine or hot chocolate after to warm us up."

"We are, are we?" Ramsay replied doubtfully, though he'd agreed to it during their walk the previous evening.

"You promised," Eliza reminded him.

"I did so we will, but you'll have to wheel me around in a chair when I finally break a leg," Ramsay retorted. "You forget, I have a doctor's note saying I'm an invalid."

"Doctors know nothing," Eliza replied. "You're fitter and stronger than all of us."

Skiing wasn't so hard this time. Their practice the day before had provided enough training to make it almost enjoyable, Ramsay thought, as they skied back to the bonfire to join the small crowd around it.

"Still on two legs, Tom," Colin said, grinning over his cup of hot chocolate.

"Just," Ramsay replied. "You two should join us. You soon get the hang of it."

"No fear," Colin and Doris said together. "We've had a sleigh ride, and we'll do another after our hot drinks. Then we're retiring inside to read."

"Is it a murder mystery again, Dad?" Eliza asked.

"It is. Lord Peter Wimsey."

"Soon, you'll be reading of our cases," Eliza told him. "If Tom doesn't write them, and he says he won't, then I will. How hard can it be, after all?"

"I'm sorry your father ever encouraged you to read his murder-mysteries, Elizabeth," Doris said. "I fear that's what has made you so keen to get mixed up in real ones."

"So, it's your fault, Colin," Ramsay said, grinning. "I

suspected some deep-rooted problem in Eliza's mind. It's probably psychological, everything is these days."

"Mystery books are how I know this is my future," Eliza responded, a little crossly. "I have a feel for these things. And it's how I know we'll be solving a case right here and very soon."

Ramsay didn't reply. It would only encourage her. He sipped his hot chocolate while looking at the group around the fire. The three young couples were drinking mulled drinks, cider, beer, or wine. The Chambers had hot drinks too, but of what, Ramsay couldn't tell from the opposite side of the bonfire. Wright was with Redhill, both drinking mulled beer. Ramsay knew that because he'd heard them ask for more. *It's lucky heating the drinks drives off the alcohol or Eliza might get her wish this afternoon.*

"They're not playing fair," Eliza whispered to Ramsay, nudging his arm to get his attention.

Ramsay looked and glimpsed a hip flask, presumably with alcohol in it, being passed between the young couples.

"That will lead to trouble," Ramsay said gloomily.

"Or excitement," Eliza retorted. "But we couldn't have that, could we?"

His attention was drawn away by the two elderly women arriving at the bonfire. They'd been given cups of hot chocolate and were soon engaged in conversation with Wright and Redhill. Ramsay was pleased they hadn't come to talk to him. They may be nice people, but their negativity about everything made them poor company.

A loud guffaw and giggling erupted among the three couples who handed their glasses to the barman and moved away from the fire. Ramsay and Eliza watched as they began rolling snowballs, preparatory to creating a snowman.

"It is good snow for snowmen," Ramsay said, approvingly.

"We should make one too," Eliza agreed.

As they watched the snowman being built, they soon saw why the couples couldn't stop giggling. The snowman became a snowwoman with a womanly figure and with accessories brought from the Manor, it made a recognizable model of Miss Dove.

"They aren't nice people," Colin exclaimed, horrified at the jeering laughter directed at the increasingly upset elderly woman.

The barman also understood the cruelty of the snowwoman and harsh words were spoken by both sides, the barman and young people, who protested it was just a joke.

Ramsay walked across the snow to confront them. "Take this down or change it into something harmless. Miss Dove's done nothing to warrant this treatment."

For a moment the young men eyed Ramsay speculatively. Then Nick Pugachev said, shrugging, "You're right. She's a harmless creature, unlike her friend."

With this, Ramsay returned to his group who watched the snowwoman soon become a generic snowman, with all the usual accessories; a carrot nose, coal for eyes, and an old pipe to match his scarf and flat cap.

However, the two elderly ladies, Miss Dove in tears, had already left the bonfire, and the remaining guests and barman were grimly silent. The young people took the hint and left to return to the toboggan hill.

"I knew that drink would cause trouble," Ramsay said, when they'd gone. "I only hope it doesn't cause more as the day wears on."

"I'm glad they can't go shooting," Doris added. "Who knows what might have happened."

"Here's hoping Chambers and Wright don't get belligerent as well," Colin said. "Look at the way Wright is staring at him."

Ramsay looked. "I say we drink up and we all go for a sleigh ride. That way, if they do, I don't have to get between them."

"And we'll be back to solve the murder," Eliza said. Her eyes blazed with excitement.

"It won't take much solving," Ramsay retorted. "Two men drink too much, and one hits and kills the other. It happens all too often, late every Saturday night up and down the country."

"But *why* does one of them kill the other?" Eliza asked, as they began walking toward the sleigh ride station. "That's the story here and we don't know it. You say manslaughter or maybe accidental death, but it could be murder."

Ramsay nodded. Normally, he'd find her ghoulish passion amusing, but this time she was too near the truth.

On their return from the sleigh ride, they found Wright and Redhill had gone inside and the Chambers still at the bonfire. They looked unhappy, but they always did. Beside them stood the Phillipsons who looked equally glum.

"The sleigh ride is free," Ramsay told them, as they waited for their hot drinks to be poured.

The three Chambers looked at him as if he'd said something rude. Ramsay couldn't make sense of them at all, but Phillipson nodded, saying, "Maybe we should. What say you, Julia?"

His wife mumbled what must have been agreement for they began to walk.

"Is there room for five in the sleigh?" Chambers asked.

"Four," his son said. "I'm not going."

"Come with us, Gregory," his mother pleaded, but he shook his head, drained his glass, and left for the hotel.

The Chambers and Phillipsons made their way to the sleigh.

"This might be it," Eliza cried. She fidgeted in her excitement.

"Still no murder," Ramsay replied. He watched the four unhappy people walking across the snowy lawn and noticed Mrs. Phillipson already closer to Chambers who was walking some way behind his wife. Phillipson stopped, turned, and the group came together again. *I hate to admit it, but I can't help thinking Eliza is going to be proved right sometime over these next days. There's too much anger swirling around. Maybe if the other guests had arrived it might have been different.*

Ramsay and Eliza decided on toboggans for the rest of the day. After exchanging their skis and retrieving Bracken, who brought his friends, Larry, Barry, and Harry, they set off for the hill.

For a time, all went well. The young people apparently held no grudge at Ramsay's earlier interference, and they all enjoyed racing down the hill with the dogs chasing after them.

The first unpleasant moment came when the Pugachevs' toboggan, on reaching the bottom of the hill, slammed into Marcus and Sarah's sled as they pulled it back to the hill. Marcus furiously reminded the Pugachevs of his wounded arm.

The two men glared at each other, fists clenched, before Pugachev said, "Sorry, it was an accident." As no one was hurt, the tension slipped away, and the two couples towed their sleds up the hill talking amiably.

Lunchtime came on. Marcus and the other young man,

Oliver, using their coat belts, hitched Barry and Harry to their sleds and, standing on the back of the toboggans yelling 'mush', they headed home. However, Larry and Bracken also wanted to join in the fun and the two amateur sled dogs swerved toward each other, the sleds followed, crashed into each other, and the two young men landed on top of their fiancées. Sarah let out a blood-curdling scream, which sent Ramsay and Eliza racing to the rescue.

The young woman lay crying in the snow while Marcus offered copious apologies in desperation.

"Never mind that," Ramsay snapped. "Get back to the Manor and ask for medical help."

"There isn't a doctor," Nick Pugachev reminded him.

"Someone will know First Aid. Meanwhile, we must make Sarah as comfortable as we can until we know she can be moved."

Marcus and Oliver set off running and Ramsay and Eliza tried to quiet Sarah. Before help arrived, however, she sat up by herself and claimed she could climb onto the toboggan if someone would pull her back to the Manor. Ramsay agreed and helped her slide onto the sled.

"Shuffle up and lie down," Ramsay said, when she didn't move further. "That way you won't lose your balance and fall off when we move."

Sarah did as she was asked, holding her right arm across her chest with the left hand. Ramsay began tugging the sled, while the others towed the remaining sleds. With the subdued dogs walking alongside, Ramsay crossed the lawn as carefully as he could manage it.

As they approached the Manor, Marcus, Oliver, and Alfred came out of the terrace doors.

"Alfred does everything here," Eliza whispered, giggling.

Alfred, it transpired, had some First Aid, and he claimed

looking after animals also gave him more insight than anything he'd been taught.

Indoors, his quick examination made him grimace. "It's best we wait until Dr. Normanton gets here. He only lives along the main street, and he's been sent for."

"You think her collarbone is broken?" Ramsay asked. His own First Aid training in the Force not completely forgotten.

"It might be, or she might just be bruised," Alfred said. "Best the doctor checks."

By now the Price-Ridleys had arrived, and they looked exactly how Ramsay felt. They questioned the young men who, shamefacedly, blamed the dogs at first. Only when Frederick told them they'd no business hitching dogs to the sleds, did they admit some error on their part.

Ramsay found himself liking the young couples less and less with every passing hour. They seemed everything spoiled, wealthy young people were believed to be.

"It's time for lunch," Ramsay reminded everyone. "We should let Alfred and the doctor decide what's best from here."

A gramophone played tunes from operettas as they ate. The band presumably lived in the village and were, consequently, home enjoying Christmas Day with their own families. Their host appeared during dessert to announce the doctor proclaimed Miss Onslow to be only badly bruised so there'd be no disruption to anyone's enjoyment of the day. After reminding them of the evening's entertainments, he left.

"I'm so glad," Doris said when he'd gone, and people began talking again. "They might have had to airlift her out of here, and I never trust those helicopter things."

"You wouldn't be in it, Mam," Eliza replied. "And I

imagine she'd be happy to know she was being taken to proper medical attention."

Doris's expression suggested she might take issue with this so Ramsay asked, "What shall we do this afternoon? I'm too tired to ski, and the accident has made me wary of toboggans."

"I brought Dad's old camera," Eliza said. "Why don't we walk out, away from the disturbed snow, and take photos? I think we might get spectacular shots of snow on the trees and hills."

"I like that," Ramsay replied, "and so will Bracken. What about you, Doris? Colin?"

Eliza's parents looked at each other before Colin said, "We're going to read."

Warmly dressed, and with Bracken for company, Ramsay and Eliza left the Manor, cameras in hand.

"Why not start in the village," Ramsay suggested. "Snow on the roofs, walls, and mailbox will all make great photos."

They returned later, cold and tired, after finishing their reels of film, to warm themselves at the bonfire. The early winter night was already drawing in and the fire showed itself at its best, lighting the faces of everyone around it, which appeared to be all the guests except the two elderly women.

"The Misses Forsythe and Dove haven't forgiven us for this morning's offense," Ramsay muttered to Eliza.

"No one will miss them," Eliza said. "You must give and take at Christmas. They're the sort who would ban it if they could."

Ramsay and Eliza joined Doris and Colin who were sipping mulled cider and trying to toast marshmallows. The one on Colin's fork slipped off into the flames and burned brightly for a moment as they watched.

"Have you actually eaten one yet?" Eliza teased her father.

"One," he replied, "and I've given the fire god about a dozen."

"Me too," Doris said, ruefully. "I don't see how anyone makes this work consistently."

Ramsay brought himself and Eliza hot mulled cider and they tried their hand at marshmallow toasting using Doris and Colin's forks. They had no more success.

"Your photography went well?" Colin asked.

"Mine did," Eliza replied, smiling. "I'm not sure Tom knows one end of a camera from another. It will have to be me who takes our crime scene photos."

Ramsay grinned, sheepishly. "It's true. I didn't have much time for taking pictures when I worked." A pang of regret made him grimace. That was only half true. The last photos he'd taken were of his wife and children the summer before the bombs hit their home. The photos still existed somewhere in his house, but it hurt too much to look at them.

"You see now why he needs me on his investigations," Eliza said. "I'm the money manager and the technical specialist. He'd be lost without me."

"Is this true, Tom?" Doris asked.

Ramsay laughed. "Nobody paid us for solving the smuggling murder, and we didn't take any photos, but other than that, I suppose, I could almost agree."

"We'll need my photos on this case," Eliza said.

"You used all your film, remember," Ramsay retorted.

"I used the film I took with me today. I've kept some for the case."

Ramsay sighed and shook his head in disbelief. She

really was convinced there would be a murder or some such crime and nothing would change her mind.

"Be careful what you wish for, Elizabeth," her mother said, seriously. "It may come true."

Their host joined them before Eliza could reply. He reminded them of the evening's entertainments, the hypnotist, the Lord of Misrule, and the live band.

As the host left the circle of light from the fire, heading back into the darkness between it and the terrace doors, Doris turned to the others and said, "I wish they hadn't resurrected that Lord of Misrule. I don't mind admitting, he frightens me."

12

CHRISTMAS DINNER AND MURDER

Ramsay, Eliza, Bracken, and the Danesdales entered the ballroom together for the pre-dinner cocktails. Everyone was assembled, even the Misses Forsythe and Dove. Brightly lit chandeliers twinkled, and their light reflected the colors of the looping garlands strung across the ceiling. Mirrors on the walls, edged with holly, also reflected the lights making the room dazzle the eye.

"It must be such a disappointment to the Price-Ridleys," Colin said, repeating his earlier thought. "They've gone to so much trouble and all for what? A dozen people who look lost among such magnificence."

Ramsay agreed, adding, "And many of those here aren't the people to enjoy it all." He nodded to the two elderly ladies who seemed to be tut-tutting without moving their lips.

"Nor the Hooray Henrys who only have eyes for the bar," Doris said, pointing at the couples lounging there and gulping down everything the barman handed them.

"You can't say the Chambers or Phillipsons are exactly thrilled either," Eliza added, "or the two old men, Wright and Redhill. In fact, unless we show our appreciation, no one will."

The band began playing a selection of music, old standards and some of the more melodic songs of the day. Nick Pugachev began singing to *I'm Dreaming of a White Christmas* when the band began adding more Christmas themed tunes into the set. The other young people joined in and Eliza too. When none of her party, or the others in the room, joined in, Eliza walked across to the bar and sang with the impromptu choir who welcomed her with broad smiles and unsteady hugs.

"They've had too much to drink already," Colin said.

Ramsay nodded. "Aye, but it is Christmas."

"I hope Eliza will be sensible," Doris said, anxiously. "She's not used to strong drink."

"It will be good for her to join in with people her own age," Ramsay replied. "After all, it can't be much fun at nineteen hanging around with older people. We aren't any of us partygoers."

"Eliza can get carried away with things," Colin explained. "That's why we're happy she's taken to you. We've removed her from police custody more than once."

"You mean her donkey protest?"

"That and others," Doris said. "She's easily led by what people tell her is a good cause."

"I think we're safe here," Ramsay said, smiling. "After all, none of them can leave the hotel. All they'll have is a bad headache and embarrassing memories in the morning."

The Danesdales didn't look convinced. Ramsay sighed inwardly. *The young people are singing Christmas songs, what harm can there be in that?*

The singing ended when Frederick introduced Mesmerizing Marvel, the hypnotist. After the previous evening's fun, the younger crowd eagerly volunteered to take part and act out childish scenes at his command.

"This is the embarrassing memory part you mentioned," Colin whispered.

Ramsay nodded, while Doris replied, "They aren't hypnotized, they're drunk."

Mesmerizing Mike ended his show, and the host announced dinner would be served as soon as everyone became seated in the dining room.

The candle-lit dining room seemed dark after the ballroom. On the dais, suffused by a subdued red glow, the Lord of Misrule sat, already enthroned. *I hope nothing happens to drive the two old ladies away.*

Eliza didn't join Ramsay and her parents. She sat with her new friends where the party was in full flight. Ramsay couldn't help but feel he too would like to be twenty again.

The first course arrived, was eaten, and cleared away before the 'lord' made his first new command, ordering Eliza to approach his throne and kneel, which she did without hesitation. He spoke quietly to her, and she responded.

"My devotee demands Tom Ramsay sing *The Skye Boat Song*," the 'lord' demanded, staring at Ramsay.

Silently cursing Eliza, Ramsay decided to comply because the consequences of not doing so would likely be worse. Although he enjoyed singing for himself, and Eliza, he never sang in public. He took a gulp of his Planters Punch and sang.

Eliza, released from her place on the dais, smiled sweetly at him as she returned to her spot. The meal continued, enlivened by similarly harmless impositions, which did indeed, in Ramsay's mind, create a livelier atmosphere.

Dark Deeds on a White Christmas 89

As the servers removed the last dishes, the 'lord' announced there would be games.

"Sardines," cried the too merry, flushed, Paul Chambers, leering at Julia Phillipson. Loud cries of 'yay' and 'nay' ensued until the 'lord' held up his hand and shook his head, much to Ramsay's relief. It was too soon for such intimate contact between barely introduced bodies.

"Charades," the 'lord' announced, "with only film or book titles. We're all adults here, you can be creative."

The couples at once set to whispering until the quieter two, Oliver and Celina, volunteered to go first. The 'lord' invited them to the stage, and they began.

Miss Forsythe stood and, beckoning Miss Dove, walked from the room to the wild cheering of the younger people and, Ramsay noted sadly, Eliza.

While the charades acted out became mildly risqué, they didn't go beyond what an adult audience would tolerate, and they ended when all three couples finished playing out their scenes and no one else joined in. The 'lord' surveyed his audience as if determining what they would accept before announcing Hot Cockles. This old parlor game, common enough when Ramsay had been a child, was too old for the young people to know. As Ramsay had guessed, they demanded to be told the rules.

The 'lord' explained. "One at a time, you will be blindfolded with your hands behind your back. Someone will slap your hands with their hand. You must guess who slapped you to win."

The young people looked puzzled until Sarah leaned forward and started whispering. Ramsay wished he could hear because their excitement at what she said was worrying. He knew they'd mischief in mind. He only wished Eliza didn't seem as excited as the rest of them.

The 'lord' pointed at Julia Phillipson and cried, "You first."

Obediently, Julia rose and approached the dais where she waited for further instructions. The 'lord' signaled a band member to place a chair in front of the woman and blindfold her. With this done, Julia was ordered to bend forward, place one hand on the chair and the other, open, behind her back.

The 'lord' pointed at Nick Pugachev and then at the waiting Julia. Pugachev walked forward and slapped Julia's hand. She guessed wrongly her husband had slapped her, and after being released, returned to her seat.

Sarah's hand shot in the air and, having a willing victim, the 'lord' ordered her to the front. When she was prepared, he signaled Marcus to approach. Ramsay knew at once what they'd been giggling about. Marcus slapped Sarah's behind, and all the young people cheered and applauded.

The 'lord' grinned. His makeup shone in the red light, making it a hideous leer. He chose Oliver for the next victim and on the game went until all the willing volunteers had had a turn. None of the older guests chose to have that, or any other, trick played on them.

With Hot Cockles finished, and the hotel almost in darkness, the 'lord' called for balloons to be brought to the stage. With a bag full of balloons placed before him, he ordered the guests to form two lines facing each other, one of men and one of women. He then explained the game. The men and women must pass a balloon between them using only their chin and chest. Each couple would continue until they dropped the balloon. The winners would be the two people still going when the others dropped out.

Eliza quickly moved to be with Ramsay. Unfortunately, their difference in heights led to them losing their balloon before Eliza enjoyed all the opportunity of affection she'd hoped for.

With the balloon game over, a game of Hide and Seek began, which left the room empty but for the 'lord', Ramsay, Marcus and Sarah, who were the 'Seekers', and the Danesdales. Even the two older men, Wright and Redhill, weren't in their seats. Gone to their beds, Ramsay thought.

"I'm going to the ladies' room," Doris told Colin. "I'll be right back."

Ramsay would have taken this as an excuse to retire to his own bed but his uneasiness about Eliza kept him glued to his seat. He and Colin sat, listening to the music, and watching the Lord of Misrule talking casually with the band leader and, in consequence, losing all his air of menace.

Ramsay observed Frederick Price-Ridley enter the room, look about, see Ramsay, and make straight for him. Ramsay's heart sank with a thud. His worst fears had been realized. The couples had played some unpleasant trick on Eliza, and he was needed.

Their host arrived at the table and spoke quietly. "Mr. Ramsay, you're a retired police officer, you said. You must come at once. We have a situation that needs to be managed, and you are best suited to do that." He turned to Colin and said, "You should come too, Mr. Danesdale. It concerns your wife."

"What?" Colin cried, too loudly.

"Quiet," Frederick hissed, waving down Colin's agitation. "She's not harmed, and I don't want to alarm everyone or have them come near her."

13

A BODY ON CHRISTMAS DAY

THE THREE MEN left the room together and, once clear of the room, hurried down the dark corridor that led to the kitchen. A rope had been hastily strung across the corridor, separating them from a dark bulky shadow on the floor ahead with Alfred guarding the shape. They stopped dead to make sense of what they saw.

"It's Mr. Chambers," Frederick explained. "He's been stabbed. I have the remaining staff rounding up the guests and taking them back to the dining room. You may want to talk to them, Mr. Ramsay."

Ramsay agreed he would and stepped over the rope to examine the body. Chambers lay on his back with a single stab wound to his chest. No knife could be seen. There was more blood than he'd have expected, which suggested Chambers didn't die immediately. Partial footprints in blood beside the body led toward the kitchen in a shaky trail.

"Who found the body?" Ramsay asked Frederick.

"Mrs. Danesdale, or at least, she was with the body when Ellen, one of our kitchen maids, came out and found them both."

"Where is Doris?" Colin demanded.

"She's in the kitchen," Frederick told him. "We thought it best she doesn't wander the hotel covered in blood. She seems dazed by it all."

"I must go to her," Colin cried, pushing past Frederick.

"Only with Mr. Ramsay," Frederick said, restraining him. "This will take careful handling."

The three made their way past the body, avoiding the scene, and entered the brightly lit kitchen where Doris sat on a stool with a woman, Ellen presumably, standing beside her. Doris held a bloodied steak knife.

Colin stepped forward but Ramsay intervened. "We must do this carefully, Colin. Doris may have implicated herself in a murder."

Seeing Colin, Doris began to rise. Ellen stepped forward and whispered into her ear. Doris stared at the knife in her hand, as if seeing it for the first time, before crying out and letting it go. It fell to the floor and lay still.

Ramsay and Colin approached her. Ramsay picked up the knife using his handkerchief, while Colin put his arm around Doris's shoulders.

"I didn't do it, Colin," Doris whispered.

"Of course, you didn't," Colin replied. "Nobody could think you did."

Ramsay heard this but didn't say anything. *The police will immediately think she did. She was holding the knife and covered in blood, what else could they think?*

"Frederick," Ramsay said, turning to the owner, "is the photographer still in the hotel?"

"Yes. You think we need photos?"

"I know we do," Ramsay said. "We need the doctor back too."

"I've phoned for him," Frederick said. "I haven't yet phoned the police."

"Then do that right away," Ramsay replied. "I'll talk to them. I'd like Inspector Baldock to investigate, if he's available."

"Is he a friend?"

Ramsay shook his head. "No, but we worked together on the murder case in Robin Hood's Bay and, while we don't get along personally, we do as investigators."

"You will investigate then?" Frederick asked. "I'll pay for your services. You were here. You know what has gone on. The police won't understand, I fear."

Eliza will be pleased, Ramsay thought, but he said, "We will. My assistant, Eliza, and I have been watching and, I must say, with some foreboding, the events of the past days."

"Oh. I thought Eliza was your girlfriend," Frederick said, surprised.

Ramsay smiled. "We are very close, but I'm too old for that nonsense now."

Frederick shook his head in disbelief. "I'll go and phone the police and call for you when I have them on the line."

Ramsay wrapped the knife carefully in a clean napkin and placed it in his pocket. A quick look at Doris's blank expression told him she wouldn't be able to give clear answers for some time.

"Ellen, it is Ellen, isn't it?" Ramsay began, speaking to the woman who was staying close by Doris.

"It is, sir."

"What did you see or hear as you left the kitchen?" Ramsay asked.

"I didn't hear anything, and the corridor was dark after the kitchen's bright lights, so I almost fell over Mrs. Danesdale as I began walking along the corridor to the dining room. I intended to remove anything the guests might have finished with, now that they were all playing games."

"And then?"

"I saw Mrs. Danesdale crouching over the body of a man. I couldn't see who at that moment. She turned and looked up at me. She had a knife in her hand. One of our steak knives, which is odd because they weren't in use tonight. Turkey doesn't warrant such blades."

"Did she say anything?"

Ellen shook her head. "No, sir, nothing. Then I saw her chin, neck, and dress were stained with blood. It gave me quite a turn." She paused, waiting for his next question.

"What did you say or do?"

"I bent closer to look at the body. It was Mr. Chambers, and he looked dead. Mrs. Danesdale still held the knife, so I didn't like to go closer."

"You thought she'd stabbed him?"

"I don't know that I did, sir. She looked horror-struck. If she did, it might have been an accident or maybe self-defense. He was a nasty man."

"And then?"

"I didn't want to upset her, so I backed away and said I'd go for help. I'm not sure she heard me because she didn't say anything; she just looked at me, lost, like."

"And you found someone?"

Ellen nodded. "Yes, sir. I found Doreen and told her to find Alfred. He came to help."

Good old dependable Alfred. Why was he nearby? Because he does everything around here is why. I'll have to alert Baldock about that or they'll suspect him. "And then?"

"Alfred helped Mrs. Danesdale to her feet and into the

kitchen. He asked me to stay with her and went to find the owner," Ellen replied.

"Did Mrs. Danesdale say anything while you waited with her?"

Again, Ellen shook her head. "Not a word. She's just sat there like she is now. Shock, I suppose."

"Aye, very likely," Ramsay replied. "The doctor will tell us more when he arrives, which I hope will be soon. Meanwhile, maybe you would make a cup of tea, strong, hot, and very sweet. That may revive Mrs. Danesdale."

"I don't like to leave Mrs. Danesdale, sir," Ellen replied, firmly. "Alfred said I should stay in case she needs help. He knows First Aid, you see."

"You will be just there," Ramsay pointed to the stove, "and Colin and I will stay right here beside Mrs. Danesdale. She won't be alone or out of your sight."

Ellen accepted that and, without taking her eyes off Doris or the two men, began making tea. Before the kettle boiled, Frederick and the village doctor arrived in the kitchen.

Ramsay was introduced to the doctor and asked, "Have you seen the body?"

The doctor nodded.

"What did you think?" Ramsay pressed him.

"We should talk somewhere quieter, Inspector."

"I'm retired now," Ramsay replied, "but you're right. While you examine Mrs. Danesdale, I'll go and find the others. Some of those playing Hide and Seek may have heard or seen something." He left the kitchen and made his way back to the dining room, where he found Alfred watching the assembled company. Ramsay smiled. Alfred reminded him of sheepdogs watching the flock when they'd been corralled into their pen. *I need Bracken here.*

"Have you found them all, Alfred?"

"I have, sir. Though they're getting restive. They'll have to be told something soon," Alfred replied.

"I'll tell them now," Ramsay told him. He stepped into the center of the room and briefly outlined what had happened, being careful not to give any details. He finished by saying, "As many of you know, before my recent retirement I was a police inspector. Mr. Price-Ridley has asked me to manage affairs until the police get here, which may be a day or so." He paused to see if there were any objections raised. There wasn't and he continued, "I'd like any of you who may have seen or heard anything this evening that might have a bearing on this tragedy to come forward and give the details to me."

No one spoke. Ramsay continued, "Many of you will have been hiding near the entrance to the kitchen in the past thirty minutes. Didn't anything sound odd to you?"

Oliver said, "I was near there, but I only heard the clattering of crockery and pans and people talking. Nothing that sounded like someone dying."

There was a murmur of assent from others.

Ramsay looked at each of them slowly, trying to elicit a response that never came. "Very well. It's late. Go back to your rooms and lock the doors. If this is murder, the murderer may not believe you all saw and heard nothing. Remember, you may not have seen them or not known you'd seen the murderer, but the murderer may have seen you. I repeat, lock your doors and don't leave your rooms until morning."

Alfred invited them to leave by a route that didn't take them past the kitchen corridor. As they filed past Ramsay, he heard the fiancées demanding male protection for the night. He smiled. *Never let a good crisis go to waste.*

"What about us?" the band leader asked.

"I suggest you return home together," Ramsay said. "I don't think anyone who remained in the dining room is in any danger, but I can't know for certain. I hope the police will be here tomorrow so be prepared for them to interview you. If they can't be here, I or my assistant, Miss Danesdale, will be around to take your statements. The same goes for you, Lord of Misrule."

The 'lord' nodded unhappily. "I told Mr. Price-Ridley this wasn't a good idea. I wish I'd never taken him up on it."

"Why did you then?" Ramsay asked.

"For the money, of course," the man replied. "The Forestry Commission's pay isn't so grand I could turn down the chance of an extra few bob."

"More than a few shillings over Christmas, I imagine," Ramsay said, grinning.

"Aye, but I'm not married so no kids," the man replied, "and there's nought much to do around here at Christmas if you don't."

"You played the part really well," Ramsay replied. "Unfortunately, your role may be thought to have a bearing on this. Go home for now. We'll talk tomorrow."

"I won't be here tomorrow," the man said. "I told the boss a few minutes ago."

Ramsay nodded, grimly. "I understand. How did he take it?"

"I think he were relieved," the man replied. "Me quitting, I mean. I think he'd already decided it couldn't go on."

"I, or the police, will still want to interview you," Ramsay said. "Good night."

When they were gone, Ramsay made his way to the room where the Labs and Bracken were resting happily among the straw. Ramsay opened the gate and he and

Bracken returned to the body and the doctor. "Well?" Ramsay asked.

With the building quiet, the doctor felt able to speak more freely. "This doesn't look well for Mrs. Danesdale, but he was almost certainly alive when she found him. He died when she removed the knife."

"But did she thrust it into him?" Ramsay asked.

"It's hard to say for certain," the doctor replied. "It slid between his ribs so it wouldn't need a lot of force, but she wouldn't know that, would she. A second question is, did she know removing the knife would open the wound and cause him to bleed out. It gushed out so much, she's covered in it."

Ramsay nodded, unhappily. He'd thought the same. "Anything else?"

"He may have spoken," the doctor said. "There's blood around his mouth which suggests maybe heavy breathing or speaking."

"Has she said anything to you?"

"Nothing. She's in deep shock. I've given her a sedative, and Ellen and Mr. Danesdale are taking her to her room."

"Her husband and daughter can keep watch tonight," Ramsay said. "She may be better in the morning."

"She'll likely need longer, Inspector. You must be prepared for that. Anyway, I bid you goodnight. I'm away to my own bed, though it'll be a wild walk to get there." The doctor turned away, fastening his overcoat against the weather outside.

Ramsay returned to the place where the body lay, and Frederick and Alfred were waiting.

"Do you have any chalk to mark the location?" Ramsay asked them.

Alfred nodded and hurried away. As he did, Ramsay

urged Bracken to take the victim's scent and follow it. As he expected, the victim came from the dining room to this dark part of the corridor. He and Bracken returned to the body. Bracken picked up a new scent, and he headed for the kitchen. Alfred returned, and Ramsay stopped Bracken. "In a moment," he told his friend. "For now, I have to direct operations."

Speaking to Alfred, Ramsay said, "We'll put him in the cold storage room until the police and ambulance arrive. It's not ideal, but we can't leave him here. For now, would you chalk out his silhouette before we move him."

Alfred nodded and crouched down. He drew a line closely around the body. Ramsay watched, as he'd done many times before on murder investigations.

"The police can't get here tonight," Frederick replied. "I spoke to the station in Scarborough and asked for Inspector Baldock, as you suggested. When they got him to the phone, he said you were to take charge until he, or another officer, arrived but that wouldn't be until the roads were cleared tomorrow."

"Then we must do the best we can. Photographer?"

Frederick nodded. "I've asked the photographer to join us. He should be here soon."

The photographer arrived almost as Frederick finished speaking. Ramsay directed him in what photos he and the police would want to record the scene, all the while thinking how upset Eliza would be in the morning when she learned her photography skills weren't needed.

When the photographer was finished, and Ramsay had recorded as many notes as he thought necessary, Alfred and Ramsay carried the body to the cold room. Frederick cleared space for it away from the food.

"Our guests must know we took care their food wasn't touched," Frederick explained, anxiously.

"You don't think the murder may be their biggest concern?" Ramsay asked, grimly amused.

"Quite frankly, Inspector," Frederick replied, "I don't. But the two together would be too much."

This jaundiced view of human nature rather accorded with Ramsay's experience down the years, and it didn't surprise him. Perhaps everyone who worked closely with the public observed the same strange reactions people had to horror.

"Now we wait for the police," Ramsay said. "Meanwhile, I'll take one last look at the scene before I turn in."

With the others gone, Ramsay took Bracken back to where the body lay and said, "Now, what did your nose find before?"

Bracken followed a scent he knew well from the body to the kitchen, walking right up to the chair where Doris had been sitting.

"Sadly, that doesn't help, Bracken," Ramsay said. "Anything more?"

They returned to the silhouette on the floor before Ramsay said, "I'm an idiot. Here Bracken, what does this tell you?" He took the knife from his pocket, unwrapped the handkerchief, and let Bracken sniff it.

Once again, Bracken took him to the chair in the kitchen, and Ramsay's heart sank. *It really is Doris,* he thought.

They returned to the corridor, but this time, Bracken turned away from the silhouette and trotted farther along the corridor before stopping at the junction with the walkway to the outside rooms, sniffing, and returning to the silhouette.

"Someone else was here?" Ramsay asked.

Bracken nodded. Unfortunately, Ramsay could only infer that meant 'yes', and he could only surmise who, as they went to his room to sleep. *Could it be Alfred? Or Ellen? Or Doreen? Or the doctor? Or the murderer?*

14

AFTERMATH – BOXING DAY, DECEMBER 26

Early next morning, long before the sun rose, Ramsay knocked on the door of the Danesdales room. Eliza opened it. He asked after Doris, and then told Eliza of all that had happened the previous evening after the body was found. His assumption she wouldn't be pleased that he'd used the hotel photographer, when he knew she'd kept film especially for this eventuality, proved to be correct.

"You still have lots of scope for your talents," Ramsay replied, in answer to her protests. "We need photos of the knife, the corridor, the place your mother sat last night, the body in the cold store, and any new evidence we find."

"I'll get my camera and we'll start now," Eliza said, letting him into the room to wait.

The hotel was as silent as the grave as they carefully examined the areas Ramsay had mentioned.

"We need to know everyone's location and why Chambers waited here in the corridor," Eliza said, staring at the chalk outline on the floor.

"We'll interview everyone when they're up, but we might learn a lot just by searching before the staff arrives and starts making breakfast. For instance, how did the knife get out here from the kitchen?"

"When you think about that," Eliza replied, "it looks like a kitchen worker might have done it. A guest would be seen walking in, taking a knife, and walking out."

"It may have been taken earlier," Ramsay said. "After all, there'd been steak on the previous evening's menu."

"Then someone meant to murder him," Eliza cried. "It wasn't a chance, unpleasant encounter in a dark corridor."

"Maybe," Ramsay said, placidly. "I'm just saying we can't rule anyone out yet."

"Mam has no reason to kill him, and she didn't have steak that night," Eliza pointed out.

"We must keep an open mind," Ramsay said. "If it's seen we're diverting suspicion from your mother, we'll lose our ability to help." He couldn't forget that Colin said Doris disliked Chambers for something that had happened in the past. *Maybe that something happened again?*

"I'm just saying," Eliza retorted. "Now where do we start?"

"The kitchen and the steak knives," Ramsay replied, leading the way into the room. The steak knives, matching the one he had still wrapped in his pocket, weren't as far from the door as he'd have liked. In a busy moment, someone could have seen them through the door windows, stepped inside and out again without being seen.

As they headed back to the corridor, Eliza asked, "You stayed in the dining room. Who was there with you?"

Ramsay showed her his notebook. "I've noted all I can be sure of. If I'd known about the murder, I'd have taken more notice. Who did you see looking for hiding places?"

"I was with the two couples when we left the room, but they went to hide together," Eliza replied. "Only the

Pugachevs came toward the kitchen, I think. Oh, and I saw Wright heading toward the lobby, presumably returning to his room."

"He and Redhill left together," Ramsay remembered. "You didn't see Redhill?"

Eliza frowned in concentration. "No, I didn't. But there's a Gents beside the lobby. Maybe he went in there."

"Probably," Ramsay said. "Bracken and I will look in there. You find any hiding places you know of. The murderer found the perfect occasion to act. I wonder if they knew Hide and Seek would be chosen? Did they suggest it?"

"Marcus and Sarah shouted it out to the Lord of Misrule," Eliza remembered. "I don't think they wanted anything other than a place to cuddle up close and cock another snook at the Miss Forsythes of this world."

Ramsay laughed. "Then the Lord of Misrule treated them as they deserved by making them the seekers."

Eliza smiled. "That's what the others said too."

"The two old ladies had left the room by then," Ramsay reminded her, "but there's another possible culprit – Miss Forsythe."

"What?" Eliza cried. "Why?"

"When she was complaining to Joyce the other morning," Ramsay replied, "Chambers said something to her. I don't know what, but it must have been offensive; it made her furious. Not angry like we've seen her over the late-night shenanigans but seriously angry. Murderous, even."

"But still," Eliza retorted. "Miss Forsythe?"

"You shouldn't judge a book by its cover," Ramsay said. "Not so long ago, all kinds of people did things in the war you wouldn't believe."

"If you say so," Eliza replied, disbelievingly, as she

walked off to begin hunting for possible hiding places near the crime scene.

Ramsay looked in the Gents toilets and, as he'd expected, saw nothing to suggest Redhill had, or had not, been there. "What do you say, Bracken?"

Bracken shook his head, leaving Ramsay to wonder if that meant he didn't think anyone connected with the body had been in there or he was just searching for a scent.

They returned to the door and Ramsay estimated the distance from the door to the body and the kitchen. *Can a frail, elderly man like Redhill cover that distance, stab someone, and get away unseen?* He thought not.

Another thought came to him. *What was Doris doing there? She went to the Ladies Room but where the body lay wasn't on the route.* He didn't like the place this thought took him.

When he arrived back at the kitchen door where Eliza waited, she demanded, "Well?"

"Well, yourself," Ramsay retorted. "What did you find?"

"Nothing. And you?"

"The same. However, I'll add both Wright and Redhill to the list of possible suspects until we can confirm otherwise."

"I wish we knew exactly when he died," Eliza said.

"Did you note the time when you saw people?"

Eliza frowned. "You're right. I didn't, so knowing when he died wouldn't help at all."

"Anyway, the doctor said he may have lived for some minutes after being stabbed. We don't know for sure when he was stabbed, or even where," Ramsay finished, as another idea presented itself. "We need to look for small blood spots in the corridor and kitchen."

They began searching, making their way out from the chalk lines in each possible direction. They found none.

Bracken found an interesting trail from the body to the lobby, which he and Ramsay followed until Bracken lost it among the scents of all the people who'd passed through there.

"If he was stabbed somewhere else, it must have been in the kitchen and the spots were overlaid by your mother's and Ellen's footprints," Ramsay said.

"Which brings us back to the kitchen staff, and most likely Ellen, knowing the kind of man Chambers was," Eliza replied.

"Possibly," Ramsay said. As he spoke, they heard footsteps approaching. "The kitchen staff are arriving. We can ask them."

None of the morning staff, however, had been working the previous evening so, after explaining the need to keep out of the roped off areas, they let them go to begin breakfast.

"I hope they're quick," Eliza said, as they returned to the dining room to wait. "I'm starving."

Ramsay smiled. Frederick's dim view of human nature was confirmed. While they waited, he wrote his notes of everything he and Eliza had seen and heard the previous night and in their search this morning.

"I don't know why you're bothering to write all this," Eliza told him. "Baldock will arrest you simply because of the coincidence of your being here. He's big on there being no such thing as a coincidence."

Ramsay laughed. "It's true. I should put my name at the top of the list. That might keep me safe. Reverse psychology, you know."

"I'm not sure he cares about psychology, Tom," Eliza replied.

As they waited and talked, tables were set, and the smell

of frying bacon began to make itself known. Other guests entered the room, subdued, and in the case of the young people, hungover.

"I'll talk to them now, as we wait," Eliza told Ramsay.

She joined the three couples, and they were soon in deep conversation. Unfortunately, Eliza seemed to be talking more than the others were. Ramsay shrugged. Everyone would soon know all there was to know so it made no difference what she said. And it would be worth it if she learned anything from the couples, now they'd had a night to sleep on events.

Ramsay ordered porridge, the thought of a fried breakfast being too much today. His meal arrived while Eliza continued talking to the young people. More of them were talking now, however, so she'd loosened them up. He was nibbling on toast and sipping tea by the time she returned.

"Did you learn anything useful?" Ramsay asked, as she sat across the table.

"It's hard to say," Eliza replied, taking a piece of his toast and buttering it. "Each couple remembers where they were; it was as I said, two of them in cramped places enjoying themselves, so each individual gives the other an alibi, and Marcus and Sarah feeling left out in the dining room. The Pugachevs saw Oliver and Celina hide but didn't see anything after they themselves hid. None of them knew I'd left the room with them so how much weight we can give their statements, I don't know."

"You did learn where they hid?"

"I did and we can decide if their hiding places would have given them easy access to the kitchen and corridor," Eliza replied.

"None claim to have seen any of the other guests?"

"They only have eyes for each other," Eliza said. "Very romantic but not very helpful, I'm afraid."

After their meal, Ramsay and Eliza examined the couples' hiding places. They were well away from where the crime happened.

"I think we can rule them out for now," Ramsay said. "Though there's something Nick Pugachev isn't telling us. I'm sure of that."

Ernie Wright approached the breakfast room, and they stopped him before he entered it.

Ramsay asked, "Could we talk to you about last night?"

Wright frowned. "I've just been told. I didn't know anything about it."

As he spoke, Bracken began a low growling before Ramsay told him to be quiet. For some reason, Bracken had taken a dislike to Wright from the first moment they met. *They say dogs can always tell.* This sign from Bracken might have been more helpful if he hadn't also taken a dislike to Paul Chambers, which Ramsay could understand, and Oliver Trubshaw, one of the quietest of the young people, which Ramsay couldn't understand.

"You saw and heard nothing unusual as you went to your room?" Eliza asked Wright.

"With the band playing and those young tearaways shouting, what could I hear? My hearing isn't great at the best of times."

"What about Mr. Redhill?" Ramsay asked. "You left together; I think."

"We did but he took a moment to rest, and I stopped off at the Gents. There in the lobby." Wright pointed at the discreet door in the paneling. "When I came out, he'd gone."

"So you wouldn't know if he saw or heard anything?" Eliza pressed him.

"I wouldn't. You have to ask him," Wright said.

"You and Chambers had a fight only days ago," Ramsay reminded him.

"And you think that means I killed him?" Wright interjected, angrily.

"Not at all. Everyone had some quarrel with the man so far as I could see," Ramsay replied. "I wondered what it was about?"

"Nothing that happened here," Wright began, still upset. Then he relented. "Very well. At the start of the Great Depression, Chambers bought the company both my parents worked for. Dad on the shop floor and Mam in the office. Chambers only got to buy it because he promised the union he would save the company and the jobs. The union backed his bid, and the deal went through. Weeks later, they learned he'd already sold the company to a man who wanted the land for development. Everyone lost their jobs."

"There was a lot of that kind of thing going on those days," Ramsay said. "I'm sorry it happened to your family."

Wright's face was ashen. "It killed them. Both my parents were dead in less than two years. Dad killed himself with the shame of not being able to provide for my brothers and sisters and me. Mam just faded away with worry and overwork. We were farmed out to relatives and some of us ended up in care."

"Did you know he would be here? Is that why you came? For revenge?" Eliza asked.

Wright shook his head. "I didn't know, but I recognized him the moment I saw him. I did alright for myself, but my brothers and sisters didn't. I'm bitter and I said so. He thought it was just business and mocked me for what I told him he'd done to us."

"You responded angrily, and that's why he hit you?" Ramsay asked.

Wright's face flicked from ashen to red as his anger returned. "It should have been me hitting him, but he got his punch in first. Then we were separated."

"You have to tell the police this when they arrive," Ramsay said. "If you hide it and they find out later, they'll be suspicious."

Wright nodded. "They'll always be suspicious of someone in a fight with the victim. But it'll all blow over. I didn't kill him." He continued into the breakfast room leaving Ramsay and Eliza to talk.

"He hasn't got an alibi," Eliza said. "And he was in the area around the time of the murder. It's going to take more than honesty to persuade Baldock it isn't Wright."

Ramsay laughed. "Well, so far, you've had Inspector Baldock arresting me and Wright and it's not yet the end of breakfast time."

Eliza grinned. "I think he could arrest Mam, Dad, and me too. I don't know what made Mam so against Chambers, but I suspect it must have been bad. Baldock doesn't know that I don't know what Mam had against him so he'll assume I killed Wright for revenge, you can be sure. And Dad, who wouldn't hurt a fly, will be a suspect too because Baldock will think whatever happened to Mam will have festered in Dad's mind and exploded into murderous rage last night."

"Whatever you think of Baldock," Ramsay said, shaking his head, "he's an experienced officer who won't simply lock up everyone who has a motive. To be honest, I doubt there's anyone in the hotel who liked the man. Even Bracken knew him for a bad 'un."

"I was right about there being a murder, and you'll see

I'm right about Baldock arresting the first person he suspects," Eliza protested.

Ramsay heard Joyce call from the reception desk, "Inspector." She held and waved the phone at him. He hurried across to the desk and learned Inspector Baldock wanted to speak to him.

Ramsay took the phone, and said, "Good morning, Inspector."

"If you say so," Baldock grumbled. "Tell me there's been another 'coincidence'? You know my views on coincidences."

"I'm afraid so," Ramsay replied. "I'm sure they've told you the general outline of the case. I'd like to provide you with more, only not here in the lobby where anyone can hear. Can I phone you back?"

Baldock gave him a number to call, and they hung up. "I'll speak to him from my room, Joyce. Can you make sure there's no one listening in on the line, please."

Joyce looked upset at the suggestion but agreed to watch the hotel reception switchboard until he returned.

In his room, Ramsay and Eliza sat around the phone's handset providing Baldock the background they'd seen and heard, as well as the thin evidence he and Eliza gathered before he phoned.

"I know you want me to say I'll keep an open mind, Ramsay," Baldock said, when Ramsay finished, "but we have a woman holding the knife that likely killed him, and she has history with him. You can ignore that, but I can't."

"I understand," Ramsay said, waving Eliza to say nothing for she looked about to explode. "When will you and the forensic team be here?"

"As soon as my assignment to the case is confirmed, you can be sure I'll be aiming to be there. However, the road patrols say the road into the dale is closed, and the weather says more snow today."

"I hadn't heard the weather report," Ramsay replied, glumly. "Tell me what you want done, and I'll do what I can. We have a photographer and a local doctor so I can start the investigation."

"Interview everyone and we'll talk later," Baldock said. "Get the photographer to take photos beyond the immediate vicinity of the murder. It may be days before I get there, and I'd like a fresh record before everything gets muddied."

"Can't you helicopter in?" Eliza asked. "They did a lot of things with helicopters two winters ago."

"We don't have a police helicopter," Baldock replied, "and it would cost a lot to hire one for me and the team, but I'll ask. There may be one taking food to livestock on the moor that I can hitch a ride on."

With the call ended, Ramsay turned to Eliza and said, "We need a room where we can interview people, and notebooks and pencils. Can you ask Joyce for that?"

"What are you going to do?" Eliza asked.

"Tell everyone in the breakfast room they're going to be interviewed by me until the police arrive. They may need some persuading. Frederick can help there."

Back at the reception desk, Ramsay and Eliza found Joyce and Frederick in agitated discussion. Ramsay outlined his talk with Baldock and what he'd been asked to do.

"They won't like it," Frederick replied, when Ramsay asked the host to accompany him to the breakfast room.

"I know," Ramsay replied, "but it must be done while everyone's memories are fresh."

"Why can't Inspector Baldock interview everyone over the phone?"

"Because it would take all day, most of the police budget,

and he wouldn't be able to see their body language or facial expressions," Ramsay said. "Interviewers get a lot from those two responses."

"Very well," Frederick said, unhappily, "but I won't be party to coercing anyone who refuses. To them, you're just another guest, not a police officer, remember."

Frederick and Ramsay's misgivings were overdone, however. All the young people agreed and that encouraged the others. In the end, only Mrs. and Gregory Chambers said they would wait and talk to the real police.

"I understand," Ramsay said, smiling, "and when Inspector Baldock phones to say when he'll be here, which I hope will be soon, he perhaps can talk to you both over the phone."

They shrugged, though they looked uneasy. *Baldock should have seen that response.*

Eliza and Joyce had an interview room ready by the time Ramsay made his schedule of the willing interviewees. The interviews didn't take long. Eliza and Ramsay's notetaking was easy because no one heard or saw anything. When the last of the witnesses left, and they'd started closing the room, Gregory Chambers walked in.

"I'll tell you what I know," he said, sullenly. *His natural manner.*

"Please do. You must have been among the last to see your father alive," Ramsay began.

"I don't know about that," Gregory replied. "He decided to play Hide and Seek, and we decided not to. We knew why he wanted to play, of course."

"Why?" Eliza asked.

"You know why," Gregory replied. "The Phillipson woman. He wanted to hide with her."

"Did they leave the room together?" Ramsay asked.

"More or less," Gregory replied. "Both left after her husband left. She claimed she didn't want to play either -- until he'd gone."

"We haven't spoken to the Phillipsons yet," Ramsay continued. "You didn't see your father after he left the room?"

"Nope. I didn't and I'm not sorry."

"Why is that?" Eliza asked.

Gregory shrugged. "He never liked me. Something about me rubbed him the wrong way."

"I imagine you left home the moment you could?" Ramsay suggested.

"I ran away. He was a brute. I don't know why Mother stuck by him."

"I heard something about this trip being a reconciliation, is that true?" Ramsay asked.

Gregory laughed. It wasn't a pleasant sound. "Mother would have it he was mellowing and wanted to be reconciled. The moment we met here in the hotel, he lost his rag and cursed me to high heaven."

Perhaps it's the long hair, garishly colorful clothes, and the straggly beard, Ramsay thought, smiling inwardly. What he said was, "Older people often have a problem with the young. Could it just be the fashions he didn't like?"

Gregory snorted. "I could have turned up in a pinstripe suit and bowler hat, he still wouldn't have welcomed me."

"But you came here," Ramsay pressed.

Gregory shrugged. "He was paying. Mother insisted. I came. I should have gone back to London, but I didn't want to spend Christmas on my own and here I could eat well. I'm almost skint, you see. He gives me an allowance that hardly covers the rent in London."

"I take it he wanted you to come and work in the business," Ramsay said. "That's how it often is with self-made men and their sons."

"He did and I wouldn't. Bad enough him bullying me at home without letting him do it all day, as well."

"What did you want to do?" Ramsay asked, unable to imagine anyone employing the man.

"I write plays," Gregory said. "If I had more money, I could get more of them put on. As it is, I'm struggling to make a living."

"Getting back to last night," Eliza said, "did you hear anything you thought odd? Arguments or anything?"

Gregory shook his head. "I finished the last of the wine and the band kept droning on with old band music. No, nothing."

"When you left the room, which way did you go?" Ramsay asked.

"Mother and I went straight out into the lobby and along the corridor to our rooms. And, again, no, I didn't see or hear anything I thought odd."

"You and your mother left and walked together the whole way to your rooms?" Eliza asked.

"Yes, we can give each other an alibi, if that's what you want to hear."

After asking if he could think of anything else and being told there wasn't, Ramsay thanked him and suggested he persuade his mother to also make a statement.

When he'd gone, Eliza asked, "Did you see them leaving?"

Ramsay nodded. "It's as he said. They finished the wine bottle and then left together." *Could they have murdered Paul Chambers together?*

15

INTERVIEWING THE WITNESSES

Gregory's words must have swayed his mother because as Ramsay and Eliza were drinking morning coffee in the dining room, Mrs. Chambers asked to talk to them privately. They agreed and returned to the interview room with their coffee and their new witness.

Her story concerning the evening matched that of Gregory, so Ramsay decided to learn more about the family background.

"Gregory is our only child," she said, "and you might notice he doesn't resemble his father very closely. That's what Paul thought anyway. He became suspicious from the moment our son was old enough to have an appearance that wasn't babyish. It grew worse with time."

"Is he Paul's son?" Eliza asked.

Mrs. Chambers flushed and cried, "I was never unfaithful to my husband. I'm a good Orthodox wife."

"Orthodox?" Ramsay queried.

"My family is from Russia," she said. "We fled during the revolution. I, of course, wasn't born then. I was born here, in Leeds."

"And your husband?" Ramsay asked.

"He is an atheist, though he claimed to be Orthodox when we married in church."

"Then he is from Russia as well?" Eliza said, puzzled. This had never been suggested before.

"He too fled the communists," Mrs. Chambers replied. "He was lucky. He got away with much of his family's wealth. Sadly, his family died in the revolution or soon after. It left him a very unhappy man."

"Is that why you've been so patient all these years?" Ramsay asked.

She nodded. "You can't know what it was like for those who escaped. They find no peace in their lives. They even blame themselves for being alive when their families aren't. My father felt the same."

"Yet he and you have done well since coming to Britain," Eliza said. "That must be some comfort. And having a son. Shouldn't that have helped?"

"Paul did well because he arrived with money, his family's money," Mrs. Chambers said. "His father had given it to him when they were being held by the communists. Paul escaped that night, and next day he watched, from a distance, his family being executed."

"That would be a character-changing moment for anyone," Ramsay said.

"He said so and I believed him," Mrs. Chambers replied. "This was in the Crimea, when it fell to the communists. Paul got on one of the last ships taking survivors of the White Russian Army into exile."

"It was one of the first news reports I really remember," Ramsay said. "That would be about 1920-ish?"

Mrs. Chambers nodded. "They landed at Istanbul, but that country too was in an upheaval after the Great War, so

Paul took a job on a British merchant ship and eventually settled here."

"Mr. Wright felt aggrieved about Paul's handling of a business in the Great Depression," Eliza said. "Can you tell us anything about that?"

"I knew nothing about it," Mrs. Chambers replied. "When I asked him that night, after the quarrel, Paul said he did all he could to save the business. He said few people were buying its products anymore, and the factory and equipment weren't suitable for making products that were being bought. And everyone was given the severance pay they were entitled to. He couldn't be responsible for the actions that Mr. Wright's parents took later."

"Aye," Ramsay replied. "It was a terrible time for everyone, right enough. There were no jobs for ordinary folk. It's how I ended up in the police force."

"Mr. Wright accusing your husband of bad faith toward the workers in that company must have hurt him badly, I imagine," Eliza said.

"Paul wasn't the sort to admit to being hurt, but I think it did. He had strong feelings, you see. With age, he's become more understanding of others, I think. His anger toward Gregory, for example, faded and he was coming around to accepting Gregory as he is."

"Does Gregory agree?" Ramsay asked.

"You've spoken to him so I'm sure you know he doesn't. But I know, knew, Paul better than anyone, and I noticed a change."

"What will happen to your business now?" Eliza asked.

"I shall put the businesses up for sale," Mrs. Chambers said. "I've no head for business and nor does Gregory. I'm sorry Paul's legacy should be sold but it will be for the best."

"You'll have enough to live on?" Ramsay asked.

Mrs. Chambers laughed. "More than enough, Mr. Ramsay, and no I didn't kill him to get the money. If I'd wanted to, I could have murdered him at any time these past ten years."

Ramsay smiled. "The police will ask again when they get here. You should know it's a routine question that's always asked when someone comes into a lot of money through the suspicious death of another."

"I do understand, and I'm not afraid of the question or the answer," Mrs. Chambers replied. "I didn't kill Paul, and they'll find no evidence to suggest I did."

"You went straight to your room when you left the dining room last night?" Eliza asked.

"Gregory and I left together, and we were together when we arrived at our rooms," she replied. "After that, I have no alibi but nor did I leave my room."

"You didn't want to play Hide and Seek?" Ramsay asked.

"I'm too old for childish games," she replied. "Paul wanted to play because he hoped for some close contact with that woman. I would only be in the way."

"Was he having an affair?"

"I expect they were having sex," Mrs. Chambers said. "There have been a few such women down the years, hoping to get rich off him. I expect her husband put her up to it."

"You must see this will be another reason the police will suspect you," Eliza said.

"Of course, and my earlier reply is the same. I didn't kill him and neither you nor they will find any evidence I did. He wasn't going to leave me for this silly woman; he knew what she was up to. It had happened before and ended quietly. It would have done this time, as well."

"Is there anyone you think might have wanted to harm him?" Ramsay asked, wrapping up the interview.

"Paul described Nicholas Pugachev's father as an 'enemy'," Mrs. Chambers said. "I pressed him to explain but he wouldn't. It concerned me because he called some businessmen 'rivals' or something like that, but he'd never called any of them an 'enemy'."

"This was since he saw Nicholas Pugachev here?" Ramsay asked.

"Yes. That very first night when the young ones were drunk and noisy. Pugachev clearly recognized Paul, and Paul knew him."

Ramsay thanked her and she left the room.

"I think she's trying to deflect the blame," Eliza said. "She has two good motives for murder and, as for saying she could have done it any time, well, that doesn't wash with me. Here she could point the finger at others and muddy the water."

"What you say is true," Ramsay said, "but we must talk to Mr. Pugachev again. His name sounds Russian, and we now know the Chambers are Russian. Maybe there's something more we don't know."

"I'll go and find him," Eliza said. Then seeing Ramsay's doubtful face, added, "It will be better coming from me. The group and I were getting along fine last night, and you saw how easy they were with me this morning. You'll make it all formal and frighten him off."

"It's because you were getting along, I'm concerned. They may turn against you when we start asking difficult questions."

"It's too soon to worry," Eliza said, brushing his objection aside. "We have questions and only he can answer them."

Ramsay considered and then agreed. "Be sure you don't alert him about why we want to talk to him."

"I'm not an idiot," Eliza said, sliding out of the door and racing off down the corridor.

She returned five minutes later with a puzzled looking Nick Pugachev, who asked Ramsay the moment he came through the door, "What's this about? Eliza is being very mysterious."

"It's nothing," Ramsay said, encouraging him to take a seat. "We talked to Mrs. Chambers, and she told us your father knew the victim. We wanted to ask more about that."

"Oh, it's no secret. My father and Chambers are, were, in business in Leeds. Their paths crossed frequently, and my father didn't like him. Not one little bit. He said he was a 'bad man'."

"You don't know why he thought that?" Eliza asked.

"I think just the way he treated everyone," Nick said. "You witnessed what he was like here, and this is Christmas, when he's on holiday. Imagine him as your boss?"

Ramsay laughed. "It's true. I wouldn't stay anywhere he was in charge. But are you sure that's all and not something very personal or historical?"

"I don't think so," Nick replied, puzzled. "Why?"

"We just learned the Chambers are Russian emigres and your father being one as well, we wondered if there was a political or historical side we didn't know about?" Eliza asked.

"Father never mentioned it when we spoke but then I didn't ask either."

Ramsay puzzled, said, "How did your father know Chambers was here?"

"I told him," Nick replied. "That first night, Mater

phoned the hotel to see if we'd arrived safely. I told Father about seeing and recognizing him."

"And what did he say?" Ramsay continued.

"That I should keep away from him. He'd told me this before, so it was what I expected him to say."

"Do you know Gregory Chambers?" Eliza asked. "You're about the same age. Did you go to the same school, maybe?"

"My father sent me to a school where I'd learn to be an English gentleman," Nick said. "No one could ever mistake the awful Gregory for any kind of gentleman."

"So, you don't know him?" Ramsay said, looking for a definite answer.

"That's correct. I knew Chambers senior by sight and reputation but not the junior one other than seeing him in his father's company when he was very young and when I was too."

"Can we have your father's phone number? I'd like to find out if there was more than just Chambers' behavior behind it."

Nick thought carefully before saying, "You can get our family phone number from the phone book, so I may as well give it to you. But you can't seriously think my father made his way here through the snow, killed Chambers, and left without being seen? How would he do that? On skis?"

"Maybe he had someone here who could do it for him?" Ramsay said, innocently.

Nick went beet red. "Now wait a minute…"

Ramsay smiled and waved down his protest. "I don't really think you had anything to do with it, but you should understand the police will think what I've said is a possibility and you should be aware of it."

"Then what do you mean?"

"I mean there could be someone here who had a good

reason for what happened, and your father may be able to shed light on that," Ramsay replied.

"You mean Mr. Wright, I suppose," Nick said, nodding. "Well, he just might. Here's our number," Nick added, scribbling on a paper napkin and handing it to Ramsay.

When Nick was gone, Eliza said, "He could be the killer, you know. His wife would give him an alibi for the time they were supposed to be hidden."

"I know," Ramsay said. "And now he must be wondering that too. We need to phone his parents before he does."

16

POLICE AREN'T COMING

When they reached Mr. Pugachev on the phone, he confirmed what his son, Nick, said. Chambers was a bad man because of the way he treated people. Pugachev didn't know anything about Chambers in Russia during the revolution. Ramsay hung up the phone and told Eliza this.

"Pity," she said. "Is that all he said? You had a long conversation."

"He told me about the Russian community," Ramsay replied. "It seems the community didn't like Chambers either. His real name was Rosenberg, by the way."

Eliza sighed. "It would have been nice to have a motive from the distant past. It would be just like a book or film."

"It doesn't mean it can't be from the past," Ramsay reminded her. "Look how Ernie Wright felt about him."

Eliza shook her head. "He was angry and said something Chambers didn't like. Is that enough anger for murder?"

Ramsay considered. "They only had a minor scuffle, that's true, but the story behind it isn't minor. Still, you're probably right, it doesn't feel like it's enough. We just can't rule it out, that's all."

"Shouldn't we phone Baldock now?" Eliza asked. "Before he calls us."

Ramsay dialed Baldock's number and was immediately connected to the inspector who answered in his usual terse fashion, "Baldock!"

"Good morning, Inspector," Ramsay said brightly, knowing it would annoy the man.

"Oh! It's you," Baldock replied. "What have you got for me?"

"We've almost finished the first interviews," Ramsay replied.

"And?"

"And nothing yet," Ramsay said. "We still have to interview the Phillipsons and the owners as being likely witnesses. When might you and the team be here?"

"Not today," Baldock growled, angrily. "The weather is closing in again, the council are focusing on the main roads, and the Chief won't pay for a helicopter."

"I hadn't heard the weather forecast," Ramsay admitted. "How close could you get? Maybe we could send the sleigh."

"If tomorrow is no better, we should arrange that," Baldock said. "For today, finish the interviews and keep the body isolated."

"We've cordoned it off in the cold store," Ramsay told him, "but that won't stop a determined villain from tampering with it, if they have a reason to do so."

"Do you think they might have?"

"Not really," Ramsay replied. "There's not much to learn from the stab wound. It's a single, simple thrust that, had the knife been left in the wound, he may have survived. Unfortunately, Mrs. Danesdale didn't know that and removed it thinking she was helping him."

"Is that what she says? Have you spoken to her?"

"Not yet, the sedation is only just beginning to wear off," Ramsay replied.

"Then you can't know what she thought when she pulled it out," Baldock said. "She may be your future mother-in-law, Ramsay, but she's the most likely person to have murdered him."

"My mam barely knew the man," Eliza, listening in, protested. She was pressed close against Ramsay with her ear as near the handset as she could get it.

"Your mother filed a report against him twenty years ago for his persistent sexual advances," Baldock replied. "We have the files. Nothing came of it because your parents began using a different food supplier and the local police warned him off. Maybe she didn't mean to murder him. Maybe, he began winding her up and she snapped."

"No!" Eliza cried. "Mam would never hurt anyone."

There was silence on Baldock's end of the phone as he considered his answer. Finally, he said, "I understand how you feel, Miss Danesdale, but we can't really know what goes through people's minds all the time. You must gather the evidence calmly and without prejudice. If you can't do that, leave it to Mr. Ramsay."

Sensing Baldock knew more than he was prepared to say, Ramsay wrapped up the call with a promise to phone in the evening.

"You see?" Eliza cried, eyes blazing with fury. "He's just going to pin it on Mam and move on."

"Your mother is in a difficult position," Ramsay admitted. "We all know that. We need to gather the evidence and find the real culprit. That's what you wanted, wasn't it? A good old-fashioned mystery?"

Eliza calmed a little and said, "Not with my mother as the murderer though."

"Then we'll see if she's able to talk to us now," Ramsay replied, "and, if she isn't, we'll talk to the Phillipsons. He may have seen his wife and Chambers hiding together, gone looking for a weapon, seen the knives through the kitchen doors, grabbed one, and stabbed Chambers. There, how's that for a simple end to the mystery?"

Doris was awake but confused when they returned to the Danesdales' room. Colin shook his head when Eliza demanded to speak to her mother.

"Not yet, Eliza, and not in that tone of voice," her father said, firmly.

Ramsay took Eliza's elbow and guided her back to the door. "We have plenty more people to talk to. Colin, keep Doris quiet and resting."

"He's protecting her," Eliza said, as they hurried off down the corridor. "He'll make her look even more guilty if he's still doing that when the police arrive."

"Your dad is helping your mother recover, and that's the best thing she can do at this time," Ramsay replied. "The sedative will wear off soon, and she'll be able to talk sensibly, which is what we want."

At the door of the Phillipsons' room, Ramsay knocked and gave his name, when asked who was knocking.

The door opened and Mr. Phillipson, wearing a thick dressing gown, peered out. He looked hungover.

"Can we talk for a moment?" Ramsay asked. "I've been asked by the police to interview everyone because they can't be here today to do it themselves."

"My wife isn't very well."

"Then we can talk out here in the hall for a few minutes, and we can come back later when your wife is feeling better," Ramsay said.

"I'm a woman," Eliza said, abruptly. "She may not want to see a man, but I'm sure she'd be fine talking to me."

Phillipson hesitated and then nodded. Eliza pushed past him and into the room.

He really is hungover. I'd just allowed them the perfect way to be sure their stories agreed with each other, and he gave it away. And him a lawyer too. Or maybe they're just innocent?

"What do you want to know?" Phillipson asked, leaning heavily against the door frame. He *was* hungover. Ramsay hoped that hadn't led to violence against his wife.

"Did you see or hear anything odd last night when you were playing Hide and Seek?" Ramsay asked.

"I didn't play," Phillipson replied. "I was sick of the whole thing and came back here. I didn't want to see them together." Then, realizing Ramsay may not understand, added, "My wife and Chambers, I mean."

"They did seem friendly," Ramsay agreed. "Weren't you concerned about it?"

"I told you. It sickened me. He paid me well on a previous commission, and Julia liked the life his money gave us. He wanted me to do some more work. I didn't like his behavior and said no. He thought he could up the fee and use Julia to wheedle me round. He was probably right because in the end, we did come on this trip."

"Was the money so much to your wife?"

Phillipson nodded. "She wants a cottage in the Cotswolds like our friends have. She..." he paused, before ending, "began *encouraging* him to pay that much. She swears there was never any infidelity."

"Do you believe her?"

"I did until this holiday," Phillipson replied, grimly. "Last night I told her I'm divorcing her."

"Which is why she's not well?"

"Exactly."

"Did anyone see you return to your room?" Ramsay asked.

Phillipson frowned. "Our host did. What's his name, Frederick. He wished me goodnight as I was entering my room."

"What time was that?"

"How on earth should I know?" Phillipson demanded. "I was too angry to think about anything but a divorce."

"You see, of course, that you could be thought of as having a motive for murder," Ramsay suggested.

"Divorce from an unfaithful wife is what I planned, not murdering her lover."

"And as you crossed the lobby last night, did you see anyone other than Frederick?"

Phillipson sighed and said, "I could have walked past the whole assembled company on my way to this room last night and I wouldn't have seen any of you. Don't you understand what I'm saying?"

Ramsay nodded in sympathy. He did understand, only the man was going to need a better alibi than this when Baldock got here.

Eliza arrived back at the door and slid past Phillipson and out into the corridor. "Julia wants to talk with you," she said to Phillipson.

"I'm sure she does," Phillipson said. "I don't want to listen."

Ramsay thanked him for providing his statement and guided Eliza, who seemed eager to play peacemaker, away.

"She's very unhappy," Eliza told Ramsay as they returned to the interview room.

"Is she injured, bruised?" Ramsay asked.

"Her eyes are red from the crocodile tears," Eliza

remarked. "That's what they are, believe me." She frowned. "We should arrest her for overacting."

"We have real work to do, Eliza. We're sleuths remember, not marriage guidance counsellors."

Grumbling, Eliza settled in the chair beside Ramsay, and they compared notes.

"So, Julia Phillipson says she hid alone and didn't see or hear anything unusual," Ramsay repeated.

"That's it," Eliza said. "She wasn't expecting Chambers to find her. She just wanted to be alone."

"Wasn't it *Greta Garbo* who just wanted to be alone?" Ramsay asked.

"What?" Eliza asked.

"Nothing, just a thought," Ramsay said. "She must have known going off to hide without her husband would make him more suspicious."

"She says she assured him there would be no hanky-panky; she just knew which side their bread was buttered on. He, however, stormed off."

"She talks in cliches," Ramsay said. "When he 'stormed off', she didn't think to go after him? Re-assure him?"

Eliza shrugged. "She said he was just drunk and wouldn't remember a thing in the morning."

"She saw no one from where she hid? Has she an alibi?" Ramsay asked.

"She says not. The others went on further into the building and that was the last she saw of anyone until Alfred called them back into the dining room."

"So, she has no alibi either," Ramsay said. "Maybe Chambers had been playing her along and told her last night what he thought of her. They were at the kitchen doors, she spotted the knives, rushed in, grabbed one, and stabbed him."

"You think she's capable of that? She strikes me as a cruel, malicious cat who hurts people rather than an active murderer," Eliza asked.

"Cats kill when they're finished playing with their prey," Ramsay said, "and maybe when their prey turns around and bites them."

"Sounds unlikely to me. Why would he stay around to be stabbed?"

"Perhaps he was walking away, she called to him, he turned, and she stabbed him. After all, this stabbing isn't something an expert would do. Had Doris not removed the knife, he might have survived."

"I still favor her husband," Eliza said. "Who uses Brylcreem in this day and age? I ask you? Hasn't the fashion revolution penetrated their part of London?"

Ramsay laughed. "Please don't give that as a reason when we speak to Baldock."

"Oh, I forgot," Eliza said, grinning. "He uses it too. I'm glad you don't, or we'd have to have a serious talk."

Ramsay shook his head, amused despite the implications of her words.

"The Price-Ridleys now?" Eliza suggested.

"It's lunch time," Ramsay replied. "They'll be busy. I don't think all the staff have come in today." They set off for the desk. No one was there.

"I thought it was quiet," Eliza said. "Staff too nervous to work with a murderer loose, you think?"

Ramsay nodded, gesturing to the windows looking out over the lawn. "Some of that but look out of the window. We're getting another dumping of snow."

"Baldock said we would," Eliza replied. "The weather forecast was right."

"We'll have lunch and interview our hosts after,"

Ramsay told her. "Maybe your mam and dad will be here for lunch."

They entered the dining room and made their way to their table, nodding to the two elderly ladies who nodded grim-faced back at them.

"I thought they'd be happy," Eliza whispered. "After all, doom is what they've been preaching these past days."

"Don't be silly," Ramsay replied, quietly. "They never suggested, or imagined, anything like this, I'm sure."

"Yesterday, you were suggesting Miss Forsythe could be a trained killer," Eliza reminded him. "Now she's a sweet old lady appalled by death. You should try and keep your stories straight."

"I merely suggested we keep an open mind," Ramsay said. Joyce arrived and handed him a menu. "Thanks," Ramsay said.

"I'm afraid it's a scratch meal today," Joyce told them. "The chef hasn't turned in to work."

"He's worried his skill with a knife will tell against him," Eliza said, trying not to giggle.

Ramsay frowned at her. "Does he live far away?"

"He was living in until only a month ago, found a cottage to rent farther along the dale," Joyce told them. "If we'd had any idea the weather would change to this, we'd have said no but..."

Ramsay gestured to the window. "I'm guessing he won't be here for dinner either."

Joyce unhappily agreed.

"We won't starve," Eliza said. "There must be a mountain of leftovers to eat and not everyone is turning up for meals." She glanced around the room. The three couples and the two elderly ladies were the only guests to be seen.

"They'll be hungry by dinnertime," Joyce replied, "You

can be sure of that. Mr. Redhill and Mr. Wright didn't take breakfast at all, nor did the Phillipsons."

She took their orders and returned to the kitchen.

"I'm truly sorry for them," Ramsay said. "This may put them out of business."

"More likely drum up trade," Eliza replied. "Everyone will want to see where the murder happened and sit where the victim sat and where the murderer slept. Our teashop had its busiest October my parents can remember, after you found old Harry's body."

Their orders arrived and they ate in silence, occasionally looking out of the window to see how much worse the weather was getting. When Joyce returned with toast and more coffee, Ramsay said they'd like to talk to her and Frederick as soon as they were free.

"We'll arrange separate breaks," Joyce said. "You don't need to question us together, do you?"

Ramsay assured her singly would be ideal and she left to warn her husband.

"I hate doing this to them with all the worry they're under," Ramsay remarked.

"I would have thought putting them under pressure was normal interrogation techniques in the police force," Eliza said, munching toast and marmalade.

"I don't think you have the full range of human feeling," Ramsay scolded her.

Eliza grinned and took another large bite of toast. "Maybe," she said, after finishing her mouthful, "but I do have intuition and it tells me we'll have to squeeze, or trick, an answer out of someone."

17

THE OWNERS' TALE & DORIS'S STORY

THEY'D ARRANGED the interviews for early afternoon, so Eliza went off to join the young couples in the billiards room while they waited. She excused herself by saying she might learn something in a regular conversation that she'd never hear in an interview.

She returned to the interview room at two-thirty just as Frederick was arriving.

"Thanks for giving us some time, Frederick," Ramsay said, as the owner took a seat. "You must be swamped with things to do."

"We are, but two of the kitchen maids have arrived and we're getting on top of things now."

"That was good of them," Ramsay said. "I doubt they'll get home tonight."

"We have plenty of empty rooms," Frederick replied. "We were making up beds when I noticed it was time to talk to you."

"We'll be as quick as we can," Ramsay said. "By now, I expect you've gone over last night in your mind many times so maybe just tell us what you remember."

Frederick spoke steadily, recounting what he'd heard or seen, where he'd been at various times during the evening before ending with, "The rest you know because you were there."

"Did you see anyone when you were in the lobby?" Eliza asked.

"Oh, I should have said. Yes, I wished Mr. Wright good night as he entered his room and then Mr. Phillipson a few minutes later entering his room. I was just coming out from the office behind reception, so I didn't see him cross the lobby."

"What made you go into the corridor where the incident took place?" Ramsay asked.

"I was patrolling the building, you might say. Trying to make sure the guests were behaving themselves," Frederick said. "They were very merry, and the kitchen has a lot of dangerous equipment."

"They're merry again," Eliza laughed. "I left them trying to organize 'Strip Billiards'."

"I'd better go," Frederick cried, "unless you have more questions?"

Ramsay said there were none right now and Frederick rushed away.

"Did you have to worry him more?" Ramsay asked Eliza, smiling.

"There are only friends in the billiards room," Eliza replied. "No one will be upset. A little excited maybe…" She let the thought die away.

Before Ramsay could reply, Joyce hurried into the room. "Has Frederick gone already?"

"Yes," Ramsay said. "Something came up."

Joyce too had gone over the night's events in her mind and could relate her activities without any hesitation.

"You didn't leave the kitchen and reception areas at all?" Eliza asked. "Not even to 'spend a penny'?"

"No. I was between the two all evening."

"Did you see Frederick during that time?"

"Oh, yes. He was in and out as he kept an eye on proceedings. I think sometimes he forgets he isn't in charge of an army squad anymore, and he doesn't need to patrol the perimeter."

"And Mr. Redhill?"

Joyce shook her head.

"Mr. Wright?"

"Yes. He left the Gentlemen's toilet off the lobby and went into the corridor to his room."

"Mr. Phillipson?"

"No." Joyce shook her head again. "Did they all go early to their rooms?"

"They say so," Eliza replied.

"What about Mrs. Danesdale?" Ramsay asked.

"Yes, she went toward her room."

"You didn't see her return?"

"I didn't, no."

"And you didn't hear anything unusual?"

"That's what puzzles me," Joyce said. "If he was stabbed where he died, shouldn't I have heard a quarrel, a cry of pain or anger, or his body falling to the floor?"

"The kitchen would be very noisy at the time, I expect," Eliza suggested, helpfully.

"I expect that was it," Joyce agreed but clearly still not convinced. When it became clear Joyce had given all the information she had to give, Ramsay thanked her, and they watched in silence as she left.

"She has a point," Ramsay said, when the door shut behind her. "Wouldn't your mother have cried out when she came upon the body, either calling for help or just in surprise?"

"She was too shocked."

"And when she pulled out the knife and blood splattered on her, wouldn't that have caused her to make some sound?" Ramsay mused.

"Too shocked," Eliza repeated stubbornly.

"I expect you're right," Ramsay agreed. There being no sense in arguing over something they couldn't confirm. "Now, it really is all up to your mother. Shall we see if she's ready to talk?"

Doris was up and sitting in a chair by the window when they returned to the Danesdales room. Her eyes were following the snowflakes falling and swirling outside the window, she hardly noticed them enter.

Ramsay looked at Colin who shook his head. Eliza said, "Dad, we must talk to Mam. She's the only one involved we haven't heard from, and her memories will fade if we leave it."

Her mother heard and turned, gazing at them with blank eyes. "I can tell you about it," she said, flatly.

"Thank you, Doris," Ramsay replied. "Just recount your movements last night for now. We can ask questions when you're feeling stronger." He glared at Eliza hoping that would be enough to stop her diving in with something that frightened Doris.

"That's easy," Doris replied, her voice low and empty of all feeling. "I went to powder my nose; you must remember that?" She looked at Ramsay and Eliza expectantly.

Ramsay smiled encouragingly. "We do. What did you do then?"

"The Ladies Powder Room was occupied, so I came here to our own room." She stopped, frowning in concentration.

"I left the room and began making my way back to the ballroom when I saw a movement in the corridor that leads to the kitchen." She stopped again. "It puzzled me. It looked like someone lying on the floor and I thought 'drunk'."

Her face became more animated as she prepared to speak again. "I went to help the person back to their room and found it was Chambers. I stopped, about to leave, when he said, 'help me'." Now her expression grew anguished. "I didn't want to because of the past so I thought I'd go to the kitchen, the door being just there, and get help that way." Tears spilled out and down her cheeks. "As I edged past him, I saw the handle of a knife in his chest and he said, 'help me' again. I crouched down and, thinking he meant remove the knife, I pulled it out." She began sobbing and they waited for her to recover.

"Take your time, dear," Colin said, putting his arm around her shoulders.

After some minutes, Doris began again, "I was splashed by blood, and I used my stole as a pad to stop it. He tried to speak. He said, 'Rosebud'. I didn't understand right away, then I remembered, like in that film. He stared at me and then just died. Ellen came out from the kitchen and tried to help. I couldn't move. She asked someone to get Alfred. When Alfred arrived, she told him what had happened. He helped me to stand and got me to a chair. Then went off to sound the alarm."

"And then we arrived," Ramsay said, softly.

"I don't remember much after the doctor gave me an injection," Doris said. "I think I've told you everything now."

"Mam," Eliza asked, "you said you saw a movement in the corridor. Was it a person?"

Her mother looked at her, dazed. "Did I? I suppose I did. I thought I saw a drunk slipping down to the ground."

"That's enough for now," Ramsay said. "Thank you, Doris. You've been very helpful. We now have everything everyone witnessed, and we can start piecing together the events." He rose from his chair and signaled Eliza to join him. "You rest, Doris, and we'll talk again later."

Back in their interview room, they discussed what they knew.

"Mam must have seen the killer though," Eliza said. "She must be made to remember."

"She may not," Ramsay replied. "Chambers might have lived quite a few minutes with the knife closing the wound. He could have made his own way there from somewhere nearby. We need the doctor to give us an estimate of how long he might have remained alive."

Eliza excitedly cried, "Then it's Wright. He met Chambers outside the dining room door, stabbed him with a knife he'd taken earlier to revenge himself after the fight the other day, and continued walking to his room."

"And Chambers staggered off down the corridor? Why?"

"To get away, I imagine," Eliza said. "He didn't realize Wright thought he'd already killed him."

"It's possible," Ramsay agreed, "but I don't see Chambers running away from Wright. It doesn't quite work for me."

"Maybe having a knife in your chest makes you act out of character," Eliza replied. "Anyhow, I think Baldock will agree and take Wright into custody, you'll see."

"We need to know who was in the Ladies Room," Ramsay murmured.

Eliza paused. "None of our witnesses mentioned being there," she said. "I'll ask. It will come better from me."

Ramsay laughed. "It certainly would. Some women might refuse to tell a man because he was a man, not because they were doing something illicit in there."

"I think it was a member of staff," Eliza replied, turning the idea over in her mind. "She wouldn't want to admit it because it's probably out of bounds to staff."

Ramsay nodded. "I think you're right. The staff toilets were occupied, and she slipped in there while no one was around to see. It was bad luck for her that your mother wanted to use it at the same time."

"It won't take long to find out who," Eliza said before pausing, then saying, "Hey, I've just thought of something brilliant."

Ramsay smiled. "Out with it."

"I said mam had to be made to remember and I know how to do it."

"The hypnotist," Ramsay said.

"If you'd thought of it, why are we waiting," Eliza cried. "Get him to our room and have him find out what mam saw."

"He's a stage hypnotist," Ramsay replied, "not a medical one. It wouldn't stand up anywhere, let alone in court."

"It doesn't have to," Eliza responded. "He just has to get mam to say who she saw, and we can find the evidence after."

Ramsay considered this. He knew he was old-fashioned in his thinking on these matters, but he'd always considered hypnotists in the same way he thought of psychics and psychiatrists. A lot of mumbo-jumbo and little to show for it. This time, however, the hypnotist wouldn't be charging for his services, and it just might jog something in Doris's mind.

He grinned. And Baldock would hate it. "It can't do any harm to try," he said.

Eliza beamed. "Welcome to the Twentieth Century,

Grandad." She stopped, thought, and then asked, "what did Mam mean by 'rosebud' and that film?"

Once again, her words reminded Ramsay of the age gap between them. "It's a classic movie called *Citizen Kane*. It's about a ruthless business tycoon who, as he is dying, whispers 'Rosebud', and no one knows why. The audience only learns at the end, when the old man's possessions are being burned and the camera zooms in on his childhood sled, which is called Rosebud."

"Never heard of it," Eliza said, shrugging. "The sled part sort of matches though. Maybe that's what brought it to his mind."

Ramsay added, "I wondered if what he actually said was, 'Rosenberg'. Pugachev said that was his real family name."

"You think he wanted to be remembered that way and not by his English name?" Eliza suggested.

"Something like that," Ramsay said. "Who you really are is important to people, and maybe more so when you've lived abroad most of your life."

"He could hardly go home," Eliza responded. "What now?"

"We still haven't spoken to Wright or Redhill," Ramsay reminded her. "They don't seem to be involved but we must ask."

"We also haven't spoken to the old biddies," Eliza retorted. "They won't be any help either."

Ramsay laughed. "You're quite right. We need to finish talking to the staff as well, particularly the woman Ellen says she sent for Alfred."

"It takes so long," Eliza complained. "The whole afternoon will be gone and none of it useful."

"Maybe the police will arrive and save you from all this tedious note taking," Ramsay teased her.

"Ha ha," Eliza replied. She would have continued only she saw Redhill shuffling toward the lobby. "Our first victim."

They hurried to intercept Redhill, who frowned at their arrival, and especially at Bracken who blocked his path by sitting in front of him.

"Bracken knows we want to talk with you," Ramsay said, smiling. "Come away, Bracken, let Mr. Redhill find a seat."

Bracken, however, remained firmly planted, staring at the man.

"Sorry about this," Ramsay said, taking hold of Bracken's collar. "He's still very young and hasn't quite grasped all the commands yet."

When they'd found seats, Eliza began, "We understand you and Mr. Wright left the dining room together. Were you together all the way to your rooms?"

Redhill shook his head. "I had maybe a little too much wine with dinner. I felt light-headed as we left the room and stopped to rest against the door. I did see Wright go into the toilet. He may have been still in there when I passed the door on my way to my room. I didn't see him again anyway."

"You didn't see anyone in the corridor, did you?" Ramsay asked. "From the doorway you might have done."

"If I'd looked that way, I might have done," Redhill replied. "Only, I didn't."

"Or hear anything unusual?" Eliza suggested.

Redhill shook his head.

"Well, thank you," Ramsay said, when it was clear the man wasn't going to say any more.

"I'm sorry I can't be more help," Redhill told them. "As I said, I felt unwell by then and maybe I missed a lot."

"You do have pills or something for your illness," Eliza asked, anxiously.

"They give me one week of pills every week to deaden the pain," Redhill replied. "The pills deaden my mind too, I fear. The world often seems very far away to me."

Ramsay nodded sympathetically. It wasn't comfortable interrogating someone, using up their remaining hours of life with such dark suspicion.

18

POLICE ARRIVE

SPEAKING to Baldock later that afternoon, however, irritated Eliza. She'd never forgiven him for his attitude throughout the smuggling mystery. Ramsay spent much of the phone call shushing her to prevent antagonizing the inspector.

"The snow has eased off here in Scarborough," Baldock told them. "How is it there?"

As Ramsay had checked the weather before calling, he was able to confirm the snow had eased in the dale as well. "In fact, it has practically stopped. I can see blue sky in breaks through the clouds."

"You offered a sleigh ride if I could get close enough," Baldock said. "Did you talk that over with the owners?"

"I did and they feel the sleigh could indeed reach the bottom of the hill into the dale but not up the hill," Ramsay replied.

"Then I'll bring some uniformed officers and the pathologist to the top of the hill, and we'll walk down to meet you. I'll gather people and cars. When I have them, I'll phone the Manor and we can organize how we meet."

"Have you time before darkness falls?" Ramsay asked,

anxiously. It was already after two o'clock and at this time of the year darkness began at three-thirty.

"We'll bring lights," Baldock replied, and hung up the phone.

Immediately, Eliza said, "We must get the hypnotists to mam now. Before Baldock gets here. We won't have another chance."

"We need your parents' permission, Eliza," Ramsay replied. "There's a possibility your mother could incriminate herself."

"She's innocent," Eliza retorted. "I know, even if you don't. I'll ask her." She practically ran from the room to her own.

Minutes later, breathless, Eliza gasped, "She's agreed to do it."

Frederick was soon found, and he brought the hypnotist to the Danesdales' room.

As Ramsay was closing the door behind himself and the hypnotist, Frederick asked anxiously, "Are you sure this is wise, Mr. Ramsay?"

"Not entirely," Ramsay agreed. He smiled encouragingly before saying, "Don't worry, I take full responsibility."

When he realised what was required of him, the hypnotist was as unhappy as Frederick had been and Doris had to re-assure him more than once before he agreed to take part.

Minutes passed agonisingly slowly as the hypnotist lulled Doris into a calm enough frame of mind to begin. Slowly, Doris's eyes closed and he began taking her back to the events of the evening. She responded quietly to the questions Ramsay prompted the hypnotist to ask.

Eliza could barely contain her frustration at the slow pace. She silently signaled Ramsay and the hypnotist to go quicker. They shook their heads, and the interview continued.

"You see someone lying on the floor in the corridor," the hypnotist said, "who is it?"

"I can't tell," Doris replied. "They were drunk. I went to help them."

"Who else is there in the corridor, Doris," the hypnotist asked.

Doris's expression became puzzled. "No one. In the busy hotel with everyone around, there was no one to help."

"Did you hear anything?"

"People in the kitchen," Doris replied, "and people giggling farther away."

"Nothing else?"

Doris shook her head. "Nothing. It was Chambers and I was about to turn away when he said, 'help me'."

The hypnotist looked at Ramsay warningly and Ramsay nodded, mouthing, "stop now."

The hypnotist brought Doris back from her trance. She looked about before saying, "Well?"

Eliza was too disappointed to speak so Ramsay said, "You did very well, Doris. Unfortunately, there doesn't seem to be anything more for you to remember."

"You go nothing?" Doris asked, her voice rising in panic. Colin crossed the room to sit beside her, putting his arm around her shoulders.

"What you told us earlier is what happened, love," he said. "That's good news. Don't fret. Tom will sort this out. You'll see."

Ramsay, Eliza and the hypnotist left the room together. Ramsay thanked him for his help and suggested the police too may want to use his services.

"Then they'll have to be quick," the man replied. "The

moment the road is open, I'm leaving. I'm not staying locked in hotel with a murderer on the loose. He may think what we've just done has unmasked him and bump me off next."

Ramsay laughed. "We don't plan to tell anyone about this, so he'll only know if you tell everyone."

At the Reception, Ramsay and Eliza learned Baldock had phoned the hotel and organized rooms for the night with Joyce and Frederick. Alfred prepared the sleigh and, when he judged the time to be right, he set off out of the hotel drive and onto the road. Wrapped in thick woolen coats, gloves, a hat and swaddled in blankets, he cut a comical figure to Ramsay and Eliza watching from the Manor's front door porch.

When the sleigh drove out of sight and its lights could no longer be seen twinkling through the trees that screened the grounds from the road, they returned inside, where the bright lights and decorations still gave the appearance of a happy event.

Seeing Ramsay's quizzical gaze at the decorations, Joyce at the desk sighed and said, "I know. It's unseemly to have them still up but we can't spare a moment from keeping the food cooked and served and beds made."

Ramsay nodded. "I wasn't criticizing, just remembering how excited we all were only a day ago."

"You must be used to this, Mr. Ramsay, surely?"

"Not at all," Ramsay said. "I've been called to places where bodies have been found, and even found one myself, but never been a part of the unfolding drama that led to the death."

"It should be a help in solving the mystery, then," Joyce replied.

Ramsay frowned. "You'd expect so but somehow it isn't. I

was here and even near and yet I saw and heard nothing. Since we arrived, I've witnessed lots of things that might have led to murder but there are so many, I can't yet separate the one from the others."

"And we can't be sure that any of them did," Eliza reminded him. "It could be something quite out of the blue."

"Unlikely, surely," Joyce said. "Who could have come in here from outside last night when the weather was so bad?"

"The staff did," Eliza reminded her.

"You think the staff?"

"We can't rule them out," Ramsay interjected, hastening Eliza away. "After all, he wasn't a nice man."

They went back to the interview room where they put their notes in order, together with the reel of film, which Eliza had taken of their evidence.

"Baldock may get in," Eliza said. "Will he get out when he wants to, that's the question."

Ramsay had been staring at their copious notes for some time, and he suddenly said, "We should copy all these for our own use."

"They're our notes," Eliza protested. "He can have his men copy them, if he wants them."

"It doesn't work that way," Ramsay replied. "He can take them as evidence. We need to get writing." Picking up a pad of hotel paper, donated by Joyce for their use, Ramsay began writing.

Sighing, Eliza began doing the same with her notes. "They'll be no good to him," she said, mutinously as she scribbled. "I can barely read them myself, so he won't be able to at all."

Ramsay smiled at her and said, "Then take more care in

the copying so I have a chance of reading them when I need to."

They were finished writing long before they heard the sleigh bells announcing the arrival of the police.

"They must be frozen," Ramsay said.

"I hope so," Eliza replied. "That way they'll have time to think before doing anything rash."

Ramsay laughed. "Come on. We'll greet them at the door. Remember, don't mention the copies we made of our notes. He'll take them too, just to stop us having access to them."

Ramsay was right about the cold. The police were frozen, even with the extra blankets Alfred had taken for them. The sleigh began turning around, ready to leave again, and Ramsay asked, "Are there more of you?"

Baldock dusted snow from his coat and growled, "The sleigh could only take three with our equipment. The doctor and two more constables are coming with the medical stuff."

"Are they waiting outside?" Ramsay asked, horrified.

"Nah. They're with the cars. They're fine. Now, where's this body?"

Ramsay, Eliza, Joyce, and Frederick led Baldock and his two men to the cold room and unlocked it. "Do you have spare keys?" Baldock demanded of Frederick.

"We do," Frederick answered, "and we need them. This is our hotel's cold room. We're in and out throughout the day."

"It's kept locked otherwise?"

"Yes," Frederick said. "Only those I give the key to can go in."

"Give me a set and you keep the other. Same rules apply, only those who are given a key can enter and woe betide any of your staff who interfere with the body."

Frederick replied in his best officer-class voice that none of his staff would dream of doing anything of the sort, saying, "We're decent people here."

Baldock grunted and examined the body. He carefully pulled the jacket away from the shirt to examine the wound more closely. "A lot of blood," he said, at last. "Not an expert thrust."

Ramsay, who understood this comment to be directed to him, nodded and said, "Unless the victim moved to avoid the blow, or parried it a little, it was an amateur's effort."

"Apart from Mr. Price-Ridley here," Baldock gestured at the owner, "are there any actual ex-servicemen on the guest list?"

"None who'll admit to it," Ramsay replied. "Even the staff, who are mostly women, were working on the land during the war, so the whole cast of characters are 'amateurs' when it comes to knife crimes."

Baldock straightened up and let the jacket fall back onto the victim's chest. Addressing the Price-Ridleys, he said, "Show us to our rooms, while we wait for the doctor to get here."

Locking the cold room as they left, the group returned to the lobby.

"It's afternoon teatime, Inspector," Ramsay said. "Eliza and I will be in the drawing room if you care to join us later."

Baldock grunted, non-committally, and followed Joyce along the corridor where Ramsay's room was located.

"Nice neighbors you're getting," Eliza teased him as they made their way across the lobby to afternoon tea.

"Keep your friends near and your enemies nearer, isn't that what they say?" Ramsay replied.

They'd barely finished their tea and treats when Baldock

joined them, ordering tea from Ellen who was serving that afternoon.

"Where are your notes and the knife?" he demanded as he sat down at their table.

"We have an interview room where we've kept everything," Ramsay replied. "And it's kept locked before you ask."

"Glad to hear it," Baldock replied. Grudgingly, Ramsay felt.

"I heard the sleigh arrive with the rest of your team," Ramsay told him. "I expect Joyce is settling them into their rooms."

Baldock nodded. "I saw them. I've told the doc I want his report on the body by dinner time."

Ramsay frowned. He'd prefer a job done right, rather than just right away. "And your forensic people?"

"Same," Baldock said, nodding to Ellen as she delivered the tray with tea and scones. When Ellen was gone, he continued, "Which is why I want that knife. It may tell us something."

"They'll have it the moment they're ready," Ramsay replied. "We're hoping for something from it too."

"Something other than my mother's fingerprints, he means," Eliza interjected, growing tired of this neutral fencing the two men were engaged in.

"I hope for your sake, and your mother's, there are other fingerprints on the knife," Baldock replied, "but from what you've told me this is a hotel steak knife. Other fingerprints aren't necessarily the great solution you think they are."

"They would be a start," Ramsay said. "There are so many possible suspects in this case. The person who found the victim is only one of many."

Baldock shrugged. "Let's not jump ahead of the evidence." He drank his tea quickly, eating a buttered scone with the same restless energy he generally displayed. "I'm ready," he said. "Take me to the interview room."

19

RAMSAY PATROLS THE GROUNDS

AFTER RAMSAY and Eliza led Baldock to the interview room, they were ordered to hand over the keys, which Ramsay did. As they made their way back to the lobby, they saw Baldock's forensic people examining the crime scene in meticulous detail.

"Do you think he listened when I explained about Wright?" Eliza asked.

"Only enough to dismiss it as your attempt to save your mother," Ramsay said. "I'm taking Bracken out for a walk. Care to come?"

Eliza nodded. Her expression flitting between gloomy and angry in turns. "It will be better than waiting here. We should ask Mam and Dad if they'd like to join us."

That hope, however, was squashed by the police constable standing guard outside the Danesdales' room door. "Sorry, Miss. No one in or out. Inspector Baldock's orders."

"I need my coat, hat, and gloves from the room," Eliza replied. "Can I at least ask my father to hand them out?"

With that agreed and executed, they went to Ramsay's

room for his outdoor clothes and on to collect Bracken, where they ended up with four dogs instead of one.

Outside, a pale wintry moon shone in a bright clear starry sky. With the dogs tugging on their leashes, they set off to the lake, which looked frozen. Eliza gingerly made her way out from the edge until she was confident the ice could take their weight.

"Come on," she called to Ramsay. "We can make a slide." Shuffling the snow off a section and backing up, Eliza took a run and slid to the end of the clearing, laughing uproariously when her leading foot stopped dead at the snow, and she fell sideways into it.

Ramsay watched anxiously until she'd clambered to her feet.

"It's solid," Eliza called, stamping a foot on the ice. "Come on."

Ramsay slowly made his way out to where Eliza was lengthening the slide. He examined the exposed ice, and it did seem thick enough for adults, something he couldn't remember seeing since being a child in Scotland.

Eliza slid down her cleared path and stopped short of the snow. "Now, you. I'll hold the dogs."

Bracken, however, was eager to join in the fun and Ramsay unclipped his leash. "Hold Larry, Harry, and Barry," he told Eliza. "I don't want them running off when we promised to look after them."

Ramsay self-consciously ran and slid down the icy lane. He didn't fall over and was amazed he hadn't. Bracken jumping up to congratulate him, however, did make him wobble.

"Down, Bracken," Ramsay said, pushing his friend off his chest. Now Ramsay was free to notice, he could see others coming to join them, led by Alfred with lanterns and a snow shovel. "We have company," he said, gesturing to the newcomers.

"They have skates," Eliza cried indignantly. "Alfred can make them a rink away from here. I cleared this. They can clear their own."

While the three couples sat on a lakeside bench putting on their skates, Alfred cleared them a rink nearer the shoreline.

"We should get skates," Eliza said.

"You should get skates," Ramsay replied in a determined voice. "I've never skated, and I'm not learning now. Besides, these dogs need a walk."

"I will," Eliza said, handing over the dog leashes and running across the snow to the couples. Ramsay watched as she then ran off to the hotel.

"Come on, boys," Ramsay said to the dogs, "we're on our own for the rest of the walk."

He gave the dogs lots of leash and they happily tracked rabbits and other creatures invisible to Ramsay. He'd circumnavigated the park by the time the moon slipped behind the trees and the Manor. "Someone *could* have come from outside, Bracken," he told his faithful companion trotting manfully through the deep snow. "That gate and the lane we saw must lead somewhere."

Bracken's expression said he agreed, but with all the snow on the ground he could find no scent.

"The fresh snow would have hidden any vehicle tracks," Ramsay mused, continuing his train of thought.

As the light faded from the sky, the hotel lamps and oil lamps Alfred had placed around the makeshift ice rink, guided Ramsay back to the Manor. A bonfire was beginning to burn as the guests began recovering from the horror.

Avoiding the skaters, Ramsay took the dogs to their

room by the back way. With that done, he and Bracken walked out to view the road and found it still covered in unmarked snow as far as the lights would show him.

"Pity," Ramsay told Bracken. "I'd hoped we would be rid of Inspector Baldock and his merry men tomorrow. That doesn't look likely."

Bracken growled his opinion at Baldock's name.

"I know," Ramsay said, "but just because someone doesn't like dogs it doesn't follow they're a bad person."

Bracken's expression said, 'he couldn't see how it wouldn't.'

They continued around the building where they met the skaters returning from the lake. Ramsay greeted them and they cordially replied. The past twenty-four hours seemed forgotten. Bracken, Ramsay noticed, greeted them too and most stroked him as he brushed against their legs, except Nick Pugachev. Bracken avoided him and he, in turn, made no attempt to engage with Bracken. *Another example of Bracken liking those who like him, or a sign Bracken thinks Pugachev a bad character?*

Ramsay could accept Bracken being partial to some and not to others but, in this case, the one he wasn't partial to happened to be the only one of the six who had a link to Chambers. The Pugachev family and son had sounded genuine when he'd spoken to them, but they would wish to appear innocent, especially if they weren't.

"You should have joined us," Eliza cried, when she reached Ramsay and Bracken. "It was marvelous."

"Marvelous if you can skate," Ramsay replied. "Bracken and I investigated the perimeter of the grounds and found a gate leading to an outside lane."

"Still," Eliza said quietly so they weren't overheard by

the others, "a lane wouldn't have been cleared when the main road hasn't been."

"We have a sleigh and skis," Ramsay replied. "Maybe others have too."

"In England?"

"There are people in England who are more familiar with snow than the English," Ramsay said.

"Oh," Eliza exclaimed. "You mean Russians. But they're all refugees from the nineteen-twenties. They wouldn't still have skis now. That's nearly fifty years ago."

"It's unlikely, I agree," Ramsay said. "Just one more possibility we have to keep in mind."

"If they won't let me into my room to wash and change for dinner," Eliza said, as they reached the point where they needed to go their separate ways, "can I bring my clothes to change in your room?"

Ramsay smiled. "You better had. We can't have you changing in the Ladies Powder Room."

Eliza ran up the stairs and Ramsay and Bracken made their way to his room. Ramsay paused outside the door. "Would you prefer to visit Larry, Harry, and Barry this evening, Bracken? It might be better than watching me dance."

Bracken clearly thought this a great idea. When they arrived at the dogs' room, Bracken and the Labs greeted each other like friends who'd been apart for years, and Ramsay took that as a sign he could safely leave his friend for the evening.

"I'll be back for our walk later," Ramsay said. Bracken hardly noticed.

Back in his room, Ramsay quickly washed and changed. He was adjusting his tie to his satisfaction when a knock came at the door. Eliza stood outside with her clothes and towel when he opened it. "Still won't let you in?" he asked.

"Idiots," Eliza snapped, as she entered and threw her dress on the bed. "What do they imagine we'll get up to while I'm changing? Mam and Dad are having dinner served in their room, in case you're wondering."

"I guessed they would be. I'll be in the bar, when you're finished," Ramsay said. "Don't be too long." He walked to the bar and sat in deep thought with his favorite Scotch. *How likely was it the Pugachevs knew something about Chambers that required him to be killed? And why now?*

Eliza, wearing her chic gown, took Ramsay by surprise when she spoke. "I'm ready."

"You look lovely," Ramsay replied, rising, "but are you sure the room is warm enough for that dress?"

Eliza shrugged. "Sarah wears her dresses every night to dinner, and she hasn't died of pneumonia yet."

Ramsay offered her his arm and they entered the dining room like something from a movie, Ramsay thought, noting that Eliza was right. Sarah did wear similar dresses to dinner, and she was again tonight. It felt all a bit grand for Ramsay.

"Good evening, Mr. Ramsay," Joyce said, bringing them a menu. "You do look very dapper tonight. Both of you."

"He does, doesn't he," Eliza agreed. "He's finally making an effort, I'm pleased to say. One day, I'll have him trained."

"There are times," Ramsay said to Joyce, "when I feel I should hand her back to her parents."

"Ah," Joyce said. "That's what I came to tell you. We hear, from the constables, Inspector Baldock is taking your mother into custody, and she'll likely be charged with murder, Eliza."

Eliza jumped to her feet. "How could he be so stupid?" she demanded of Ramsay.

"The evidence points to Doris," Ramsay said. "He could hardly do less. It's early days. We'll talk to him after dinner and ask why."

"Apparently there's only one set of fingerprints on the knife, Mrs. Danesdale's," Joyce said.

"One of those constables is very indiscreet," Ramsay said.

"I don't think it's a secret," Joyce replied. "Everyone seems to know."

"I want to talk to Baldock now," Eliza said, turning away.

Ramsay grabbed her arm. "Wait," he told her. "We'll get more information from him if we don't go there in a temper."

It took Eliza a moment to accept this and sit. "I don't want anything to eat," she told Joyce. "I can't."

Ramsay ordered his meal and Joyce left them.

"You were the one who asked for that idiot," Eliza hissed.

"With the evidence that exists, any inspector would have done the same," Ramsay said. "If only to help your mother understand the predicament she's in."

"Oh! He's being helpful, is he?" Eliza responded savagely.

20

ELIZA'S MOTHER IS CHIEF SUSPECT

AFTER DINNER, Eliza changed back into everyday clothes, explaining to Ramsay that if it came to a fist fight, she didn't want her dress spoiled. She set off to confront Baldock, with an amused Ramsay along to keep the peace. They found Baldock in their interview room, reviewing the information coming in from his men.

Inspector Baldock listened patiently to Eliza's re-iteration of the evidence against Wright, namely his humiliation by Chambers days earlier, his grievance against Chambers over the death of his parents, and his proximity to the murder scene at the time the murder must have taken place.

When Eliza ran out of breath, Baldock replied, "I haven't ruled out anyone, Miss Danesdale. However, your mother was found crouched over the body, holding the murder weapon and the only fingerprints on it are hers. For now, that's enough for me to charge her."

"And browbeat her into submission while she's in shock over finding the body," Eliza yelled.

Baldock frowned. "Your mother may well be in shock at *what she's done* rather than *what she found*. And I will interview her with her lawyer present; there'll be no coercion, I promise you."

Eliza, taking her cue from Ramsay's expression, bit her lip and remained silent. Ramsay asked, "You read the notes from our interview with Mrs. Danesdale so you know she is clear she found the body?"

"Well, she would, wouldn't she?" Baldock responded. "Look, I understand your feelings, I really do, but you must let me do my job. If Mrs. Danesdale is innocent, that will come out in the investigation."

"Did the Forensic people find any new evidence?" Ramsay asked, hoping to hear they'd found some evidence for a third person in the corridor.

"None, I'm afraid," Baldock replied. "If the murderer isn't Mrs. Danesdale, they left nothing behind to show their presence."

"The corridor was clean and dry," Eliza reminded him. "There wouldn't be footprints or anything like that."

"Thank you, Miss Danesdale, I had thought of that." Baldock's voice remained cool, though with just the tiniest hint of sarcasm in it.

"What are your plans for the rest of today and tomorrow?" Ramsay asked.

"I plan to have everyone's room searched this evening and return to Scarborough tomorrow with my prisoner."

"What?" Eliza cried. "Why?"

"Why what?" Baldock replied.

"Why take my mother away from here? Why search our rooms?"

"I'm searching the rooms as part of the widening search around the crime scene," Baldock replied. "And I'm taking your mother to Scarborough because that's where I'll be for the next days and where she can have legal representation while I interview her."

"Will the road be open or are you using the sleigh to get out?" Ramsay asked.

"The council say they'll have the road open by the morning. Why? Are you thinking of leaving?"

"I'm not but many others may be," Ramsay replied. "Someone should tell them." He was thinking of the two older women.

"I told the owners. I'm sure they'll let everyone know," Baldock said.

"We never interviewed the Misses Forsythe and Dove," Eliza interjected. "Have you?"

Baldock nodded. "We have and they say they saw and heard nothing. Now, I have work to do so you two should go back to your holiday and leave this to us now."

Outside the door, Eliza turned to Ramsay, saying, "I don't like him. He'll investigate nothing and no one because he has an easy victim."

Ramsay said, "Then we need to re-double our efforts to find the real killer. If what you say is true, we're your mother's best hope."

"Where do we start?"

"People will want to leave tomorrow," Ramsay replied, "so we need to talk to them again tonight. Particularly Ernie Wright, as he's the most obvious suspect after your mother."

"Did you believe him about why he's searching our rooms?"

Ramsay laughed. "No. I think there was something missing from Chambers' body, and they want to find it."

"That's what I think too," Eliza replied, "What could be missing?"

Ramsay shrugged. "His watch, wallet, or a lucky or significant object, would be my guess."

"I saw his watch," Eliza replied, thoughtfully. "Did you see his wallet when you examined the body?"

"I didn't, but I assumed he left it in his room. After all, he wouldn't need it at the Christmas Dinner."

"His wife didn't tell us it was missing," Eliza remembered, "and she would have done, I think. So, I'd say a lucky charm, or a significant object is the most likely reason."

"We need to ask his wife and son, as well as others who might have seen something in the days leading up to his death."

"I didn't see anything, did you?" Eliza asked. "Would we notice, if he did wear a lucky charm?"

Ramsay shook his head. "I didn't see anything on him other than a large signet ring. As for others, Miss Forsythe and Miss Dove both wear crosses on their necklaces. Marcus has a St. Christopher ring as well as a signet ring. Pugachev has a ring with what looks like an icon on it. And so on. We do notice but only recall it if our memories are jogged."

"Sarah wears a St. Christopher necklace as well," Eliza added, thinking hard. "The other two girls have something similar, only I can't identify what right now."

"We ask everyone about Chambers' jewelry, starting with his wife and Wright, and we also keep our eyes peeled in case one of them is wearing something we recognize as being worn by Chambers recently."

"Do we interview them together or separately? Us, I mean?" Eliza asked.

"Separately first, together if we get something that looks important. We compare notes in the bar at nine," Ramsay said. "I'll start with Wright."

"We need a list, or we'll annoy everyone," Eliza pointed out. She scribbled down all the people they'd interviewed and showed it to Ramsay. He noted down the ones he felt best suited to interviewing and crossed them out on Eliza's list. She scanned the remaining names, nodded, and said, "I'm off."

At nine, Ramsay was waiting at a table sipping his favorite Glenfiddich when Eliza arrived.

"What did Wright say?" she demanded.

"He told me what he said last time," Ramsay replied, "as you'd expect. He wears a signet ring with his initials on it and nothing else. He doesn't remember Chambers wearing anything like a significant object."

"You should have pressed him more," Eliza grumbled. "He's the one. I know he is."

"Possibly. Now what did you get from Mrs. Chambers?"

"The police told her not to say anything," Eliza replied. "I got nothing from her."

Ramsay smiled. "That confirms what we thought, I think. Something that should have been on his body, wasn't."

"It must be an object that meant something to the murderer," Eliza said, excitedly. "Chambers was flaunting something that belonged to someone else, and the murderer recognized it."

Ramsay nodded his agreement. "We need to talk to the photographer. He may have photos that include Chambers. If the murderer saw it, it may also be visible on a photo."

Eliza became thoughtful for a moment. "I think this means it really was a spur of the moment killing. The murderer suddenly saw, or was shown, the object and immediately killed Chambers to recover the object. This wasn't someone coming from outside or coming here with the intention of killing him."

"Unfortunately, that again makes your mother one of the most likely suspects," Ramsay said. "We're building a case against her."

Eliza shook her head. "I don't think we're making things worse because I suspect Baldock already figured this out the moment he heard of the missing object."

"Were any of your witnesses helpful about jewelry?" Ramsay asked.

"None of them. What about yours?"

"I think Julia Phillipson may be able to help, if we can separate her from her husband," Ramsay replied. "They're back on speaking terms and, when I questioned them, they were together. They said they never noticed anything but something about her expression makes me wonder."

"We must get her alone then. What about Redhill?"

"He too said no more than he told us before," Ramsay replied. "He seems uninterested in everything that's happening, which I find odd."

"I don't," Eliza replied. "He looks like he has only days to live. Why would he care?"

"Maybe you're right," Ramsay agreed. "I spoke to the photographer on the phone, and he's agreed to bring us the photos he took before everything closed down. We must hope the road is open tomorrow."

21

FINALLY, A REAL SUSPECT

The first vehicle into the dale, following closely behind the council's bulldozer, was the photographer. He lived closest and hoped to sell photos to the guests before they left. When Ramsay, Bracken, and Eliza were summoned by Joyce, the photographer occupied the hotel's office.

They examined every photo he'd taken that night, put aside any with the victim visible, until they were sure they'd seen them all. Taking these back to Ramsay's room, they left the photographer to offer his remaining photos to the guests.

The first guests to leave were the two elderly ladies who'd summoned a taxi as soon as they were informed the road would be open. Ramsay had one last try to procure something from them concerning the night of the murder; they were adamant they were in their room with the radio on, listening to a Christmas broadcast. They knew nothing about the murder. He believed them.

The next to leave were the Phillipsons who finding the only local taxi willing to come into the dale had just left with the elderly ladies in it, demanded the hotel take them to the nearest train station. The Mesmerising Marvel demanded he be allowed to join them, and the stolid, reliable Alfred had been called to drive them all in the hotel's Morris Minor shooting brake. While their baggage was being loaded and with Mr. Phillipson at the car supervising Alfred in the correct way to handle luggage, Eliza took the opportunity to hustle Mrs. Phillipson into the Powder Room.

Amused, Ramsay watched Alfred's expression as the last of the bags were loaded and decided the Phillipsons better tip well. The Powder Room door opened. Mrs. Phillipson exited as her husband came in search of her, and then they too were gone.

When silence descended on the lobby, Eliza peered out from around the Powder Room door. With the lobby clear, Eliza rejoined Ramsay, her eyes shone, and her smile couldn't have been wider.

"Well?"

"A kind of brooch he used as a tie pin," Eliza whispered, looking about her. "It had a black eagle with two heads and other things on it. 'Like our royal regalia', she said."

"The double-headed eagle was the Romanov family crest," Ramsay mused. "Maybe his family were minor royalty – or just royalists, perhaps. It would explain why he had to leave, if his family were related or well-known supporters."

"It might explain his manners," Eliza muttered. "He treated everyone like serfs."

"We must find that pin," Ramsay said. "I wish now I'd asked Miss Forsythe and Miss Dove to empty out their cases."

"And the Phillipsons," Eliza added, then shaking her

head, added, "No. She wouldn't have told me about it if they had it."

They had to stop mulling over their new evidence when they spotted Baldock, Doris, Colin and a constable descending the stairs.

"You're making a terrible mistake, Inspector," Eliza told him as they reached the foot of the stairs. "And we'll prove it very soon."

Baldock didn't reply. Nor did he stop Eliza from hugging her mother, who was still oblivious to everything around her, and saying, "Don't worry, Tom will find the real culprit." She turned to her father and noticed he was carrying two cases. "Are you going too, Dad?"

"Your mother will need me to organize things for her defense," he replied. "And I want to visit every day. I can't do that from here. You and Tom stay and find the real culprit and we'll all be together at home again soon."

The small unhappy group exited the hotel, with Bracken trotting unhappily behind, and into the two police cars waiting outside. Ramsay and Eliza watched them leave. Bracken returned, clearly puzzled at this unexpected event.

"I hope they crash and Mam escapes," Eliza muttered.

"Your mother is in no fit state to live outdoors on the moors in this weather," Ramsay reminded her. "Now we have work to do. If we find that pin on Wright, it should be enough to have your mother released."

"We'll need help from Joyce," Eliza said. "He won't let us search his belongings if he has it."

"The police searched his and everyone's belongings," Ramsay reminded her, "and they didn't find it. Where might it be hidden until it was safe to pick it up?"

"Anywhere!"

"Not anywhere the cleaners might find it. Not anywhere

the kitchen staff might find it. Not anywhere guests might stumble across it," Ramsay replied. "Somewhere clever."

"The cold room," Eliza cried. "Or inside something he wears or has with him at all times, like a spectacles case or a book."

"He smokes a pipe so a tobacco tin," Ramsay added. "They searched the cars, but he came by taxi so that's out. He always sits at the same table at meals and stool at the bar. We can start with those."

After ensuring the bar and dining room were empty, they set to work on the chairs, cushions, tables, and nearby fittings. Even Bracken found nothing. The cold room too turned out to be free of hidden objects, though it did give Bracken the opportunity to rejoin his friends and follow them outside for a run in the snow. Joyce assured Ramsay neither Wright nor any other guest had been given keys and he'd never been seen in there when staff were present. The same objection applied to the equipment storage room.

"It's on him then," Eliza said. "We need to search his room when he's out."

"Lunch is on its way," Ramsay replied. "I'll take our table and you search his room when he's safely in the dining room if Joyce will loan us the key for thirty minutes."

Joyce thought this an awful idea and said so. Fortunately, Frederick arrived during the discussion and said, "We might agree to this provided it is you, Mr. Ramsay, who searches."

"Why not me?" Eliza demanded.

"Because Mr. Ramsay was a police officer, and I'm confident he knows how to do this without arousing suspicion," Frederick said, bluntly.

"We accept," Ramsay replied. "When he enters the dining room, Eliza will take our seat. I'll take the spare key and search his room."

Dark Deeds on a White Christmas

"I'll ask Ellen to drag his meal out," Joyce said. "A little longer between courses should give you the time you need."

"Don't tell her why," Ramsay pleaded. "The fewer people who know of this, the better."

"The police searched everyone's rooms, though," Frederick said. "Why do you think you'll find whatever it is you're looking for?"

"The police are gone," Ramsay said. "If it was hidden, it's now safe to bring out and admire."

"What is this thing?" Joyce asked, baffled.

"We'd rather not say," Ramsay replied. "Later, when this is over everyone will be told. Now, we'll let you go back to work, and I'll return just before noon."

They left the lobby heading for Ramsay's room. "While we wait, we'll examine every one of those photos. Maybe we'll spot that pin. It might help us find it, if it's hidden cleverly."

It didn't take long. The tiepin was clearly visible on several photos though without a magnifying glass, hard to examine.

"I have one," Eliza said. "Now I can enter my own room we can use it to examine these photos."

"Why have you a magnifying glass?" Ramsay asked, as they hurried upstairs with the photos inside his jacket.

"I bought it for our cases," Eliza replied, reddening.

Ramsay laughed. "You're the eternal optimist. I'll give you that."

"I'm the realist," Eliza said, "and we'll be on our tenth case before you wake up."

They were still bickering when they arrived at the Danesdales' room.

"That's it all right," Ramsay said, when they were safely

in the room and examining the photos through the glass. "We need the photographer to blow this up."

"He's still in the office taking orders," Eliza told Ramsay. "At least he was when we were talking to Joyce because I heard him."

The photographer took their order of four blown-up photos of the pin, entering it into his notebook. "Others are ahead of you. Do you need this right away?"

Ramsay nodded. "How much to do these first and bring them back here today?" The price wasn't too high, and Ramsay agreed.

"I'll be back before dark," the photographer told them. "The weather is supposed to be bad again overnight."

By the time the photographer had taken the last of the photo orders, it was lunch time. Ramsay and Eliza took up a position where they could watch the door and, through it, Wright's seat. It wasn't long before Wright appeared. When he entered the dining room and took his usual seat, Eliza left Ramsay to take up her place at the lunch table too.

Ramsay had already been given the master key, and he set off quickly to his task. Unfortunately, Redhill appeared out of his room and Ramsay lost valuable time going into his own room to wait for the corridor to clear. When it was, he rushed to Wright's room and began searching before anyone else arrived to stop him.

His hands flew across the tobacco tins on the desk and flitted through the man's soap bag before giving up on those in disgust. He rifled the drawers of the bedside table and the chest of drawers opposite the foot of the bed. He pulled cases out from under the bed and searched those. Wright's slippers were under the bed as well and he shook them, but nothing fell out. A chamber pot lay beside Wright's slippers, fortunately it was empty, and it also didn't contain the tiepin.

On the dressing table in front of the mirror lay a fine silver set of brushes, combs, and scissors. Ramsay picked up the hairbrush and examined it closely. He'd heard of things hidden in the false backs of brushes. The hairbrush back was unmovable, the clothes brush wasn't. He flicked the tiny catch with his thumbnail and slid the back off exposing the cavity. The tiepin was nestled inside.

Replacing everything as he found it, he opened the door, checked the corridor, and left quickly for his own room, where he phoned Baldock. The inspector answered with his customary growl. A growl that grew louder when he learned what Ramsay had done.

"You had no right doing that," Baldock reminded him.

"We had to find that pin," Ramsay said. "You need to come here and search again."

"How can I be sure you didn't just plant it on Wright?" Baldock demanded.

"When you find it, it'll have Wright's fingerprints on it," Ramsay said. "By the way, it's damaged. I think it took the brunt of the knife thrust, which is why Chambers wasn't killed instantly."

"I'll be there in forty-five minutes," Baldock said. "You be sure he doesn't go back to his room."

"I'll do my best," Ramsay said. "You know the Phillipsons and the Misses Forsythe and Dove have left, I imagine. You will be continuing to include them in the investigation going forward?"

"Ramsay, I shouldn't have to say this," Baldock replied. "I do know my job. Just because they aren't under your feet at the hotel doesn't mean I've lost sight of them. You keep your eyes on the ones you're still tripping over."

Ramsay chuckled. "I will, have no fear. Oh, one more thing. What is it you're not telling us about Doris?"

Baldock paused so long, Ramsay wasn't sure he hadn't left. Eventually, Baldock said, "Don't tell Eliza right now, this may never come out if Wright is the killer."

Ramsay agreed and Baldock said, "When she was a child, Mrs. Danesdale threw a bucket of whitewash over a boy who kept teasing her. Whitewash then was made of lime, and it blinded him for life."

"She was just a child," Ramsay protested.

"It shows she has a temper, and a prosecutor will use it," Baldock replied evenly. "Also, she'd assaulted Chambers back in the day. He didn't press charges because his own behavior would have come to light but, again, Doris Danesdale is no shrinking violet and stabbing Chambers in a fit of rage will sound very plausible to a jury."

"I understand and you're right," Ramsay said. "Well, it's still not her, it's Wright, and if you're here quickly enough, you can prove it."

Hanging up the phone, Ramsay put on a dinner jacket and made his way to join Eliza. He grinned when he saw her absentmindedly crumbling bread between her fingers.

"Where have you been," she hissed as he sat beside her.

Whispering, Ramsay told her of all that had happened. Her anger disappeared and her expression was now joyful.

"Don't look at him," Ramsay warned, when she was about to smile triumphantly across the room at Wright. "We need him to stay right here in the dining room until the police arrive."

Forty-five minutes crawled by, as they nervously ate their meal and watched while Wright began preparing to leave the table. Before he could rise, Joyce arrived at his side and began talking to him.

Ramsay breathed a sigh of relief and surreptitiously glanced at his watch until Joyce and Wright had no more to say. However, before she'd left the room, Frederick was there, heartily asking Wright if his meal had been to his satisfaction and would he be staying for the band tonight. When Wright appeared to say he wasn't, Frederick proceeded to explain how, with the road open, all the band would be playing and well worth hearing.

Faintly, from outside, they heard police cars' bells and Ramsay smiled. He whispered to Eliza, "I think it's done."

The front door opened and then Baldock's voice boomed through the lobby calling for the receptionist.

Joyce hurried to meet him, and they spoke briefly. Joyce hesitantly pointed to the dining room and a moment later, Baldock was striding across the room to confront Wright.

After a brief discussion, Wright followed Baldock into the lobby and out of sight. The dining room became silent a moment and then everyone burst into excited low chatter that grew quickly into astonished excitement.

They were all still in that state when, fifteen minutes later, Baldock, Wright, and a police constable were seen leaving the hotel for a police car.

"Mam's safe," Eliza cried, beaming.

"For now," Ramsay replied.

"Them arresting her was madness," Eliza said. "She's the mildest person in the universe, after Dad. She would never hurt anyone."

Ramsay thought it best to agree. *Eliza would never believe her mother capable of what she'd already done, let alone what she might have done.*

22

TIMING IS EVERYTHING

ELIZA'S HAPPINESS grew even greater when, after her afternoon of skating with the young people and then tobogganing with Ramsay and Bracken, she received a message from Joyce as she returned to her room. Her father had phoned to say they were both at home. Eliza's only disappointment was learning they didn't want to return to the Manor. Her mother couldn't yet face that.

The Danesdales didn't have a phone in the house, so Eliza wasn't able to phone them back and snow was beginning to fall again. Driving home to support them might have to wait.

"Though," she told Ramsay, "the holiday spirit has gone out of the place and an early return might be best. After all, there's nothing more we can do here."

"You go," Ramsay said, both pleased and saddened she didn't want to continue their stay. "Until I hear Wright has been formally charged, I'm going to keep working on this case. Something's not right."

"He had the pin," Eliza said. "He hated Chambers. He

was in the vicinity when the murder occurred. What more do you want?"

"Why did he have the pin?" Ramsay replied. "He's not Russian. It has no meaning for him."

"A trophy or a keepsake, what does it matter?"

"You're probably right," Ramsay said, "but I think we'll find out more if we keep digging. For you, being home with your mother is where you should be."

"You're trying to be rid of me," Eliza replied, glaring at him. "We're partners. If you're staying, I'm staying."

"Then we should ask ourselves, who would want that pin?" Ramsay asked.

"Nick Pugachev or his dad," Eliza replied, "and also Mrs. Chambers and her son, Gregory."

Ramsay nodded. "The pin is only of value to someone who believed in its cause, I think," Ramsay agreed. "It didn't look to me like it was valuable for itself."

"It might be made of silver," Eliza mused. "But even if it is, it wouldn't be enough to kill for."

"The two Chambers wouldn't have needed to take it," Ramsay said. "It would come to them with his personal effects, which only leaves your friend Nick Pugachev."

"More likely his father, I'd say," Eliza told him. "Nick grew up here."

Again, Ramsay agreed, yet said, "You keep mixing with the three couples and gently interrogate Nick Pugachev."

"But how did it come to be in Wright's possession?" Eliza suddenly cried. "If Nick took it from the body, how did Wright come to have it?"

"I think something like this: Wright was passing the end of the corridor, watched Pugachev stab Chambers and tear the pin from his body. Pugachev stuffed the pin in his jacket pocket, where it wouldn't be seen, only it didn't go in properly. Maybe the design caught on the fabric. Whatever the reason, the pin fell to the ground as Pugachev hurried off and Wright took it."

"Blackmail," Eliza said.

Ramsay nodded. "I think so. He blamed Chambers for the deaths of his parents and may have thought getting some compensation from the community Chambers came from as justice. Something like that."

"You think Wright will be released?" Eliza asked, anxiously.

"If there are any fingerprints on the pin that aren't Chambers or Wrights and he tells a good story of how he came by it, yes," Ramsay replied.

"Then Mam might be back in custody," Eliza cried.

"You'll have wormed the truth out of Nick Pugachev by then, I have no doubt of that."

"I'll find them and start right now," Eliza said and hurried off to search for the couples.

Ramsay too headed for the lobby. From the door, he saw guests skating, tobogganing, and even a stately sleigh ride with Redhill as the only passenger. Ramsay was still watching when Eliza hurried past him, dressed for the outdoors.

"I'll have the answer out of him by nightfall," she whispered as she passed.

"Gently does it," Ramsay warned her, but she was already halfway across the snowy drive heading for the lake where the Pugachevs were expertly skating. *Maybe skating is in their Russian blood.*

When Ramsay spotted the sleigh return, and no one waiting to board it, he thought, *Poor Alfred, stuck sitting on a sleigh in the cold with no customers.* Hurrying back to his room, he dressed and walked out to the sleigh. *The perfect chance to re-interview the man who does everything around here.*

Alfred greeted him warmly and Ramsay knew he'd guessed right. The man was bored out of his mind.

"It's quiet with everyone gone," Ramsay said, settling himself into the seat and blankets provided for the passengers.

"Now they've taken Mr. Wright into custody, will Mr. and Mrs. Danesdale come back?" Alfred asked.

"I'm afraid not," Ramsay told him. "The experience was too much for Mrs. Danesdale."

"Aye, poor lady. She were horror-struck that night. I were in the war and experienced one or two cases like that."

"And now the police have taken Mr. Wright into custody," Ramsay continued. "They must think we're all in on it." He laughed to show he wasn't serious.

"Yon fellow will enjoy being the victim," Alfred said. "I never once met him, but he would try to persuade me I were being exploited and should join a union."

"You certainly do a lot of the work around here," Ramsay told him.

Alfred nodded. "I like to be busy, right enough. That's no business of anyone but me."

"Then you've found the perfect job," Ramsay laughed. "You're doing something different every time I see you."

"Who would want to spend their life doing the same thing every day?" Alfred asked, then added. "That's no way for a man to live."

"I suppose that was part of why I liked the police," Ramsay replied. "Always something new happening in the neighborhood."

"Aye, I suppose," Alfred said, in his low steady voice. "I don't reckon they'll convict Mr. Wright though."

"Why not?"

Alfred turned and gazed at Ramsay. "You met him, talked to him, didn't you?"

"You don't think him the type to kill someone?" Ramsay hazarded.

"Him? Nah! He'd pull the wings off flies, but kill a man? No!" Alfred shook his head to emphasize his point.

Ramsay's assessment of Wright had been exactly that, which is why he liked his blackmail theory. It fitted Wright's character better.

"Still," Ramsay said, "he told me he was a Union Steward and that can be a rough business."

Alfred laughed. "He's a steward in a union of office workers. No doubt he'll claim to be the victim of police brutality when he gets back to work. He'll be a hero, you'll see."

"You may be right," Ramsay agreed. "Now you've had time to think about it, does anything strike you as odd? Something maybe you thought all right at the time, but now doesn't?"

"Nay, I were too busy to worry about what the guests were doing," Alfred replied. "What I can say is it happened very fast. I'd just passed by that corridor only minutes before, and I saw no one."

"You couldn't say how many minutes, I suppose?"

"Nay," Alfred laughed. "I wasn't keeping track of the time. Why? Are you thinking it might have been old Mr. Redhill?"

Ramsay laughed "Not really. It's just that, if it was one minute, it would have to be a young person. Two or three minutes, brings in the middle-aged ones. Five minutes or more might bring even Mr. Redhill into the picture." *And the possibility of two people, one stabbing, one stealing.*

"I could tell you later," Alfred said, thoughtfully. "I

remember what I did and where I was when Doreen called me to the body. I can re-trace my steps and time myself."

"Do, please," Ramsay urged. "As soon as possible."

"If you'll wait with the sleigh when I park it and tell anyone who comes I've just gone to the Gents, I'll do it right now." As he finished speaking, he drew the sleigh to a halt where it waited for guests.

When Ramsay agreed, Alfred climbed down from the driver's seat and ambled off to the Manor. Ramsay smiled. *If he walked at that speed on the night of the murder, anyone could have done it.*

No one came for the sleigh, which disappointed Ramsay for he was toying with the idea of being the driver. So he had mixed feelings when Alfred came ambling back.

"I'd say four, maybe five, minutes," Alfred said, in answer to Ramsay's unspoken question. He climbed back into the driver's seat and settled down to wait.

"Someone as frail as Mr. Redhill could have done it then," Ramsay said, sadly. "I was hoping to at least rule him out."

"You can rule out the band members and the Lord of Misrule," Alfred reminded him.

"I already had," Ramsay agreed. "I saw all of them myself."

"I were at the back of the stage and could see all those still sitting," Alfred continued. "But I told you all that."

"You noticed Redhill and Wright leave, didn't you?"

"I did. They left together. Once they were out of the door, I couldn't see them then, of course."

"That's my difficulty," Ramsay replied. "Wright went into the Gents just outside the door. Redhill wasn't seen. Why not?"

"He's so slow, he may not have made it out into the lobby when your witness saw Wright," Alfred said.

"It's true, and Mr. Redhill stops so often for a rest, he likely was just out of sight. It's annoying."

"He would be able to see into the corridor where it happened, if that were the case," Alfred said. "Which means the murderer had quite a bit less than five minutes, unless the murderer is Mr. Redhill, of course."

Ramsay nodded, saying, "The difficulty with Redhill is his frailty. Chambers would brush him aside long before it came to knives. It must be one of the young people. Likely Chambers had been too handsy with the girls and one of the boys took exception."

"He were a dirty old man, right enough," Alfred said. "He shocked more than one of the kitchen staff. We're not used to that kind of thing around here. Not often anyway."

"No one mentioned that," Ramsay said, annoyed.

"We don't like to speak ill of the dead," Alfred responded.

"But that's withholding evidence," Ramsay protested.

"And it isn't our job to help snoops either," Alfred replied. His words were cutting but said without any anger or malice. It was just a fact of life.

"Did you tell the police?"

"I didn't because it wasn't me that were shocked. I've no idea if the lasses did," Alfred replied.

His calm statements frustrated Ramsay. *How many investigations had ended without a successful conclusion because communities wouldn't trust the police?*

23

MONEY MATTERS

RAMSAY WAS at their dinner table waiting for Eliza, when Mr. Redhill shuffled into the room. With Wright gone, he would be alone at his table. Ramsay crossed the room and asked if he'd like to join Ramsay and Eliza, saying, "Perhaps better than eating alone tonight."

Redhill considered his answer carefully. "Perhaps not for dinner," he replied, smiling. "Your pretty, young companion won't thank you for inviting me. But I would like to talk to you. In the bar, later?"

Ramsay pressed his invitation to sit with them for dinner, without success. In the end, Ramsay agreed to a drink in the bar, before returning to his seat.

Eliza, when she joined him for dinner, wasn't any happier with her afternoon than he had been with his.

"Nick says he never noticed the tiepin Chambers wore," Eliza told Ramsay. "He claims never to have looked at the man closely, he despised him that much."

Ramsay found that hard to believe. "What about his wife?"

"She saw it, and his signet ring," Eliza replied. "Sarah did too. Marcus, like Nick, couldn't believe anyone would look at jewelry a man wore."

Ramsay laughed. "I believe that. If I wasn't trained to observe, I'd never notice things people wear either."

"The girls would have mentioned the pin to the boys, though, wouldn't they?" Eliza suggested.

"But did the boys listen?"

"I bet Nick did and, when he talked it over with his father, he was ordered to take it. I didn't much like Pugachev senior when we spoke to him. I thought he sounded shifty."

Frederick brought them the menu, explaining the kitchen was short-staffed again because the weather reports for evening and overnight were bad.

"Then we may be cut off again tomorrow," Eliza suggested. "Oliver and Celina will be upset. They wanted to leave today while the road was open, and the others persuaded them not to go."

"They'll soon have the road cleared tomorrow. The first time through is always the hardest," Frederick replied. "Your friends will be able to go."

Eliza grimaced. "I hope so."

When Frederick had moved on, she said quietly to Ramsay, "You might have noticed Oliver and Celina were tobogganing and not skating?"

Ramsay nodded.

"Well, Celina claims her ankles are too weak for skating, but the truth is, they've fallen out with the other two couples. There may be fireworks tomorrow if we're shut in."

"We may learn something if that happens," Ramsay said. He looked at the table where the three couples were sitting. It was certainly much subdued compared to earlier in the holiday. *Could he and Eliza use this to their advantage?*

Ellen brought in their first course, which gave Ramsay time to ponder this important question.

"I'll stay close to them tomorrow," Eliza said, between bites, "and maybe I'll learn something to our advantage."

"Can we do anything to bring on the break-up?" Ramsay asked. "Have you any ideas?"

"They're talking of going shooting again," Eliza replied. "Frederick has a Land Rover ready to take them. I could borrow one of their guns and lightly 'wing' Oliver." Eliza laughed.

Ignoring Eliza's satiric suggestion, Ramsay replied, "They'll be cold, especially the ones watching and not taking part. Maybe work on that. Play up the men's callous disregard for their female partners, that sort of thing."

"It might work, though the boys did offer the girls a turn with the guns last time, so it won't be an easy argument to make."

"By the time they've been out for an hour or more, I think it will work. If not, the conversation might suggest avenues to explore, gaps to widen."

Eliza nodded, her mouth too full to speak. Finally, she asked, "What about tonight?"

"The band is setting up, there'll be dancing. Maybe you can do something with that."

"Aren't you glad now that I'm your partner?" Eliza asked. "After all, you have no way of talking to those people except as a policeman or a parent. And they wouldn't respond to either."

Ramsay smiled. "You win. You're the perfect partner."

Eliza took his hand and squeezed it. "I am, and so are you. You're just not ready to accept it yet." She paused, then added, "And I've done some sounding out for a commission."

"What?" Ramsay cried, startled.

"When I put away my skates, Frederick was nearby. I suggested the hotel needed a satisfactory end to this mystery, now the police were just arresting anyone they suspect. He said they'd already considered having private detectives working for him to be sure the hotel's name isn't tarnished. He said, he'd spoken to you?"

Ramsay nodded. "He did suggest it. I didn't follow up on the suggestion."

"Why not?" Eliza cried. "They want help. We should help. And we should be paid for it."

"Eliza," Ramsay whispered angrily. "The police are not fumbling, and we are no more likely to solve the mystery than they are. *And*," he said dramatically, "we can't be certain of keeping the hotel's name out of anything."

"Pooh. I didn't say we could, nor did I guarantee we'd catch the murderer. I just raised some thoughts he might want to consider, and I think he agrees having us on his side would help. I think he'd already been thinking that way."

Ramsay groaned. "I'm not going to be able to look him, or Joyce, in the eye again for the rest of the holiday."

"I'm sure you didn't feel that way when your police pay was handed to you each week," Eliza said, puzzled. "It's in their interests as well as ours for us to solve this."

Seeing he wasn't going to change her mind, Ramsay decided he'd better straighten it out with Frederick after dinner; he dropped the subject.

After dinner, Eliza wanted to dance, which they did until he finally said he was going to bed. Eliza pretended to be very understanding of his age and offered to help him to his room. Ramsay wanted to box her ears but smiled grimly instead.

"Maybe we should have hot cocoa in your room," Eliza suggested, as they made their way to his room.

"If you don't go back to that ballroom and ingratiate yourself with those couples, I won't be responsible for my actions," Ramsay replied.

She kissed him and left, waving gaily back to him as she returned along the corridor to the ballroom.

In his room, Ramsay phoned reception. "Can I speak to Frederick," he asked, when Joyce answered the phone.

"He's bedding down the dogs for the night, can I help you?"

"Has Frederick explained about Eliza's suggestion regarding money?" Ramsay asked, cautiously.

"Oh, yes," Joyce said. "We'd like to talk more about that tomorrow. Things will be a bit tight here with all that's happened, but we do see the sense in it. What are your usual rates?"

As Ramsay had never seriously expected to be charging anyone for solving mysteries, and he had nothing else to go on, he told her what he'd charged in the pet case.

"Well," Joyce said, "Frederick and I will discuss it tonight and we'll see what we can do."

Stunned, Ramsay said, weakly, "Thank you," and hung up the handset. *Apparently, the secret to getting paid for your work was simply to ask for it. Eliza right again.*

Remembering his promise to Redhill and hoping the man hadn't given up and gone to bed, Ramsay hurried back to the bar.

"Sorry about that," Ramsay said, with considerable relief on seeing the man still waiting. "Eliza would dance, and then I had to phone Inspector Baldock. I talk with him on a schedule you understand, and... well, I'm late."

Redhill gave his weary smile and said it didn't matter.

"Do you have something particular you wanted to say?" Ramsay asked.

Redhill frowned. "There was and now I can't remember what. It's these pills they give me. My mind is like cotton wool much of the time. Have a seat and it will come back to me."

At the bar, Ramsay bought Redhill a second drink and himself a whisky before returning to sit beside the man.

Thinking it might jog Redhill's memory if they talked, Ramsay asked, "Do you often spend time alone at hotels or was it the Christmas event you wanted to enjoy?"

Redhill chuckled so softly Ramsay barely heard him. "I'm spending what would have been my children's inheritance, if I had children." He paused, then continued, "I'd better explain. Eighteen months ago, I had a business and worked every hour God gave me until, one day, I felt strange and went to the doctor. I expected a 'take two aspirins and lie down answer'. He told me I had less than six months to live. I should retire and enjoy myself with the time I had left."

"I'm sorry to hear that," Ramsay interjected.

Redhill brushed Ramsay's words aside with a wave of a trembling hand and continued, "I sold my business and took a villa in the South of France. For six months, right through that winter, I did everything I'd never done before, drank wine, ate too much food, listened to local songs, and even," he chuckled, "fended off some predatory females."

Ramsay laughed. "That sounds like a proper vacation."

Redhill nodded. "I came back for my six month checkup and again I was told I had less than six months to live, and I should make the best of my time. Unfortunately, I'd spent so much in the previous six months, I couldn't afford

France. I went to Spain, a lovely little fishing village on the Costa Brava."

"Lots of people are going there now, I'm told," Ramsay commented.

Redhill nodded, smiling sadly. "I took boat trips with an old fisherman and asked how he felt about the new hotels being built along the beach. He said, they all loved it. They'd become what Jesus told his disciples, 'no longer fishermen but fishers of men'. What he meant was, instead of going out every evening and early morning to catch the few remaining sardines and pilchards in the sea, they were taking holiday-makers out to fish for tuna and were growing wealthy by their standards."

"I suppose it is good that way," Ramsay agreed. "It will devastate our own holiday towns here in England, though."

Redhill agreed. "We don't have the sun in England. You can't blame people for wanting to see it. It was what I did, when the doctor said retire."

"You came back though?"

"If I hadn't returned for my twice a year doctor appointment, how would he tell me I had no more than six months to live?" Redhill laughed. It wasn't a happy sound.

"You couldn't afford Spain again?" Ramsay suggested.

"Not easily. Still, it was late summer, and I needed to sell my house and wind up other affairs, which left me at a loss for the winter. Then someone told me of this 'Traditional Christmas Feast' at Harkness Manor and here I am." He slumped back against his chair as if exhausted by so much effort.

"Sadly, it hasn't been as happy as advertised," Ramsay said.

"But it has been exciting," Redhill replied. "I've never

been involved in anything like this in all my years. Which is what I wanted to ask you; I've finally remembered."

Ramsay waited patiently while Redhill thought about what he wanted to say.

"How likely is it that Mr. Wright is charged with murder and, if he isn't, how likely will your travel companion, Mrs. Danesdale, be charged?"

Ramsay answered carefully, "I can't be sure of either of them. Inspector Baldock doesn't take me fully into his confidence, I'm afraid. That he has good evidence is clear but to make a case requires much more than that. Why?"

"Neither looks like the murdering type, I suppose," Redhill replied. "Perhaps that's always the way, is it?"

"Not in my experience," Ramsay replied. "Had you grown fond of Mr. Wright? You were seated together most nights."

Redhill smiled his sad smile. "Not fond. He was much too sure of his opinions. And he had many strong opinions. I just don't see him as the killer, I suppose."

"You didn't know him before you came here?"

"I didn't," Redhill replied, "though we live not so far from each other apparently."

"If you were in business locally, you would know Paul Chambers, I imagine," Ramsay suggested.

"I knew of him and what I knew I didn't like. We were in completely different lines of business, I'm pleased to say."

Ramsay continued, "You would meet Chambers at business events and conferences, wouldn't you?"

"I would if I chose to, which I didn't," Redhill replied. He continued, "I grow so tired in the evenings, so I think I'll go to bed now. You've set my mind at rest over the two suspects, Mr. Ramsay, thank you." He rose unsteadily to his feet and shuffled away.

Poor man. I fear the doctor has it right this time, Ramsay thought as he watched him leave. He was about to follow when the door between the bar and the ballroom flew open, and Eliza bounced through.

"You were supposed to be resting, not interrogating witnesses without me," she whispered.

"I couldn't let you do all the work," Ramsay replied. "Are you having any success?"

"I'm not telling you," Eliza retorted, "until you tell me."

"I'm tired," Ramsay said. "We can recap all we've learned in the morning. Good night." He smiled, kissed her cheek and set off.

Eliza was walking at his side immediately. "What did he say?"

"He asked if I thought Baldock would be able to charge your mother or Wright with what evidence he had."

"You've been sitting with him for hours," Eliza protested. "There must be more than that?"

"Everything else just led up to that question."

"What did you tell him?"

"I said it would depend on new evidence turning up," Ramsay replied. "Now, I'm at my room. You go back and continue interrogating the Hooray Henrys, particularly Nick Pugachev and Gregory Chambers. Something is there, I'm sure of it."

* * *

ELIZA RETURNED TO THE OTHERS, who were slouching around a table stacked with drinks and empty glasses. They were listening intently to another of Gregory's stories of life in London, which Eliza still found hard to entirely believe.

"You've met Mick Jagger?" Sarah asked Gregory, who'd been talking about a party he'd recently attended.

Gregory nodded. Eliza thought he looked like those dogs you saw in car windows with the nodding heads.

"What's he like?"

"Great guy," Gregory said. "He says he might fund my next play, if he likes it."

"Have you met Paul McCartney?" Eliza asked.

"I go to all the parties," Gregory said. "When you're in the arts, you're in with the crowd. In London, it's all about art, music, painting, fashion, movies, and, of course, theater."

"Sounds to me like it's all about money," Oliver said

"Money's the reward for getting the art right, that's all," Gregory replied. "We're about life, man. We're the new world of art, not your sordid old world of moneymaking for the sake of it."

"Is McCartney going to fund you too?" Eliza continued.

"Nah. He's not the intellectual of that group," Gregory said. "Lennon, though, he will, I'm certain."

"Do you know Jean Shrimpton?" Sarah asked, her eyes shining.

"I could introduce you," Gregory replied, "if you come down. Models are making big money now. More than you'll ever make strutting your stuff here in Yorkshire."

Oliver grinned triumphantly. "Art for art's sake."

Gregory was irritated. "What didn't you understand when I said, 'reward for doing it right'?"

"I understood perfectly," Oliver replied, his expression contemptuous.

"You told us your father's allowance wasn't enough for you," Marcus said. "So how do you live while you wait for Lennon and Jagger to fund your plays?"

"I do some acting," Gregory responded. "And I buy and sell some pills."

"Pills?" Eliza cried.

"Yeah. We have pills for everything in London, and it'll only get better. Soon, you'll take a pill and write a masterpiece or climb a mountain or whatever you want to do."

"I thought it was weed you all smoked," Celina said. "That's what you told us yesterday."

"We do. It's why we can see the future and you can't, yet. Once you join us and your mind is opened, awakened, you can't ever live in this backward way we live now."

"We can't all smoke your Wacky Baccy though, Greg," Nick told him. "There are millions of people and only a little dope."

"As people waken, the fields growing crap like sugar, which kills you, will be growing weed and everyone will be living the life we should all have had if it wasn't for the rich," Gregory replied.

"I'm from a farming family," Oliver said. "Weed won't grow here. How will people pay for their food if everyone is living the way you say?"

"You can't see it yet," Gregory said. "No one will be working to live. People will grow food and exchange it for what pleases them. Everything will belong to everyone."

Eliza laughed. "You mean I can wear Sarah's necklace when I want to?"

"In your dreams," Sarah said, grinning inanely.

"Yes, that's it," Gregory cried. "No more personal possessions."

"What if I don't want to share my necklace?" Sarah asked, no longer grinning.

"You and Eliza would share a joint or two and you'd

share," Gregory replied, earnestly. "You'd want her to experience the same pleasure in it as you have."

"What if I want it too?" Celina asked. "This won't work."

"I wish I had some weed with me," Gregory said, sadly. "Then you'd see the future and how easy it all will be."

"Celina's point is a good one though, Gregory," Oliver said. "Does she just share a joint or two with Eliza and then she gets to have a turn with the necklace?"

"Yes, yes," Gregory said, excited. "That's how easy it is."

"And the weed," Nick asked, "it's just growing wild, is it?"

"I said," Gregory retorted, irritated again that his audience wasn't fully joining into the glorious vision of the future, "wherever it can grow, it will be grown, and people will pick and pack it for their own and others' pleasure."

"I'm surprised you haven't had the police at your door," Eliza said, her brow furrowed in thought.

Gregory sniggered. "I can handle the fuzz. I'm a storyteller, remember. They can't lay a finger on me."

"They have been at your door?" Eliza persisted.

"Sure, they've hassled me," Gregory boasted. "They know I sell a few pills, but they can't prove I'm a dealer, cos I'm not."

"You sell drugs?" Oliver asked, incredulous at what he was hearing.

"Only some uppers, nothing heavy," Gregory said, airily. "We all do a bit. Buy more than we need when we have cash, sell some when we're low. It's how we party all day and night."

"You say the police know this?" Oliver asked, still unable to believe what he was hearing.

"Like I said, man," Gregory responded, angrily, "I'm a writer. I can tell a story they believe, and they go away frustrated."

Eliza almost laughed at Oliver's expression, which said he clearly didn't think Gregory's storytelling skill was displaying well today.

"Handy for you your father dying then," Oliver said. "Now you can fund your own plays, buy more drugs to sell, and become the star you think you should be."

Gregory's expression changed from irritated to sly. "When something has to be, Lady Luck plays her part."

"Or you make your own luck," Nick said, grinning.

Gregory's sly expression became positively demonic. "You can't seriously think I killed my father," he replied and laughed. "I'd be the number one suspect if they hadn't found Eliza's mother holding the knife."

"You're still *my* number one suspect," Oliver said.

"Well, like in so many things, you're wrong," Gregory replied, smiling drunkenly around at them all.

His gaze held at Eliza for a moment, and he winked. The gesture shocked her. Eliza jumped. Her skin crawled. Revulsion flooded her mind, and she felt physically sick. *He's playing with us. He did it! And he's playing with us.*

Before Eliza rushed from the room, as she wanted to, Marcus suddenly spoke. He'd been so quiet until now, she'd assumed he was completely drunk.

Slurring his words, Marcus said, "Follow the money, that's what they say." He lapsed into silence once again.

"Listen, man," Gregory replied. "In London, we have plenty of murders, and most of them aren't about money. It's about sex. Sex is what drives us all. Sex kills people and countries. It flattens mountains and builds monuments in their place. Everything is about sex. When you're awakened, you'll understand. People have drilled down into every other part of life and made the world what it is, but we haven't even begun to explore sex. It's the last taboo and when we do plumb those depths, the whole world will change."

"Is that from one of your plays?" Sarah asked. She was still watching Gregory in fascinated attention.

Gregory nodded, beaming at being understood by one of his captive audience. "It's my latest. It's being considered by a couple of producers. I'm just waiting to hear back from them."

Eliza became aware of Gregory's attention transferring from her to Sarah. She had to stop that if she was to get the evidence she needed to incriminate him. Eliza cried, "That's how I feel too, Greg. We're all suffocated by our inability to talk about it. It should come naturally to us, only we have all these inhibitions."

Gregory turned back to Eliza and excitedly replied, "Exactly. We need to shed these inhibitions like old clothes. Throw them off, revel in our nakedness."

"That's what I like about modeling," Sarah told him. "We're born naked and spend all our lives wrapped up like mummies. The catwalk is where I'm most free. Crazy as that sounds."

Gregory turned back to Sarah. "You feel it. Eliza feels it. I feel it. One day, everyone will, and we'll all be free."

Nick broke into the rising crescendo of excitement, saying, "Wasn't it Lenin who said sex should be as natural as drinking a glass of water?"

Gregory nodded. "And would be if it weren't for this oppressive social system we've inherited from our past. We'll smash it and live happily ever after, like a fairy tale."

"Exactly like a fairy tale," Oliver replied. "It's not real life."

"It will be," Gregory replied. "One day, even a doubter like you will live it."

"We need more drinks," Marcus spoke again.

"If we're shooting in the morning," Eliza reminded them, "we probably should stop drinking."

Marcus laughed. "If I'm still drunk in the morning, I might have my revenge on whoever shot me last time." His eyes swept blearily around the group.

Nick, the unspoken leader of the group, said, "Eliza's right. We don't want another accident."

The group rose unsteadily to their feet. Eliza stepped forward to help Gregory. She was sure he could manage himself, but she needed to return his attention to her and away from the 'divine Sarah', who remained annoyingly divine even when drunk.

Eliza's suspicion Gregory wasn't nearly as drunk as he'd appeared soon became confirmed. He clearly liked having a young woman hold his arm, steadying him, and they set off down the corridor toward his room.

"Sarah could see it," Gregory said, leering at Eliza. "She saw how good it will be."

Eliza laughed. "Sarah sees herself walking around naked and everyone admiring her. She's in favor of anything that lets her do that."

"But that's it!" Gregory cried. "Everyone doing what they want, for their own pleasure."

"Would Marcus be pleased if men were ogling his girlfriend or wife?" Eliza asked.

"He would in the future I'm talking of," Gregory responded, his hands grasping at Eliza.

She slapped him and he stopped fumbling for a moment. "And would other women be happy when they can't compete?"

"They'd smoke some more weed, and they'd understand we're all beautiful," Gregory replied, slurring his words. His expression became sly, and he added, "*You* wouldn't need to be jealous." His hands began wandering again.

Eliza fended him off all the way to his room, where she pushed him inside with relief. "Goodnight, Greg. We must be up early for the shooting in the morning."

Gregory smiled craftily. "Then you'll see what I can do."

He closed the door and Eliza walked away considering his words. *Might he do something stupid if given a gun? Just to impress her?*

24

ELIZA LEARNS SHOOTING

RAMSAY AND ELIZA were able to exchange only the briefest of greetings at breakfast, as Eliza sat with her new friends. He grinned when he noted she'd taken a chair between the Pugachevs and Oliver and Celina, leaving Gregory sitting away from her. He was less happy at the way Gregory's eyes followed her every move and the hunger blazing in them. *Eliza might have to shoot him, if he doesn't control himself.*

After waving Eliza off to the moors with the shooting party, Ramsay returned to the drawing room hoping that Mrs. Chambers would be there. She wasn't so he began searching and found her in the library.

"Good morning," Ramsay said, as he began inspecting the books available to be borrowed by guests. They were a motley collection of books, mainly paperbacks that guests had left behind.

"Good morning," Mrs. Chambers replied, in quelling tones.

Ramsay selected a book, a Georgette Heyer mystery, *Why Shoot a Butler,* and sat himself in an easy chair as if to read. He flicked through the pages and waited until he felt her gaze on him, expecting him to speak.

"Did you suspect the dispute between your husband and Mr. Wright might come to this?" Ramsay asked, without preamble.

"Obviously not, or we would have left the hotel the moment we saw the man."

"I interviewed Mr. Wright, and I didn't imagine this either," Ramsay answered, as if talking to himself. "I'm usually a good judge of character, or I thought I was."

"It seems we were both wrong," Mrs. Chambers said. She'd laid her book aside now and appeared anxious to say something, if he asked the right question.

"You and your husband got along well?" Ramsay asked. "I know you had your son as a rub point but outside that?"

"Not really," she replied. "We both had tempers and things often became heated."

"But you stayed with him?"

"I said we both had tempers," she said, as if speaking to a rather slow child. "We understood each other even if we weren't always best friends."

"That must have upset Gregory when he was small."

She nodded. "It did. He often tried to come between us, trying to save me, and would be hurt. Not seriously hurt, more emotionally hurt."

"I'm a placid kind of fellow and an ex-police officer," Ramsay continued, "so this sounds alarming to me."

"Then you can't imagine how boring, how spiritless, that sounds," she replied, grinning. "Life is for living, Mr. Policeman, not just existing."

"I heard that phrase a lot when we were interviewing people, and all too often it was when we were trying to explain a body in the mortuary."

"And you have another body, and you, or the police, have cleared it up."

"You don't sound unhappy at your husband's death," Ramsay said.

She shook her head. "Once, maybe, not now. It's been too long."

"You must have loved each other then, surely?"

"I suppose so but that was over twenty years ago, nearly a quarter of a century," she replied. "Can you remember how you felt twenty years ago?"

I remember I felt too much and vowing I'd never allow myself to feel again. Ramsay hoped the pain didn't show on his face. "Perhaps not," he said. "You stayed with him though?"

"I said we understood each other, and we did. I'm not happy he's dead, but I'm pleased my marriage is over while I'm young enough to enjoy the rest of my life."

"What does Gregory think about it? He went shooting with the others today, I noticed."

"The same as I do. Sorry to lose his father but pleased he can now live his life as he wants. My husband could be an oppressive personality to live with."

"You have no fear that it might have been Gregory who killed your husband?"

She shook her head. "He often threatened to kill his father but, unlike his father, Gregory is a very weak man. He could never have brought himself to do it."

"Not even in a momentary fit of rage?" Ramsay asked.

"We can never be sure what anyone will do under such circumstances," Mrs. Chambers replied. "He has the Chambers' temper so perhaps he might if Paul had prevented him getting away. Paul liked to tease Gregory. He was a cruel man if he sensed weakness."

"From what you've said, I'm amazed someone hasn't murdered him before now," Ramsay said.

She took a moment to reflect before saying, "Ask your police friend to look up the disappearance of a man called Mercer, Liam Mercer. He made the mistake of attacking my husband once and injuring Paul quite badly. No one in our city made that mistake again."

"Your husband killed him?"

"I'm sure he had people abduct Mercer, and then I suspect Paul killed him very slowly. Paul wasn't squeamish about violence. He said he'd seen so much of it in the Revolution, it no longer had any hold over him."

Revolted, Ramsay made his excuses and left her to continue reading. He returned to his room and phoned Baldock. When Baldock was brought to the phone, he relayed everything he'd been told.

"Nice family," Baldock said, when Ramsay finished speaking. "I'll have the lads do some digging and see what we find. You're not thinking it's his missus or the son, are you?"

"No," Ramsay replied. "I'm sure if it was, she wouldn't have told me any of this. She's sure we have the murderer and feels relieved she can unburden herself on someone. I dare say, she also hopes to gain some sympathy for Wright who has, after all, set her free. I suspect she thinks she owes him that much."

* * *

ELIZA SQUEEZED into the backseat of one Land Rover, along with Oliver and Celina. After the previous night's discussion, she considered Oliver her best hope for rescue, if she should need it. An old-fashioned man may be irritating sometimes and yet necessary to have nearby when things went wrong.

Up on the moors, the snow had been blown into ravines and gullies, leaving wide expanses of heather exposed. Here the pheasants would be sheltering and feeding, unaware of the mass slaughter planned for them.

"You haven't fired a gun, Eliza, I remember you saying?" Celina asked.

"I haven't, and it's kind of you to let me try."

"You're welcome to my turn all morning," Celina said, smiling. "If it were up to me, the pheasants would live happily ever after."

Eliza laughed. "With me taking a turn at shooting, at least some of them will."

"Your friend, Gregory, too, I imagine," Oliver interjected.

"He's not my friend," Eliza protested. "It's just he and I are the only two people our age who are on our own."

"I doubt he has any friends," Oliver replied. "There's something of the night about him. He makes my skin crawl."

"That's not nice, Oliver," Celina cried. "He wants what's best for people. Isn't that what we all want?"

Oliver snorted and returned to looking out the steamed-up window.

The Land Rover finally stopped, and they stepped outside into the biting cold. The icy wind that cleared the snow, nipped their exposed skin. Each hurriedly wrapped their scarves across their mouth and nose. The wintry sun reflecting from wide swathes of pristine snow blinded them and they dived back into the vehicle for the sunglasses they'd been advised to bring and hadn't believed they'd need.

As the men gathered their guns and ammunition from the back of the Land Rovers, the women and Gregory huddled together behind a vehicle, sheltering from the wind.

"Only men could think this fun," Sarah grumbled.

"They have all that hostility," Gregory interjected. "This lets it loose without hurting people. In the future, they'll smoke and be mellow. None of this will happen."

Eliza was torn between a cutting remark and continuing to keep Gregory talking in front of witnesses. "It doesn't seem to do that for you people down in London, Greg. From what you've been telling us."

Gregory frowned. "The incidents I've been caught up in were with people who haven't yet joined our revolution. We have to defend ourselves until they come aboard."

Eliza nodded, approvingly. "I see that, yes. It must have cost you emotionally to do what you had to do when you're already part of the violence-free future." She hoped what she said didn't sound cynical.

Gregory didn't notice. "It did, believe me. Both times, I needed to meditate with my favorite grass to recover my spirit."

Muriel Pugachev, who hardly ever spoke, suddenly said, "This new world can't come soon enough for me. I hate the cold." They could see why. Her lips were blue, and she was shivering despite the thick fur coat that reached her ankles.

Eliza and Celina sympathized quickly before Gregory could use her words for another advertisement on the delights of drugs, which he no doubt hoped to sell them.

Eliza, replying to Gregory's earlier words, said, "Then we can be sure you had nothing to do with your father's death. You haven't needed to smoke or meditate, have you?"

Gregory grinned slyly. "I didn't kill him, but I wouldn't have needed too much consoling, if I had. He was one of the worst of the old breed. A supporter of the Czarist regime. That's why he fled Russia – to escape justice."

"Surely he didn't say it that way?" Eliza asked. "Or did he change his mind about it all later in life?"

Gregory shook his head. "He was proud of what he did. I read about the revolution and knew him for the monster he was. And why the people rose against them. I told him what I thought of him once."

"What did he say?" Sarah asked.

Gregory looked triumphant. "He stared at me like I was mad. I could see his mind trying to make sense of having a son who would have supported the Reds, if I'd been there. Then he laughed, and said, 'Good'."

"What do you think he meant by that?" Eliza asked. For herself, she thought his father would have been pleased to shoot Gregory. It would be interesting to hear what Gregory thought it meant.

"He meant we'd be on different sides, as we always would be," Gregory replied. "It meant he need never consider me as his son. It meant his rejection of me was as natural as mine was of him. That conversation set me free."

Eliza studied him as he spoke. *Is he lying when he says he didn't killed his father? Did he mean his mother had and he only assisted? Is he just playing a part, which is what he always seems to be doing.*

Nicholas, Marcus, and Oliver were now walking toward the organizer of the morning shoot, so Eliza led the others to join them.

The organizer outlined the arrangements and ended by repeating that they were to stay on the marked paths to and from the Hides, wicker and heather barricades, behind which they wouldn't be seen by the pheasants. Reminding them the snow may be many feet deep in places and someone who fell in a ravine might not be rescued easily, the organizer set off.

Following the man, they trudged out in single file to the Hides that they'd shoot from when the Beaters drove the pheasants up into the air in fright. They'd barely started, when Sarah announced, she was returning to the vehicles and needed a key to get into one. Muriel said she'd go with Sarah. A driver returned with them, and the rest continued.

Eliza again made sure she kept close to Oliver and, as she'd expected, was placed with him and Celina at one Hide, while Gregory went on with Marcus and Nick to the next ones.

"Glad he's gone?" Oliver asked Eliza.

Eliza smiled. "After everything he's said, I don't want to be near him if he has a gun in his hand."

"Nick should never have agreed to let him take a turn with his gun," Celina said, watching the party slowly making their way to the next Hide twenty yards away.

"He felt he had to," Oliver said. "They barely know each other, but they're from the same community and they've known each other from childhood."

"Sooner Nick than me," Eliza said. "I wouldn't put it past Gregory to be harboring a lethal grudge from some incident years ago that Nick has entirely forgotten."

"He's that kind of person, isn't he?" Celina agreed, nodding.

With all the guns now in place, the organizer signaled to the Beaters, half a mile away across the moor, to begin. The signal was returned, and Eliza heard the Beaters' shouting as they struck the heather with long sticks. Soon, pheasants could be seen rising from cover and, wings whirring, flying toward them.

As they approached, Nick, whose Hide being farther

forward, fired. The bang startled Celina who ducked below the Hide wall.

Marcus and Oliver fired together, one barrel and then the second, before a moment of quiet as they reloaded. For thirty minutes the noise of yelling Beaters, whirring squawking pheasants, and the banging of the guns shattered Eliza's senses. But then, there were fewer birds and Oliver, after loading his gun, offered it to Celina who shook her head. Oliver looked at Eliza.

Eliza accepted the gun, feeling the warmth of the stock and barrels through her gloves and coat. Whatever Ramsay thought, this was another step on her apprenticeship to being a detective. Oliver helped her settle the gun stock against her shoulder and take aim. She pulled the first trigger when a bird flew across the narrow notch of the sights and to her great relief, she saw it fly on. Another bird appeared, and she pulled the second trigger. It too flew overhead.

Oliver guided her through loading the gun and she raised it back up toward the sky. After firing both barrels, Eliza swiftly reloaded and was ready again.

"You're a natural," Oliver told her, as she waited for another pheasant to appear.

"At loading maybe," Eliza replied, just before she fired again. "We wouldn't eat many pheasant tonight if we were relying on me to shoot one." She fired again and her heart sank as the bird twisted awkwardly in the sky before plummeting to the ground. Horror-stricken, she watched a dog bound through the heather, pick up the bird with its teeth, and bring it back to where the dead birds were being stacked.

"Good shot," Oliver cried.

"I've had my experience," Eliza said, handing him his

gun. "I'll stop while I'm winning." In truth, she needed time to recover.

Celina, seeing Eliza's expression, said, smiling, "Gregory would recommend smoking a joint."

Eliza nodded. "And I now have an appreciation for his advice. One might work after killing a pheasant, I don't know how many I'd need if I killed a person."

Oliver, who'd just brought down another bird, said, "You'll be amazed how quickly you grow used to it."

Eliza nodded but didn't reply. Her mind whirred like the wings of those doomed pheasants. *If Gregory is telling the truth about his involvement in two London murders, can that be why he isn't upset at being involved in another here in Yorkshire?*

The return drive down from the high moors to the Manor in the valley was a somber one for Eliza. She still felt sickened at what she'd done and, also, the possible insight it had given her into the mind of a murderer. Worse, Gregory had somehow managed to push his way into the Land Rover she chose, and she had to listen to him gloating over the two birds he'd killed, all the way back to the Manor.

"I'll buy my own guns, with my share of the family money," he told her. "I'd have more brace of pheasants than any of the others, if I'd had a gun throughout the shoot."

"I'm sure you would," Eliza agreed, through gritted teeth. "And you have so much experience of death, it wouldn't hold you back."

He laughed. "It's true," he said.

And Eliza believed him. The lust for more killing shone in his eyes and expression.

When they arrived, and she exited the vehicle, she saw the birds' bodies being unloaded from an earlier vehicle and revulsion swept over her once again.

* * *

THE SHOOTING PARTY returned in time for lunch allowing Ramsay and Eliza to share results of their morning's interrogations.

"You didn't shoot anyone, did you?" Ramsay asked, when they were safely in his room.

"I wish," Eliza said, grimly. "I wish I'd shot Gregory Chambers. What a creepy creature he is."

"He didn't molest you, did he?"

"Him?" Eliza cried, scornfully. "He wouldn't dare. No, it was the way he told me about the birds he'll kill when he gets his own guns. And how much he enjoys killing." She grimaced; her expression disgusted.

"Maybe he thinks because you were shooting too, you would enjoy being part of his cruel new life. As his wife or mistress, perhaps," Ramsay said.

"I got that impression, and, in the interest of investigating, I may have led him to think I might," Eliza admitted. She glanced at him, sensing he wouldn't be pleased hearing this.

She was right; Ramsay was not happy. "Are you mad, Eliza? He might be the murderer for all we know."

"Wright is the murderer," Eliza retorted, then slowly said, "At least, I thought he was until the drive back."

"What happened?" Ramsay said, in a tone of growing anger.

"Nothing happened," Eliza snapped back. "He just told me again they sometimes 'offed' people down in London. People who needed to be dealt with. He'd been knocking back his hip flask of rum pretty well by this time, but I think he may have been telling the truth. He says kids often run away to London and are never seen again. Is that true?"

"There's some truth in it," Ramsay agreed. "Usually, it's just too much drink or drugs and jumping off a bridge into the Thames though."

Eliza shivered. "He wanted me to show some interest, so I suggested his life sounded exciting. We arrived before he said more, but I'm sure I'll learn more from him if I give him the chance."

"Then don't."

"We're all playing billiards this afternoon," Eliza said. "I said I'd go. It will be safe enough with everyone else. He can whisper in my ear all the loathsome things he's dying to tell someone."

"I'll come with you," Ramsay said.

"You will not. He'll slither away, and I'll never hear him admit to killing his father."

"You think that?"

Eliza nodded. "I do. I think Wright may be many things, but now I'm sure Gregory Chambers killed his father. It's right there in his eyes. Creepy."

Ramsay had been anxious about Eliza going with the shooting party in the morning, he was ten times that as she set off to the Billiard Room with the young people. *Why am I worried? Billiards, after all, is a clean way of killing compared to shooting*, he thought satirically, trying to allay his heightened fears with humor.

When they were gone, he took Bracken and the three Labs out for a walk. Once again, he went to examine the lane that touched on the back of the Manor's property. On the track leading to the gate, snow was melting, and he could see through the gate that the snow was melting fast in the lane too. Tying the dogs' leashes to the securely locked gate, he climbed over to view the lane.

It ran alongside the property all the way down to the

main road, and, in the other direction, turned sharply at the gate, running straight over a low hill. He judged the distance too far for him to leave the dogs and explore. He needed a map. Climbing back over the gate, Ramsay unhitched the dogs and made his way back to the hotel.

After returning the dogs to their room, Ramsay went straight to reception where Joyce provided him an Ordinance Survey map of the area. She told him, "There's nothing along that lane beyond a neighboring farm." His inspection of the map confirmed that to be the case.

"Is the farmer a friend?" Ramsay asked her.

"We buy from him," Joyce replied. "You don't suspect him of murdering Mr. Chambers, do you?"

Ramsay laughed. "Not at all. It's just the lane would be a convenient way for an intruder to approach the Manor unseen."

"The dogs would see or hear any intruder," Joyce said. "They're on that side of the house."

To prevent any further discussion, Ramsay agreed that to be the case. Still, he wasn't convinced. The dogs were a long way from the approach an intruder would use, and with the recent storms they wouldn't have seen or heard anything. *Mr. Pugachev senior wasn't off his suspect list yet.*

25

ELIZA'S BAR ROOM BRAWL

As Ramsay prepared to go in search of Redhill to continue their conversation, he saw Eliza hurrying away from the Billiard Room. She was putting on the cardigan she'd been wearing and clearly agitated.

"What is it?" Ramsay asked, moving to intercept her before she ran upstairs to her room.

"It's those idiots," she retorted. "They're drunk."

"They're always half cut," Ramsay replied. "What's different this time."

"Strip billiards is what's different this time," Eliza said. "Sarah finally got her wish. It's all right for her, she's a model and used to parading around half naked. The rest of us, not so much."

"You did right to leave," Ramsay said.

"They'll be harder to infiltrate now, though," Eliza replied. "I think it might have been a test of who is *in* and who is *out*. I've made myself out."

Ramsay nodded, sympathetically. "Did you learn anything new from Gregory before you left?"

Eliza's agitation subsided. "I did. And I'm more certain than ever he's our man."

"What did he say?"

"Last night, when Oliver told Gregory they'd heard him threatening to kill his father the night before the murder, Gregory laughed and said, 'What of it? I was always threatening to kill him. It didn't mean anything'."

"That sounds about right from him," Ramsay said.

"Yes, but he turned away so only I could see his face and he winked at me," Eliza cried. "Everything was in that wink. It said, 'you and I know I did, but we can't let these bumpkins know'."

"You may be reading more into it than he will admit to," Ramsay told her. "You know how he's been impressing you with his tales of life in the big city."

Eliza shook her head. "He's mad. Today, he came right out and whispered it to me. He knows we talk to Baldock and yet he said it."

"Did anyone else hear him?" Ramsay asked.

"Unlikely," Eliza admitted. "He was close to me and leaned in. I thought he was going to kiss my ear."

Ramsay nodded. "He's playing games with us. He'll deny saying it, and he knows your word against his isn't any use to the police."

"You should have heard the way he said it." Eliza shivered. "He's a psychopath, or whatever it is that makes people kill others."

"He may be a bit unbalanced, I agree," Ramsay said. "Anyway, Baldock can have his mental background researched, just in case. It's time we were talking with him."

Baldock, however, when they spoke to him, wasn't impressed by anything Ramsay and Eliza had to say. "Until I hear there are other prints on that tiepin, I'm holding

Wright. And if there are no prints on the knife and he sticks to his story of finding it in the corridor, I'll release him and take Mrs. Danesdale back into custody."

Eliza was ready to start yelling at the phone, but Ramsay put his hand over the mouthpiece. "You sit still and say nothing, or you'll make matters worse," he whispered before uncovering the phone.

"You have nothing new on Wright?" Ramsay asked.

"He has one conviction for drunk and disorderly but that's years ago," Baldock replied. "He's been a model citizen these past twenty years."

"Maybe recognizing Chambers put him back on the booze," Ramsay suggested.

"Maybe you're still clutching at straws," Baldock retorted. "You'll have to do better than that."

"Look into the victim's wife and son," Ramsay pleaded.

"I do know my job, Ramsay," Baldock replied. "We're looking into all the potential suspects and we've already some interesting items and, yes, the will is in her favor, so she has a motive. And, yes, the son will expect something from his mama when she inherits, so he has a motive. They have motives but not opportunity. If the witness statements are to be believed, no one saw them anywhere near the victim at the time of the murder."

"With Wright in custody, the son is getting drunk and bragging about his lethal behavior in London," Ramsay said, "and he's hinting he was involved in this murder too."

"You've spoken to him, as I have," Baldock said. "He's a fantasist who wants to be thought a kind of gangster character. I wouldn't believe him if he walked into the station tomorrow and confessed."

"Perhaps that's his plan, Inspector," Eliza said before Ramsay could stop her.

"I'll have the team look more closely at his life in London," Baldock offered. "Now, I have work to do. If you learn more, we can talk again this evening."

When he'd hung up the phone, Ramsay asked, "What exactly did Oliver overhear the Chambers saying?"

Eliza thought back to the earlier exchange between Oliver and Gregory before replying, "Something like Mrs. Chambers and Gregory talking and what sounded like Gregory planning to murder his father."

"Nothing more specific than that?" Ramsay asked.

Still trying to recover the conversation from her mind, Eliza continued, "Mrs. Chambers was pleading with Gregory to give her more time and Gregory said something like 'No. He's growing worse not better! You heard him last night. He never wants to see me again. Well, I'll make sure he never does see me again. See if I don't.' That was the gist of it."

"It sounds more like a threat to commit suicide or leave the country than a threat to murder his father," Ramsay said, disappointed.

Eliza frowned. "Now I've said it out loud, it does to me as well. Gregory, however, when he answered Oliver, made it clear he meant murder."

"We need more," Ramsay said. "Baldock knows he'll never get a winning case out of this."

"Then I'll go and grill Mrs. Chambers," Eliza said. "She's bending the bartender's ear." Eliza left the room, leaving Ramsay to think.

Maybe, Ramsay thought, Eliza would be argumentative enough to provoke Mrs. Chambers into unguarded words. Normally, he'd be against that, but they were stuck. If Wright had a good story, and there were other fingerprints on the tiepin, he wouldn't be charged. On balance, an angry

Mrs. Chambers telling some honest truths may be what would bring an end to the case. Particularly, if she didn't want to share her inheritance with her son.

Unable to go to the bar, where he would interfere with Eliza's interrogation, Ramsay set off to the room where the dogs lived. At least with the dogs he'd have congenial company and enough quiet to think. Part way along the corridor, he heard muffled screeching and the crash of things falling or being thrown. With the mental picture of a barroom brawl involving Eliza in his head, he ran back to the lobby and into the bar. The mental picture didn't do the scene justice.

The barman was holding Mrs. Chambers firmly as she screeched insults at Eliza whose hands covered her face. Around the three were tumbled barstools, broken glass, and a purse spilled open.

Ramsay quickly reached Eliza and demanded to see the damage. When she turned up her face to his and removed her hand, he breathed a sigh of relief. The scratches were from fingernails, nothing worse.

"She accused my son of killing his own father," Mrs. Chambers yelled at Ramsay. "You put her up to this."

Before Eliza could yell back, Ramsay said, "Nonsense. Be quiet both of you." His calmness lowered the passion in both combatants enough for him to continue, "We're going to leave the bar, Mrs. Chambers, and, when we're gone, I suggest you do the same before the management phone for the police."

He assisted Eliza to the reception, where Joyce, who'd entered the bar and seen the aftermath, was opening a medicine cabinet in the office. After dabbing iodine on Eliza's scratches, Joyce placed a pad over them and taped it down firmly.

"All done," she said. "It should stay in place while you sleep. I only hope that awful woman doesn't have rabies or anything serious you might catch."

Eliza laughed grimly. "She flew at me without warning. Honestly, I had no chance. I thought I'd asked my question in a kindly way."

"Sounds like a guilty conscience to me," Joyce said, replacing everything in the cabinet. As she spoke, Mrs. Chambers exited the bar being supported by the barman. The woman's bleary eyes stared at them malevolently while she muttered incoherent curses in their direction.

"Perhaps we should put her behavior down to grief, Joyce," Ramsay said. "The less made of this the better."

"I say we dig deeper," Eliza retorted angrily. "Guilty conscience is exactly right."

"If she is the murderer," Ramsay pointed out, "she's behaving in a stupid fashion. She should be sitting quietly being nice to everyone." He shook his head, "It doesn't make sense."

"It does if she believes it's her precious son and he terrifies her," Eliza said. "After all, when she gets the money, she might be next."

Ramsay nodded. "Well, we can think about that in the morning after we've rested. Wild surmising won't help anyone." Wishing Joyce good night, he guided Eliza away from the reception, to where they might talk without being overheard.

After persuading Eliza to retire to her room and rest, Ramsay returned to the bar and helped the barman tidy the room. His actions amused the Hooray Henrys who were sitting at a table drinking, and staying as far away from the debris as they could.

Ramsay ignored their sniggering but not what he overheard them saying. They knew about the tiepin, and they knew about Wright's drunk and disorderly charges of long ago. It was a chilling moment. All Ramsay's sympathy for Eliza's injuries were forgotten as he realized they only knew the information because Eliza had let it slip. Eliza wanted desperately to be an investigator, righting wrongs and saving the people, but she was too young, too indiscreet for the job. One day, maybe, but not yet.

That evening, Ramsay spoke to Baldock alone. He recounted the events of the afternoon and suggested Baldock have his men step up their background research on the Chambers.

"I already have, based on our earlier discussion," Baldock replied, "and the fact I'm releasing Wright, pending further inquiries."

"The fingerprints on the tiepin weren't conclusive?"

"Wright's fingerprints aren't on it at all," Baldock began.

Ramsay interjected, "That just means he used a handkerchief to hold it."

"You and your friend need to get it into your heads I'm not a beginner in this profession," Baldock responded, his voice icy.

"Sorry," Ramsay said, "I got carried away."

"The only prints on the tiepin were Chambers', and they were smudged by the cloth Wright used to hold it," Baldock continued. "He says he found it in the corridor and planned to use it to get money, but he didn't know who the murderer was."

"There should be a crime of planning to blackmail someone," Ramsay growled. "That piece of evidence may have moved the investigation forward if it had been available earlier."

"You realize, of course, this takes us right back to Mrs. Danesdale," Baldock said.

Ramsay had expected this. "You won't be taking her back into custody though?"

"Unless you have some new evidence, not right away, no. We did find new background that may be suggestive. I'm sorry, Ramsay, but she's looking more and more like the murderer. It's only a matter of time before she's formally charged."

"What sort of new background?"

"When she blinded that boy, she was assessed by the 'trick cyclists' of the day and they thought she wasn't as stable as she should be," Baldock responded. "They assessed her regularly every year until she became an adult."

Ramsay didn't like the sound of this. Like Baldock, he had little time for psychiatrists who, in his opinion, were generally as mad as their patients, but juries were impressed, and judges also took their words seriously. He asked, "Has nothing come up about the Pugachevs?"

"Nothing to suggest they would murder Chambers," Baldock said. "They're model citizens, though those friends they're with are a bit grubby. Only youthful indiscretions, mind you, but not squeaky clean."

"The Price-Ridleys?" Ramsay asked, growing desperate.

"Model citizens *and* squeaky clean," Baldock replied.

"The Phillipsons?"

"According to the law, they're model citizens too," Baldock responded, drily.

"Redhill?"

"Again, a model citizen who sadly is dying of cancer," Baldock said. "As you know."

Ramsay agreed. "I spoke to him at length the other

evening. Life is unfair to so many people. Work hard and then contract an incurable illness before you have a chance to enjoy the fruits of your earnings."

"Life is hard sometimes," Baldock replied. "Still, life's unfairness isn't our bailiwick, fortunately."

Ramsay laughed. "Very true. It's difficult enough being sure about the evidence when we're dealing with ordinary human behavior." He paused, before adding, "Speaking of which, looking into Gregory Chambers' life is where I expect to find evidence that is convincing."

"You'd best be right, for your future mother-in-law's sake," Baldock responded grimly. "Good night." He hung up the phone before Ramsay could reply.

Ramsay went to sleep imagining ways to tell Eliza that Wright had been freed, and her mother was once again chief suspect. No brilliant idea came to mind, which meant straightforward simplicity remained his best option. *It just wasn't a palatable one.*

26

ELIZA'S INITIATIVE

THE FOLLOWING morning Ramsay knocked on the door of Eliza's room and, much to his surprise, found her ready to start the day with renewed energy. The pad on her face was gone, replaced by skin-tone cream.

"I hope those scratches weren't still open when you put that muck on," Ramsay said, disapprovingly.

"They weren't. Now, where do we start today," Eliza replied, as they walked to the breakfast room.

"I'll start by telling you I spoke to Baldock last night, and they've released Wright," Ramsay replied.

"No incriminating fingerprints then," Eliza said.

"None."

"Mam's not really free yet, is she?" Eliza asked, as they sat at their table and Ellen handed them menus.

Ramsay thanked Ellen, making his choice immediately. Though the English didn't make porridge properly, it was good enough for his simple tastes.

Eliza ordered toast and handed her menu back. She waited for Ellen to leave before saying, "I told you it had to be Gregory. Now you must believe me."

"You were convinced about Wright too, for a time," Ramsay reminded her. "We must judge on the evidence."

"That's what I'm doing," Eliza protested. "The evidence we had pointed to Wright. Now it doesn't. Now the evidence I have points to Gregory."

"Then we need him to say it more plainly and in front of reliable witnesses," Ramsay said.

"The others were there and heard some of it too," Eliza replied.

"Baldock says your new friends aren't as reliable as you think, except for the Pugachevs. The others have a list of minor infractions to their names," Ramsay said and smiled as Eliza's expression changed from confident to shifty. "But then you knew that didn't you?"

Eliza blushed. "When Gregory was boasting about his doings in London, Marcus and Oliver tried to keep up with stories of their own."

Ramsay laughed. "They didn't want their girls to think they weren't 'bad boys' too."

Eliza nodded, still red. "Their claims were tame, and Gregory kept raising the stakes to see if they would, or could, follow. Like a gambler who knows he has the winning hand."

"What do you know about gambling?" Ramsay asked, slipping once again into his 'wise old man' role and immediately regretting it. "Forget I said that."

"I've seen films," Eliza protested. "Anyway, Gregory soon left the others far behind. He'd done everything but the Great Train Robbery."

Ramsay laughed. "Baldock called him a fantasist and he's right. I won't be convinced about Gregory's guilt without solid physical evidence. Not even a confession will convince me after hearing this."

"Then we get the evidence," Eliza replied. "We'll set a trap. I've drawn him into indiscreet talk, I'll tell him I'm going to the police unless he pays me."

Ramsay shook his head. "We aren't placing you in any more danger. I wouldn't have let you go alone to talk to Mrs. Chambers last night, if I'd known how volatile she was."

"You don't have a say in it," Eliza responded. "I want him to show his true self and that's what I'll get."

"You might get an awful lot more than you bargained for, if he's only half as wild as his mother. Get him drunk some more, and you'll get the confession we need."

"As you rightly said," Eliza retorted, triumphantly, "a confession won't do. No one would believe a word he says."

They ate their breakfasts, each in silent determination to have their way. Neither seemed likely to get their way, however, for when they left the breakfast room, they discovered the Chambers checking out.

"There goes my plan," Eliza groaned, as the Chambers, followed by Alfred carrying their bags, exited the front door.

"There goes my plan too," Ramsay said, relieved. At least now Eliza couldn't put herself in harm's way. Before he could say more, Eliza ran across the lobby and out through the door. Ramsay hurried after.

Outside, Eliza was talking to Gregory. They were both well away from his mother, who was already in the car and away from Alfred, who was placing the last bag into it.

Eliza ran lightly back through the slush to the door where Ramsay stood, a broad smile on her face. "Ugh," she cried as she reached the door, "my feet are soaked."

"What was that all about?" Ramsay asked. He was afraid he already knew.

"I assured Gregory, I'm still interested in his exciting life in London, and we should meet to talk about it," Eliza said, her eyes shining. "I think he fell for it."

"With me standing here watching? Not likely. He couldn't be that dim."

"We'll know if, and when, he gets in touch," Eliza replied, as they turned to go inside.

"He'll be back in Leeds and on the train to London tomorrow," Ramsay said. "There are plenty of young women in London looking for excitement."

"I *might* have led him to believe he'll be rewarded if he takes me along," Eliza said, grinning. "And if he's scored with any of those London girls, it wasn't obvious from his bragging. I think he'll go for it."

Though her words made him uneasy, Ramsay remained confident he was right, only saying, "How is he to get in touch with you when you aren't on the phone at home?"

"Never you mind, Mr. Know-it-all," Eliza retorted. "Having you tagging along will kill the whole thing."

"I, or someone has to be there, to witness whatever it is you hope will happen," Ramsay replied, "otherwise we won't have the evidence."

"I'll get the others to be my witnesses," Eliza said. "They'll be at breakfast now, and I'll put it to them. They're young enough to enjoy the hunt and be in at the kill."

"You're against foxhunting," Ramsay reminded her.

"But not man-hunting," Eliza replied, laughing. "That's a fair contest." She kissed his cheek and set off for the breakfast room.

For a moment, Ramsay was puzzled. Then he remembered the younger people were going shooting again in the afternoon. Maybe Gregory, even though he'd left the hotel, still meant to be one of the party, and Eliza would be there as bait. So that was her plan; get Gregory drunk enough from his hip flask and he'd be easy to draw out and maybe antagonize into an indiscretion. Now, Ramsay needed to know where they were shooting and how to get there.

At Ramsay's request, Joyce had Frederick brought to reception, where she once again provided the map of the area. Ramsay took notes from Frederick's detailed directions of where to hide his car near enough to help Eliza, if needed. Ramsay thanked them both and went to take Bracken for his morning walk, which, Bracken insisted, would only happen if he took the three Labs as well.

Ramsay and the dogs made their way around the lake, where the ice was now melting. Large expanses of open water were filled with quacking ducks and Ramsay had to hold back the dogs who were eager to catch themselves lunch.

"Not today, gentlemen," he told them, leading them away from the lake toward the track and the lane that so fascinated him. The track now was a slippery, muddy mess, and he regretted not wearing his rubber boots. The lane too was almost clear of snow, slick black asphalt shining in the morning sun.

He wasn't going to be able to lift three Labs and Bracken over the locked gate, so he stared out at the lane, like a prisoner yearning for freedom, before sighing and turning away.

As they made their way back along the track, they heard voices, which Ramsay surmised were the young people skiing or tobogganing. Rounding a bend, he saw he'd guessed right. The couples and Eliza were tramping up the hill tugging toboggans. They were setting off back down as he and the dogs arrived at the top of the hill. Eliza waved as she slid down, shouting, "Wait for me at the top. I'll give you a ride down on the next run."

Ramsay and the dogs watched Eliza reach the bottom and begin making her way up.

"You men will have to get yourselves down," Ramsay told the dogs. "There isn't enough room for all of us on the toboggan."

Arriving beside them, Eliza swung the sled to face downhill, jumped on, and told him to climb aboard. The dogs were now excitedly jumping at both sides of the sled, licking the faces of the two riders and bumping them in their exuberance. "You'll knock us over, if you're not careful," Ramsay said, laughing and pushing the boisterous Labs away as the sled began to move. Fortunately, the dogs couldn't run as fast as the toboggan, and they were soon left behind, only catching up to the riders when they stopped.

Again, the dogs were eager to lick faces and jostle Ramsay and Eliza as they struggled to their feet. "All right, all right," Ramsay cried, pushing them away, "that's enough, boys."

"You'll have to take them in," Eliza told him. "There'll be an accident if they stay."

Ramsay nodded. "I fear you're right and most likely to one of them. They'll get their paws under the runners sooner or later. I'll take them away."

"They have lots of energy left, you might want to take them on a longer walk," Eliza said.

"You're trying to get rid of me," Ramsay said, suspiciously.

"This is no place for old men or boisterous dogs," Eliza replied, chuckling. "If that's what you mean."

"I can take a hint," Ramsay said, smiling. He gathered up the leashes and set out for the Manor. "We'll walk into the village," he told the dogs. "See how they've been coping with the snow."

They passed the Manor and headed out onto the road. It too was wet, with slushy piles on each side. Water ran down either side to the drains. Crossing the road, Ramsay spotted, in the distance, a lone car approaching the village. It looked familiar. By the time he'd reached the path at the farther side of the road, it was slowing and swung into the lane he'd been staring at only an hour ago. He took two more steps and stopped.

"I'm the most dimwitted detective in the world, Bracken," he said. "Come on. We have work to do."

He ran across the road with the dogs bounding ahead. They re-entered the hotel grounds where Ramsay decided to return the Labs to their own pen. With trembling fingers, he removed the wooden wedge from the homemade catch and ushered Larry, Harry, and Barry inside. After unclipping their leashes, he patted them and shut the gate. The three Labs gazed sadly after them as Ramsay and Bracken began running for the track that led to the lane.

Though it seemed like a lifetime to Ramsay, he soon saw the toboggan hill with all the sleds at the base and no one beside them.

"She has her new friends hiding among the trees, Bracken," Ramsay panted as they continued hurrying toward the hill. He undid the buttons of his overcoat as he ran and then tearing it off, flung it on the ground. Without the heavy coat flapping around his knees, running became almost a pleasure. They climbed the hill as quickly and silently as Ramsay was able, considering his rasping gasps for air. At the top, he peered around the bushes along the track. The farther end was out of sight because the track curved and the bushes obscured the view.

"We'll keep close into the bushes, Bracken," Ramsay

said, when he had breath to speak, "until we reach the corner. Then we'll go into the trees."

Moving along the track was harder than it looked, the slush was deep and the ground underneath, thawing. Ramsay slipped with almost every step. Finally, they were there, and he peered around the bush. No one could be seen. However, the radiator grill and bumper of a car parked outside the gate were visible, the rest of it was hidden by the wall that marked the property boundary.

"If she's gone into his car," Ramsay muttered to himself, "I'll murder her myself if he hasn't."

Leading Bracken into the trees, they continued forward. Among the trees the snow still lay deep, mounded into drifts by the wind, and it made for slow progress. Then Bracken growled low.

"Shh," Ramsay whispered. He looked about to find what Bracken had detected. Seeing nothing, Ramsay moved softly forward again, until Bracken growled louder. This time he spotted what Bracken had smelled or heard. Hiding behind a tree ahead of them stood Sarah, the model. Even her snow clothes looked like she'd just stepped out from a winter vacation catalogue.

He crept closer until he thought it best to alert her to his presence. The last thing he needed would be for her to become startled and scream. "Sarah," he whispered. It took more than one attempt to catch her attention, she was so engrossed in something happening beyond his view.

She looked at him in surprise, then waved him to come forward. Through the dark foliage of the firs, he observed Marcus hiding. He too stared watchfully forward.

"Eliza is luring Gregory into the wood, and we're to witness what he says or does," Sarah told Ramsay as he eased past her on his way to Marcus.

Ramsay nodded, though his mind was astounded that any of them thought this a good idea. He wondered if they'd considered how short a time it took to stab someone and how they would get to the victim before that happened.

Marcus heard him approaching and turned to greet him. He too appeared surprised at seeing Ramsay.

"I thought you were Sarah," he whispered, as Ramsay and Bracken reached his hideout.

"Where are they?" Ramsay demanded, scanning what little there was to be seen ahead of them.

"There," Marcus pointed to a patch of light color between two heavy branches. "That's Eliza's jacket."

"And how do you know that?" Ramsay almost exploded. Marcus might have been watching snow or an empty jacket for minutes by this time.

"I saw them arrive," Marcus said simply. "Don't worry, nothing's happening, or I'd have known about it."

Ramsay looked about for a better observation point and, seeing a gap to his right, and keeping his eye on the patch of white, he crept toward the gap. Eliza was sitting on Gregory's knee, and Gregory was sitting on a tree stump. He looked, and Ramsay hoped he was, extremely uncomfortable.

The couple were clearly speaking because their lips were moving. Ramsay, however, was too far away and heard nothing. He crept back to Marcus. "Are any of the others closer? I can't hear a word they're saying."

Marcus nodded. "We're all around this clearing. I was just unlucky Gregory picked that stump to sit on and not the nearer one. Oliver or Nick will hear, and Celina might too. We thought it safer for the girls to stay back in case he spotted one of us."

Ramsay returned to his wider view, but his movement must have been seen, or sensed, for Gregory suddenly stood and Eliza crashed to the ground. Gregory looked wildly about, saw Ramsay and ran.

Bracken took off, pulling Ramsay along with him. In the deep snow, however, Bracken's shorter legs, and Ramsay's older ones, were no match for a frightened fugitive. Gregory sprinted quickly to the track, over the gate, and into his car. He drove off as Ramsay arrived at the gate. He took the car's number, though he knew who it belonged to, and returned to the clearing.

"You idiot," Eliza yelled, as he arrived back at the group. "He was telling me how he murdered his dad, and you broke in before he'd finished."

"I heard enough to convince me," Oliver said, looking at Nick and Celina. They nodded.

"I did too," Celina added.

"Then we can have Baldock bring him in," Ramsay said, smiling ruefully at Eliza.

"We still only have suggestive words," Eliza shouted angrily. "We'd have had details, if you'd walked the dogs like I told you to. You've spoiled everything!"

27

THE NEW SUSPECT

Ramsay, Bracken, Eliza and the young couples phoned Baldock the moment they were back at the Manor.

"This better be good," Baldock grumbled when Ramsay told him they had new evidence against the Chambers. "So far, your information has been moderate at best."

Ramsay outlined the events of the day, much to Eliza's indignation. Then, she told Baldock what Gregory had said, implicating both his mother and him in the murder. Oliver and Celina confirmed Eliza's version of Gregory's words.

For a minute or more, a long silence reigned as Baldock wrestled with what he'd been told. His gut told him this was another wild theory. He imagined a courtroom lawyer telling a jury that this whole fanciful tale relied on the boastful conceit of a lovesick young man.

"Very well," he said, at last. "We'll bring them in for questioning. However, Ramsay, you and I both know young Gregory is going to deny everything and claim the witnesses are picking on him because they don't like him. This is schoolyard stuff."

"Which is why I'm so angry at Tom," Eliza cried. "Gregory was on the point of saying something real, or possibly attempting to harm me. I felt him tensing up, wanting to show what he could do, but not yet having the courage to do it. I'll never forgive Tom, never."

Ramsay practically felt Baldock's intense pleasure as he almost purred, "The police interrogation may yet save the day, Miss Danesdale. We aren't altogether clueless. And your sleuthing partner, Ramsay, has his moments sometimes. Now, unless you have more to add, let me go and set the wheels in motion."

They didn't have more, and he ended the call. The couples made their excuses and left the room, rather embarrassed to be witnessing the rift between Ramsay and Eliza.

"I'll join you in the bar," Eliza said to them, crossly, as they left.

When the door closed, she turned on Ramsay, saying, "If they don't get a confession, and those two murderers get away, it's your fault."

"I'm not having you sitting on a potential murderer's lap with his arms around you," Ramsay replied, equally as unhappy as Eliza. "You might have been killed before any of us reached you. It takes no more than a second for a stabbing."

"We weren't going to get him without some drastic action," Eliza cried. "And if he'd tried to get a knife from his pocket, I'd have seen him and escaped."

"How would you have escaped? His arms were right around you. Be sensible, woman. Having him and his mother executed for a second murder wouldn't be worth the price we, your mother, father, and I, would have paid by losing you."

They glared at each other for a minute before Eliza

shrugged and said, "Well, maybe it might not have ended well, but I moved this investigation in the right direction."

Ramsay stepped forward and hugged her. "You did, but don't do it again."

Eliza laughed. "Yes, Grandad. Anything you say, Grandad." She looked up at him and was rewarded with a kiss on the forehead. "I like you better than Gregory," she said, hugging him tightly.

Ramsay chuckled. "Is that supposed to be a compliment?"

"Possibly," Eliza replied, thoughtfully. "I'm not sure. Do you know any gruesome tales of murders and beatings?"

"Too many, sadly," Ramsay replied. "We'll keep them for another time. You join your friends in the bar."

"Won't you come too?"

"They may still say things to you they wouldn't say if I'm around," Ramsay replied. "And I'm not convinced those Hooray Henrys are as innocent as they appear."

"We have the killer," Eliza cried, pushing him away. "Why can't you accept that?"

Ramsay sighed. "I'm almost the original Doubting Thomas," he said. "There are cases from twenty years ago that I still wonder if I got right. What bothers me on this one is, I don't see creepy Gregory stabbing his father. Chambers senior would make mincemeat of Gregory, wherever and whenever they met."

"I'll do as you ask," Eliza said, shaking her head at his stubbornness, "but you're wrong this time, Doubting Thomas." She left for the bar sure it was a waste of time.

* * *

As Eliza approached the group, Marcus asked, "Have you murdered him?" The others chuckled.

"I should," Eliza replied. "We were so close to having real evidence."

"It was more exciting than shooting," Sarah said. "Though just as cold."

Celina and Muriel agreed. "I've never been part of anything like that," Muriel added. "I'll remember it long after I've forgotten the rest of this Christmas."

"You'll remember the murder, surely?" Nick said.

"I wasn't part of that," Muriel replied, wistfully. "It hardly seems real to me now."

"Gregory is a horrible little man," Celina said, "but my money would be on that Phillipson. He was rightly furious with his wife. She was so hot for Chambers it embarrassed everyone who witnessed it. And he looked a lot more likely to kill someone than poor Gregory."

"Poor Gregory," Oliver repeated. "Rich Gregory now and that's what will hang him. The motive is so huge."

"Motive, yes," Nick said, "opportunity, no. At least, no one saw either of them near the victim when the murder took place."

"Witnesses are useless," Oliver retorted. "Look at us. We three," he gestured to Nick and Celina, "were close enough to hear what was being said. Yet what Eliza told Baldock wasn't what I thought I heard. I didn't say so at the time because it would have caused confusion. I've no doubt Nick and Celina will say they heard something different, as well." He looked at Nick and Celina who nodded, unhappily.

"What makes you say that?" Eliza demanded.

Oliver was obviously uncomfortable but replied, "You made it sound as if Gregory explicitly described killing his father – a confession of murder. What I heard were general statements about killing his father. Not a confession, just more of what we've heard hints of before. I think you interpreted what he said to what you wanted to hear."

Eliza interjected, "Then you need to get your stories straight before the police ask for witness statements."

"You're proving my point, Eliza," Oliver said, "Witnesses are unreliable at best. If we make our stories the same, we'd be tripped up by any competent lawyer when questioned in the witness box."

"Not if you get your story straight now, and stick to it," Eliza cried, hotly, hearing her evidence disappearing before her eyes.

Nick shook his head. "If we all tell the same story, that will be evidence of collusion." He paused, looked at his wife and asked, "What did you hear, Muriel?"

Muriel frowned. Her expression puzzled and unhappy. "I-I couldn't be sure. I was farther away than you were, Nick, and Gregory mumbles a lot."

Eliza thought she might burst into tears; what she was hearing made her so angry and frustrated. "Then you tell the police you didn't hear anything, Muriel."

Muriel nodded. "I intend to, if they ask."

For a moment, there was silence, until Nick asked Celina, "Why do you think it was Phillipson? Other than him being angry, I mean."

"He'd left the room," Celina replied. "He might have been anywhere, like hiding in that corridor waiting for Chambers to show up."

"The corridor is well-lit," Muriel protested.

Celina shook her head. "When you go into it after leaving the brightly lit dining room or lobby, it looks pitch-black. That's what I find, anyway."

"I've thought that too," Eliza agreed, nodding. "Unless

you stop in the corridor and let your eyes adjust to the light, you wouldn't see anyone there."

"Well, I didn't see him after we left the dining room," Nick said, "and we went along the corridor."

"There's that junction with the corridor to the outside rooms," Eliza mused. "What if he hid in there and waited until he heard Chambers?"

"How would Phillipson know who he heard in the corridor, if he was round the corner?" Oliver asked.

"He expected to hear his wife as well," Celina replied. "That's how he thought he'd know."

"She left with us," Muriel said, before adding, "I think?"

"Then he'd expect Chambers very soon after," Celina said. "And maybe Chambers called her name, quietly, of course."

"That *could* be how it happened," Oliver agreed, smiling at his fiancée. "The police must have thought of it too, and they haven't had him in for questioning so I'm guessing there's a reason why not. You talk to the police, Eliza. Do you know?"

"I don't," Eliza admitted. "We tell them things. They tell us very little, other than my mother will be formally charged if no better suspects appear."

"My guess is someone saw Phillipson away from the corridor at the time of the murder, so he has an alibi," Nick suggested.

"I understood from the constable that day, they don't know exactly what time the murder happened," Oliver replied. "I think we should investigate Phillipson and find the evidence. That way we save Eliza's mother and become heroes for a day."

Nick shook his head. "If he was angry at his wife carrying on with Chambers, he'd kill his wife. Wouldn't he?"

Once again, silence descended as they thought through this suggestion. Then Marcus said thoughtfully, "I agree. He'd kill his wife. I would, if it was me."

Sarah shot him a quizzical look that Eliza found hard to describe. A look like those Julia Phillipson gave Chambers. Julia's expression had seemed lustful when everyone else was revolted by his attitude and coarse behavior. Sarah's gaze at Marcus was similarly hard to understand. It certainly wasn't anger. *I may not understand people as well as I need to*, Eliza thought.

Muriel suddenly giggled, "My guess is Miss Forsythe. She wouldn't have hesitated if she met him in the corridor and had a knife in her hand."

Everyone laughed, though they sounded a little unsure that she wasn't right.

"Seriously, though," Oliver said. "Is there a way to find out where Phillipson went after leaving the dining room?"

"We can ask the staff," Marcus said. "Only the police, Ramsay, and Eliza have already done that." He looked directly at Eliza as he said this.

Eliza reddened. "He does have an alibi in the sense one of the Price-Ridleys witnessed him entering his room. It doesn't rule him out. He might have left his room as soon as the coast became clear. No one saw him, if he did."

Muriel suggested they leave it to the police, finishing by saying, "...because from all I've heard, no one did it."

"I have a cousin who's a lawyer in London," Marcus said. "He might know something about Phillipson that would suggest a better motive."

"Then what are you waiting for," Oliver cried. "Phone him now."

Intrigued, Eliza waited with the others for Marcus's return. When he did, the result was disappointing.

"My cousin doesn't know any Quentin Phillipson," Marcus told them. "He did look him up in a directory for me and he says Phillipson works for a successful firm of Barristers who specialize in company law."

"He worked for Chambers and didn't like what he'd been asked to do," Eliza told them. "He didn't want to work for Chambers again."

"Then it's something criminal," Oliver said, excitedly. "How do we find out what?"

"The police will be looking into this," Muriel said. "We shouldn't get involved."

Nick Pugachev, ignoring his wife, suggested, "If it's about business, and the law, my father will know. He tracks everything about Chambers and his dealings."

"Phone him," Oliver cried. "We're halfway to having this case solved already."

Nick's father provided more insight. Chambers had recently been in dispute with a government department over land. The case had been tried in London, and Chambers won. People said Chambers paid people to lie about aspects of the case. They were only rumors, however. When asked if Chambers had paid people, Nick's father laughed and said, "Unlikely. His kind never get their hands dirty."

"Then there's the answer," Oliver said, firmly. "Chambers wanted Phillipson to act illegally again, and Phillipson didn't want to. Chambers used Phillipson's involvement in the previous case to force him to accept the new one he was planning. Once you've done something wrong, you're always at the mercy of the Chambers of this world."

"Was Mrs. Phillipson in on it, do you think?" Celina asked. "She seemed more on Chambers' side than her husband's."

"Which is why he killed Chambers and not her," Marcus

added. "Killing her would only make him more in Chambers' power."

"If we got all this from two phone calls," Nick said, "what have the police been doing?"

"The police don't know people who know the Phillipsons or the Chambers," Eliza reminded them. "And they don't know that your cousin, Marcus, and your father, Nick, do."

"You have their ear," Muriel replied. "Tell them and let's have this over and done with."

"I will, only you must understand nothing we've said here is evidence," Eliza told them. "It's only a place for the police to start investigating, if they haven't already."

"What do we pay them for," Marcus said, in disgust. "If Dad ever goes bankrupt, I'll take a job in the police. I thought investigating would be hard until today. It seems *I* can do it and *we* can do it."

"Why don't we?" Oliver asked. "I need a hobby and this one might pay. We can charge for our services like they do on telly or in films."

Eliza groaned inwardly. She was creating competition for the soon to be *Danesdale and Ramsay Detective Agency* and right in her own backyard.

***

On their previously arranged evening phone call with Doris and Colin, Eliza happily told her parents the case was solved, and her mother need have no more worries.

"Tom?" Colin asked anxiously.

"It may be so," Ramsay confirmed. "However, you should both be prepared for setbacks. You're still the most likely suspect, Doris, if our new leads don't work out."

Eliza growled at such timidity. "The police have no new evidence against you, Mam," she said. "They let Wright go but he's still a possibility, and they may have to let Gregory Chambers go as well, thanks to Tom's foolishness, but we'll finish this off and you'll be safe. Don't let Tom frighten you."

"Tom has more experience in these matters, Elizabeth," her mother said. "We should be guided by him."

Eliza ground her teeth and glared at Ramsay. *Save me from old people and their constant caution,* her expression said.

Ramsay was forced to smile, though he tried not to laugh.

"Eliza's point is a good one," Ramsay said. "We're raising enough doubts about the murderer to keep you somewhat safe without fresh evidence."

Eliza's expression remained thunderous, but she forced herself to speak calmly saying, "I think we've done everything we can here. Would you like us to come home?"

"Enjoy the rest of the time we booked, dear," her mother told her. "Your dad and I are enjoying the quiet."

"I need Eliza here, anyway," Ramsay said. "There's still work to be done before this is truly finished."

"He's got me spying on the Hooray Henrys," Eliza added. "Though you can't imagine such silly people hurting anyone, let alone killing them."

"They're handy enough at killing pheasants by all accounts," her father reminded her.

Eliza scoffed at such talk. "Killing pheasants with a shotgun isn't like stabbing someone with a knife."

"Yet you think Gregory did," her mother replied. "If Gregory, why not the others?"

Eliza said nothing. She didn't want to tell her parents about the tiepin and its significance to the victim and perhaps the murderer, which made it hard to explain.

"We have some thoughts about why he was killed," Ramsay said, "that might implicate the young people, or some of them at least. Until we're satisfied they weren't involved, we can't be sure who did it."

"Weren't they your witnesses for today's incident?" Colin asked.

"Yes," Ramsay replied. "If it is them, how lucky it was that we gave them the opportunity to shift the blame to someone else."

"I'm not sure I'm ever going to feel safe again," Doris said. "This just goes on and on."

Ramsay agreed, saying, "Until one day, it ends."

They ended the call and Ramsay and Eliza gazed at each other in silence.

Eliza became suddenly conscious of sitting on Ramsay's bed and needed to break the spell. "We must make Mother safe," she said.

"We will," Ramsay re-assured her. "Now, a nightcap?"

"Won't the others be suspicious if they see us together, after I spent the evening with them calling you names?"

"We don't need to go to the bar. I've a bottle of Glenfiddich." Ramsay took the bottle from the top shelf of his wardrobe.

"Mother wouldn't approve," Eliza said, looking around for a cup or glass.

"Then I'm pleased to do something *you* surely approve of," Ramsay said, smiling. He took a glass and a cup from a drawer of the dressing table, poured a small quantity into both, and handed the glass to Eliza.

"Phone Baldock now, and I'll tell him what we learned," Eliza said, sipping the whisky carefully. "I don't want to be slurring my evidence when I give it."

"Tomorrow morning, first thing," Ramsay replied. "Tonight, we rest."

Later, as Eliza returned to her room, she wished she'd told Ramsay about Phillipson. She'd wanted to, only she knew he'd say it was just hearsay and try to stop her telling Baldock. She didn't want that. Baldock would also say hearsay, but once he'd heard it, he would follow it up. He had that kind of bloodhound quality in him.

28

BRACKEN GIVES UP ON THE INVESTIGATION

NEXT MORNING, however, Baldock wasn't in a good frame of mind when they called. "Colleague's leaving party," he curtly explained, when Ramsay asked if he was ill.

"They always come with mixed feelings," Ramsay suggested.

"This one came with too many mixed drinks," Baldock replied.

Ramsay laughed. "Then we'll be brief. Do you have the Chambers in custody?"

"Not yet," Baldock said. "They should be here by mid-morning."

"Eliza learned some interesting information yesterday," Ramsay continued. "It may help in the interviews."

"Is it evidence?" Baldock asked.

"It's what people heard Mrs. Chambers and Gregory Chambers saying the day before the murder," Eliza interjected. "And it reinforces what he said to me when he thought we were alone yesterday, which I've already told you."

"Hold it right there," Baldock said. "If this isn't in their witness statements, then I don't know about it."

"It isn't," Eliza admitted, "because the young people didn't want to be any more involved."

"Withholding evidence is a serious offense," Baldock reminded her. "If I ask them to make new statements, what you tell me now better be in those new statements."

"Let Eliza say what she's been told and what happened," Ramsay interjected. "It will be useful material for the interviews. If anything comes from it, go back to those couples and ask them to add to, or amend, their statements."

Baldock groaned. "I'm listening," he said. Ramsay thought he heard teeth grinding.

Eliza recounted what the group had told her. Mrs. Chambers said she'd kill her husband, and Gregory saying she wouldn't need to. He would do it. He'd had enough of being treated like nobody. His father had always had it in for him, and it was time to end it.

"They said they heard this earlier, but they only tell you now after hearing what Gregory whispered in your ear yesterday," Baldock said. "It sounds fishy to me, and it will to a jury, if we ever get it that far."

"Your team have found plenty of background on the Chambers to back up what the young people heard Gregory say to Eliza when he thought they were alone," Ramsay responded. "These witnesses didn't know all the background, so they didn't tailor his words or make it up."

"One of them, Pugachev, knew of the Chambers when he was growing up," Baldock retorted. "He might well know stories that helped him create this overheard conversation, and the others went along with it."

"All we're suggesting," Ramsay said, "is use it in the interviews. Maybe it will rattle them. I'm sure it will."

Before Ramsay or Baldock began wrapping up the meeting, Eliza suddenly said, "I have more, Inspector."

"About the Chambers?"

"No, about Mr. Phillipson," Eliza replied, ignoring Ramsay's surprised expression.

"What about him?" Baldock growled.

"You'll say this is hearsay," Eliza said and she recounted what the Hooray Henrys had uncovered from their phone calls to family.

"I won't say this is hearsay, Miss Danesdale," Baldock replied in a dangerous tone, "because it doesn't rise to that level. This is gossip and worse, it's lawyers and businessmen's gossip. In my experience those two groups are worse than a mother's coffee morning meeting for tittle-tattle."

"You will look into it, though," Eliza said, firmly. "If it's true, he has a strong motive, and we all know his alibi isn't solid."

"Some of what you've just told me, we already know, and we're already looking into it. However, your mother is still the most likely murderer, and you need to accept that," Baldock said. "Flinging out these wild accusations about everyone at the Manor for Christmas isn't helping anyone. Now, go before I lose all patience with you two. The Chief is already angry about Wright, who has had his lawyer onto him. I don't need more lawyers bending the chief's ear to get me."

Ramsay and Eliza made their way to the breakfast room. They were the only two guests there.

"They sleep in," Eliza commented, when Ramsay glared at the empty table where the three couples should be sitting.

"Lazy beggars," Ramsay growled. He ordered breakfast and asked Eliza if she was joining him on his walk with Bracken.

"I think I should continue to be arm's length with you," she replied. "There may be more to come."

Mr. Redhill shuffled into the room and Ramsay invited him to join them, which allowed Eliza the opportunity to leave. She smiled, saying, "I'm sure you old-timers will have lots to talk about, like walking to school, uphill, both ways, with snow up to your waists. Snow today is nothing by comparison, I've been told." She left quickly before Ramsay retaliated.

"Your young friend is very lively today," Redhill remarked, watching Eliza leave.

"She's found some friends her own age," Ramsay replied. "It must get tedious trailing around with her parents and me."

"Are you a friend of the family?"

"Not exactly," Ramsay said and explained the month he spent in Robin Hood's Bay solving a murder and smuggling ring.

"I remember something about that," Redhill said, when Ramsay finished. "So that was you. And now this murder. You attract crimes, it seems."

"I hope not," Ramsay said. "Eliza is still at an age where she finds it all exciting, which is why I'm pleased she's spending time with people her own age doing the silly things people of that age do."

Redhill laughed. "I bet you never said that when they found themselves in the police station, and you had to sort out the mess."

"I didn't, of course. Only, Eliza wants a taste of the wider world. She lives in a small village with few people her age. Having those three couples around, unsatisfactory as you or I might find them, is doing her a power of good."

"She looks close to that little tick, Gregory," Redhill said. "You might have to steer her away from him."

"Why? What do you know about him?"

"Only what I've learned since being here," Redhill replied. "He writes plays down in London that no one puts on and lives a Bohemian style of life. It may be all exaggeration but it's enough to be a warning."

"Playwrights and artists in general are a rackety lot," Ramsay agreed. "Still, the wider world will call to us all sometimes. We can't shut it out altogether."

"I have and I'm not sorry I did," Redhill retorted. "Be watchful, not complacent. That's all I'm saying."

Ramsay frowned. The man clearly knew something to Gregory's discredit. "Is there something I should know about? Something in particular, I mean?"

"Only snippets of conversation and they're alarming," Redhill replied. "He's obsessed with killing. It's a fixation with him. I never hear him speak but he mentions it. Very disturbing."

"Your room is nearby?"

"Next door," Redhill said. "The walls are thick, so I don't hear the full conversation, but he and his mother are, well, obsessed. There's no other word for it."

* * *

RAMSAY SPENT a long afternoon outdoors with Bracken and the Labs. As they walked and chased rabbits that Ramsay never caught a glimpse of, Ramsay kept his eyes on Eliza and the Hooray Henrys. They spent the morning tobogganing and the afternoon skiing badly, which at least gave Ramsay some laughs as they crashed into each other or landed face first in the snow. He could only hope Eliza learned something new out of it.

Eliza, returning to the Manor as the light was fading, escaped her companions long enough to tell Ramsay they needed to talk.

"My room when you're changed," Ramsay whispered and turned away as Nick and Muriel emerged from the corridor leading from the equipment room. He and Bracken, they'd been making their way outside for a late afternoon walk, exited the main doors leaving Eliza to talk with the Pugachevs.

"Well, Bracken," Ramsay said, when he was sure they were alone, "Eliza may have learned something."

Bracken gave him the resigned expression Ramsay had come to expect these past days. *He misses his doggie friends when I take only him for a walk.*

'Why can't I make him understand,' Bracken thought, equally sadly.

Thirty minutes later, back in his room, Ramsay and Bracken were pleased when a discreet knock on the door was followed by Eliza whispering, "It's me."

Ramsay opened the door, and Eliza slipped quickly inside breathing a sigh of relief. Bracken ran to her, and she squatted down to fuss over him.

"What did you want to say?" Ramsay asked, after confirming no one in the corridor had seen Eliza enter and closing the door behind her.

"They actually heard Mrs. Chambers threatening, or planning, to kill her husband before he was murdered," Eliza replied.

Ramsay frowned. This made no sense. People didn't speak their plans to kill people out loud. "How is this different from what they said before? I think they're now just making things up."

"I thought that, but they swear it's true."

"They know you're feeding everything they say back to me," Ramsay objected. "They're using us to frame the Chambers."

"Why would they?" Eliza cried.

"Because Pugachev senior hated Chambers and probably his family too by association," Ramsay said. "I'm beginning to doubt everything they've told us."

"It wasn't the Pugachevs though," Eliza replied. "It was Oliver and Celina. They have no reason to hate the Chambers; they'd never even met them until they came here."

"What if Gregory had been as creepy to Celina as he was to you? Neither Oliver nor Celina would like that, and this is simply revenge."

"If you don't like me telling you what I hear," Eliza cried, "what's the point in me listening to them?"

"I'm telling you what Baldock will say if we tell him this," Ramsay responded. "Anyway, how was Mrs. Chambers planning to kill her husband?"

Eliza hesitated. "With poison in his Christmas dinner. I know that isn't what happened but that's what she said."

"Maybe she was just mulling over fantastical possibilities, rather than planning his death," Ramsay mused. "Who was she telling this too?"

"They assumed Gregory, but they didn't hear anyone else speaking," Eliza replied. "It was just a single sentence they heard in passing."

Ramsay's expression remained thoughtful for a moment. Then he said, "Redhill said something similar to me last night when we were talking. He said Gregory was obsessed with killing."

"There you are then," Eliza crowed triumphantly. "Three different people hearing them plotting."

"When people are angry," Ramsay countered, "they often plot murders of whoever has angered them. They don't do it, though. It's just words."

Eliza dismissed such a feeble argument with a wave of her hand. "Some do. These two did. We need to pass this on to Baldock."

Ramsay shook his head. "He believes we're desperately trying to save your mother. This will seem like more tittle-tattle than useful evidence."

"He can use it in his interrogation of them. It might unsettle them more to learn someone else overheard them plotting."

"You stay with the couples," Ramsay said. "Maybe you'll learn more. I'll speak to Baldock later and share what we've learned."

Eliza, rather unwillingly, agreed and, after checking the corridor, she left Ramsay's room for her own.

Ramsay sat for some time, stroking Bracken and deciding how to tell Baldock without losing the inspector's trust. He knew Baldock's point-of-view on this because it would be his too if he were in the inspector's place. Being fed a constant stream of circumstantial evidence that, coincidentally, took the spotlight off the most likely suspect, who just happened to be Eliza's mother, was highly suspicious in itself. He felt tempted not to phone Baldock at all.

"What say you, Bracken? Do I tell him these tales or let him proceed with his case unenlightened?"

Again, Bracken's expression was hard for Ramsay to read. Often Ramsay felt he understood his friend perfectly. This time he thought Bracken might just be bored.

"I'll tell him," Ramsay said, after a further moment of

thought, "but I'll get an earful for my trouble." He picked up the handset and dialed Baldock's number.

"What?" Baldock practically snarled when he picked up.

"Evening," Ramsay replied.

"Oh, it's you. I expect you want to hear how it's going?" Baldock said.

"I would like to," Ramsay replied. "Only if you think it safe."

"Is Miss Danesdale with you?"

Ramsay laughed. "No, and I won't share anything she shouldn't hear."

"They were refusing to say anything at first," Baldock said. "Your information, however, did get them talking, but only after their lawyer had called for and was given a private meeting between them."

"And the result?"

"Gregory is a London West End playwright, and they were working through scenes he's considering," Baldock replied. "It's a new one for me."

"We don't get many playwrights up here in the North," Ramsay said. "It would be a first for me too."

Baldock continued, "We reminded him we hadn't found such a script when we'd searched their rooms."

"Did you find any?"

Baldock laughed. "If you can call them scripts. More like mindless rambling."

"And what did he say about the lack of script?"

Baldock chuckled. He was enjoying recounting this tale. "It hasn't been written down yet. It's still in his head."

"I've two other people who heard them speaking about murder," Ramsay told him. "Oliver and Celina claim Mrs. Chambers was planning to poison her husband."

"Do you think there's anything in it?" Baldock asked.

"Without the script, I don't see how the Chambers can prove that's what they were doing. On the other hand, what we have is a lot of talk that got overheard, which is nothing more than hearsay."

"It occurs to me," Ramsay responded slowly, "they might have done all this to provide themselves with a cover story. One we can't disprove."

"If they did, they would have written it down," Baldock countered. "That would be their trump card."

"Maybe they were planning to do that, and Chambers was killed before their plans were ready," Ramsay said, gloomily.

"You're a great help," Baldock said. "If that's what happened, they aren't the murderers. You're providing information for us to follow up on and now shooting down your own line of enquiry."

"Not at all," Ramsay replied. "Just considering the possibilities. I still think they are the most likely, with motive, means, and opportunity."

"The most likely murderer is Mrs. Danesdale," Baldock retorted. "She had all three, while these two jokers weren't seen anywhere near the murder scene."

Ramsay bit his lip. Baldock was right, of course, which Ramsay found galling. Only, Doris murdering the man was so unlikely as to be practically impossible.

"That shut you up," Baldock said. "If we can't get anything on these two, I'm going to charge Mrs. Danesdale. People above don't understand why I haven't already."

Ramsay knew that experience very well and sympathized. "Those two will trip up somewhere. That kind of people always do. Too clever by half."

"You'd better be right for your friend's sake," Baldock told him. "Now get lost. I've work to do."

After promising to call again in the morning, Ramsay hung up the phone. As always when he talked to Baldock, he came away depressed. "Come on, Bracken. Let's get some fresh air. Maybe it will clear my head."

Bracken's expression suggested that would be good, only he didn't think at this stage anything could clear his friend's befuddled brain. The answer was as plain as the nose on his face, and Bracken's too.

29

PEOPLE DON'T ALWAYS MEAN WHAT THEY SAY

While Ramsay and Bracken were enjoying a milder night out on the grounds, Eliza saw Joyce clearing tables.

As she was temporarily without a dance partner, Eliza asked, "Your staff not here tonight?"

Joyce smiled, grimly, and replied, "Not enough of them. The first hint of a snowstorm now and they phone in sick."

"Let me help," Eliza said, springing to her feet. "I'm fully trained at clearing tables. When I'm not sleuthing, I waitress at my parents' tea shop."

Joyce laughed. "You're a paying guest. You should be dancing."

"I'm a spare in this crowd," Eliza said, placing dishes on the tray. "All the single men are gone, except old Mr. Redhill and he won't be dancing again, I fear."

"It's a shame for you," Joyce said. "A nightmare for us. The Chambers left without paying. They claim Paul Chambers was to pay, but he didn't, and we can't get money out of the police, of course."

"I doubt the police budget covers paying the murder

victim's bills," Eliza agreed. "The mother and son Chambers must have money at home. They'll send it, I imagine."

"They said they would, only they had to get the family lawyer to release money from the estate," Joyce said, as they each carried a tray of dishes from the dining room to the kitchen. "I hope we hear from them soon."

Eliza realized Joyce likely didn't know the Chambers had been taken into police custody and racked her brains to guess what Ramsay would do. Was there a reason not to tell Joyce? Or would this come back to haunt her like her too ready slip over the tiepin? She chose silence. After all, Joyce might guess Eliza and Ramsay were responsible for the Chambers being in custody.

"Did you ever hear Mrs. Chambers plotting to murder her husband?" Eliza asked, as they walked back to the dining room for the final dishes.

"No," Joyce replied. "Did someone?"

"They say they did," Eliza replied, "only it's so unlikely. You don't say that kind of thing out loud, do you?"

Joyce laughed. "When my evening staff called in sick an hour ago, anyone nearby would have heard me threatening to murder her, her doctor, and Frederick. And yes, I did say it out loud."

"I hope no one heard you," Eliza replied, trying not to smile.

"Only Frederick, and I've been threatening to kill him since the birth of our first child," Joyce said, smiling. "He's used to it now."

Eliza asked, "There were complications?" They began heaping the remaining dishes onto their trays.

"The doctor described it as a 'difficult birth'. For him it might have been. My own view was considerably more descriptive than that."

"You had another though," Eliza said.

"Another two and they were both fine. Still, you can see that sometimes we all occasionally threaten to murder people out loud and, yes, even in our loudest voices."

Eliza laughed. "Perhaps, you're right. I'm reading too much into an overheard remark."

They finished the tables; Joyce thanked Eliza and went off to help the people working in the kitchen.

Eliza returned to the ballroom and found herself once again in demand for a dance that needed a crowd. She joined the tail of an enthusiastic conga line and wished that, as once before, Ramsay's hands were on her waist.

Ramsay peeked into the ballroom as he and Bracken headed back to his room. He smiled seeing Eliza happily doing *The Locomotion* with the others and felt his plan to help her infatuation die away naturally was working perfectly.

30

THINGS GROW WORSE

ELIZA JOINED him at breakfast the following morning, once again looking as though she hadn't slept.

"You're killing me," she said, in reply to his breezy good morning.

"I'm toughening you up for the life of a busy private detective," Ramsay responded. "Believe me, every one of them I ever met looked just like you look now."

"What did Baldock say?" Eliza asked, gratefully taking the tea offered by Ellen who was struggling to stop herself laughing.

When Ellen left, Ramsay told her about the playwright defense the Chambers had employed.

"Oh," Eliza said, downcast. "He told me he was a writer." She considered what this meant before saying, "I never thought that might have been what they were doing. Are we wrong again?"

"Possibly," Ramsay replied. "And if we are, your mother is back in the frame. Baldock is still leaning that way. His bosses think he has enough for a case, and he reluctantly agrees."

"I never saw him as being on our side," Eliza muttered.

"He isn't the most comfortable of men to deal with," Ramsay agreed, "and he still doesn't entirely trust me, but he's too good a copper to deliberately put someone away he thinks is innocent."

"Clearly he doesn't think Mam is innocent," Eliza replied.

"Look at the evidence," Ramsay said. "There's really no choice but to test it in court if the Chambers can't be shown to be involved."

"When I sat there listening to Gregory," Eliza said, gloomily, "I never considered that he was just spinning a tale to test his audience's reaction. I'm hopeless at this."

Ramsay shrugged. "If they stick to that story, Baldock will have to let them go."

"Wait," Eliza cried, "surely he'd have the script written down somewhere."

Ramsay explained Baldock's response to that question.

"I suppose writers do think and talk it out before writing, don't they?" Eliza asked.

"Who knows."

"Even if 'they' don't," Eliza said, gloomily. "No one can swear 'he' doesn't. It's another dead-end, isn't it?"

"We'll know more after we talk to Baldock today," Ramsay replied. "Which means you need to keep digging with the Hooray Henrys."

"The only thing I'm digging is my own grave," Eliza grumbled. "I'll have cirrhosis of the liver before this holiday is over. What the heck. Live fast, die young, have a good-looking corpse, isn't that what they say?"

"Probably, now I'm going before the Hooray Henrys arrive. You need to be still at odds with me, in their minds."

He left the table and went in search of Bracken who he'd left with the Labs for breakfast.

* * *

INSPECTOR BALDOCK DIDN'T LIKE many people. And as his years in the police increased, he found he liked less and less. When his wife left and took the children, he'd been devastated. Now he found he disliked them as much as he disliked the rest of mankind. However, in this general ocean of dislike, occasionally a particularly repellant member of the human race hove into view and here he faced one of them now. Baldock seated himself at the Interview Room table and stared across it at Gregory Chambers for a solid minute before beginning.

"Yesterday, you provided some names of people who you felt would confirm that you frequently say out loud the dialogue of stories you're writing. We phoned them and those we spoke to weren't able to confirm your story. Would you like to suggest more people who might?"

Gregory shifted uncomfortably and glanced at his lawyer for guidance. The man nodded.

"I have two more," Gregory said. "I didn't want to use them because they aren't friends, as such."

"All the better," Baldock replied. "If they vouch for you, they will be more credible witnesses than friends would be."

Gregory clearly didn't think so but provided the name of the actor who lived on the same floor of the apartment block where Gregory lived, and, also, the name of a police sergeant at the nearby police station.

Baldock laughed when he heard this last one. "He can confirm your story?" he asked.

Blushing, Gregory muttered, "Yes."

Baldock left the room and gave the actor's name and number to his detective-sergeant but phoned the police station himself. He was soon put through to Sergeant Mullins and, after introducing himself, explained the reason for his call.

Mullins chuckled. "We've had a number of complaints about your Mr. Chambers over the last year or so. Usually, older women complaining about his obscene comments in their presence."

"Obscene?"

"Those are the complaints we get," Mullins replied. "I don't say he doesn't threaten strangers with murder, only, if he does, they haven't complained."

"I see," Baldock said. "And his defense is he's rehearsing parts for a play."

"That's it, exactly," Mullins told him. "It's never possible to prove he was directing the comments at the women, and we let him go with a warning. Simply walking around talking loudly about sex isn't actually a crime, though it's generally frowned on in polite society."

Baldock thanked him for the information and went in search of his detective-sergeant, who he found on the phone.

His subordinate placed his hand over the mouthpiece and said, "The phone is in the hall. They've gone to find our suspect's witness." He took his hand away and spoke, "Hello, yes North Yorkshire Police, are you Garth Archer?" The man on the other end confirmed he was, and the detective signaled to Baldock, 'Me or you?'

Baldock reached for the handset, introduced himself, and told the witness the reason for the call.

"What's the loathsome leech done now?" Archer asked.

Baldock explained and asked Archer's relationship with Gregory.

"I don't have any kind of relationship with him," Archer replied. "I'm an Actor, he's an Extra. And, he claims, an aspiring playwright who hasn't sold a play. Unfortunately, we happen to live on the same floor of this rooming house. What made it worse, he was in a crowd scene of a play I had a part in over a year ago. Now I can't lose the blighter, no matter how rude I am to him."

Baldock laughed. "You're not a friend then?"

"I didn't know he had any friends," Archer replied. "No one who's met him could like him. Why? What's he done?"

Baldock described what a witness had overheard of Gregory's speech.

Archer laughed. "Murder? That's a new one. It's usually sex. All his plays have been about sex."

"Maybe he thinks he'll have more success with a play about murder," Baldock suggested.

"It would be just like him to change to murder right at the time as the market is coming around to plays about explicit sex," Archer said.

"To sum up," Baldock continued, realizing the conversation was drifting away from the evidence he needed, "you can confirm he does often speak out loud parts of plays he's working on. This behavior doesn't strike you as being out of character?"

"That's it, Inspector," Archer replied. "I'd dearly like you to put him in prison for a nice long stretch, but I just can't do it."

Baldock thanked him and handed the phone back to his subordinate, who had clearly understood the gist of the conversation.

"We let them go?" he asked, as he returned the handset to its cradle.

"I'm afraid so, Jim," Baldock replied. "We're back with the Danesdale woman as murderer. The Chief will be pleased. He thinks we'll get a result there."

"You're not so sure, sir?"

Baldock frowned. "On the contrary, I fear he's right."

* * *

BY LUNCHTIME, Ramsay had grown tired of walking dogs and his stomach was in knots. He made his way back to the Manor, dropped off the dogs at their room, and he and Bracken returned to his room. He found his hands were trembling as he dialed the numbers.

"It's ridiculous, Bracken," he told his companion. "I've never been so anxious about any case as I am about this one." He heard the phone ringing and willed someone to pick it up.

It felt like an age before Baldock answered with his usual aggressive, "What?"

"It's me," Ramsay replied. "Any good news?"

Baldock laughed. "Depends on who is asking. For you, it's bad news."

"They're sticking with their story?"

"Worse," Baldock said. "His story is true. He does wander around rehearsing his plays out loud and frightening passers-by."

"Then you've let them go?" Ramsay asked, knowing the answer.

"We've done more than that," Baldock said, grimly. "We've released them and charged your future mother-in-law with murder. She's being picked up as we speak and will be back in a cell within the hour."

* * *

Eliza was eating lunch with the three couples when Ramsay found her. Nothing could be gained by subterfuge at this point, so Ramsay and Bracken crossed the floor to her side.

"We need to talk," he said, brusquely, "in private." He nodded coldly to her companions whose expressions were a mixture of surprise and amusement.

When they were alone in the lobby, Ramsay recounted his conversation with Baldock.

"Damn him," Eliza cried. "I must go home to Dad. He'll need help organizing lawyers and things."

"It's the New Year's Party at the Manor this evening and no lawyers will be at work this afternoon," Ramsay reminded her. "Your father will have accompanied your mother to Scarborough so there'll be no one at home. We can leave tomorrow, and nothing will be lost."

"I'm not staying here doing nothing," Eliza cried.

"There still may be something we've missed," Ramsay said. "We have this afternoon to find it."

Suddenly breaking into their conversation, Bracken sighed. They looked down at him, puzzled. Bracken gazed back at them pityingly. 'If only they'd make the effort to understand. He could understand them but not the reverse. Humans really are an unintelligent species!'

"We dismissed the idea of the staff being involved," Ramsay continued, turning back to Eliza, "because a murder usually needs more than a passing acquaintance but maybe we were wrong."

Eliza thought and nodded. "If Chambers was so objectionable to his fellow workers and business owners, maybe he offended the Manor owners or staff. After all, Mrs. Price-Ridley is a handsome woman, maybe he'd tried it on with her?"

"Tell the Hooray Henrys you have work to do," Ramsay said, "and we'll start again with our hosts."

Joyce, however, shook her head. "He wasn't a nice man," she said, "but there was nothing like that with me. What about you, dear?" she asked Eliza.

Eliza shook her head. "I thought he only had eyes for Mrs. Phillipson. We wondered if maybe someone else got pestered."

"The police asked that and none of the staff mentioned it if he did," Joyce replied.

"If it led to murder, they wouldn't mention it, would they," Ramsay said.

"I suppose not," Joyce agreed. "We can ask Ellen if she knows anything. She usually does. She's the 'mother hen' to most of our temps."

Ellen had one suggestion. A young woman who helped out that night and her husband had as well. "Doreen's a good-looking girl and her husband's a jealous man. It's why he came along to help Alfred with the logs and such."

"Doreen isn't here today," Joyce said. "Truth is, with most of the guests not arriving, and now so many gone, we barely need anyone other than our full-time staff."

"Does she live locally?" Ramsay asked. "Could we easily go and talk to her?"

"They have an old cottage just behind the post office," Ellen said. "I can't say if they'll be in today. It's New Year's Eve. They may have gone to visit family."

"It's worth a try," Eliza said, eager for any action at all. "We can take Bracken. He'll enjoy the walk."

They found the cottage easily enough, an old building with a sagging roof and tired whitewash on the outer walls. They knocked, and the door was opened by a blonde-haired young woman with keen blue eyes.

"You're that policeman guest at the Manor," she said, before Ramsay could introduce them.

"You recognize us, that's good," Ramsay replied. "We wanted to ask again about the night of the murder."

"I told the police everything I knew, which wasn't anything at all," Doreen said. "Come inside, or we'll catch our death standing here." She stepped aside and they entered.

The room was dark. A fire in an old-fashioned metal hearth gave it most of its light, though a single bulb with a small shade hung from the ceiling in the center of the room.

"Can I get you a cup of tea?" Doreen asked.

"We've just had lunch," Eliza said, smiling. "Thank you, though."

"Well, what did you want to know?" Doreen asked gesturing them to sit on the small couch in front of the fire.

"This may be embarrassing for you to answer," Eliza said, before Ramsay had the chance to speak. "We wondered if the victim, Mr. Chambers, propositioned you that night?"

Doreen laughed. "He made a saucy remark or two when I served at dinner but nothing more. His sort allus do."

"Apparently, he had a reputation with women," Ramsay said.

"I expect he did," Doreen said, shrugging. "Be sensible, an old, rich man with life slipping by. More sad than threatening, in my opinion."

"Your husband didn't hear any of the remarks?" Eliza asked.

"You leave Chris out of this," Doreen replied, suddenly angry and suspicious. "If you've been told it were ought to do with Chris, you and your informer are barking up the wrong tree. Chris never came into the dining room. He took logs from the woodshed to the furnace all evening, and that was as far as he got."

"Did you see anyone in the corridor near the time of the murder?" Ramsay asked, to divert the conversation.

"I told the police all this," Doreen grumbled. "Are you two trying to get me to say something different?"

"The police didn't share their interview notes with us," Ramsay said, "and we didn't talk to you that day. Perhaps you weren't in work then?"

"I were only hired for the Christmas Dinner," Doreen said. "Chambers was in the corridor when I returned to the kitchen. He asked for a Christmas kiss. I told him he should ask his wife. The next time I saw him, only minutes later, he lay dead on the floor, and Ellen asked me to fetch Alfred."

"You saw Mrs. Danesdale crouching over the body?" Ramsay asked.

"I did. She were whiter than the dead man. Poor lady. Shock, I suppose."

"Shocked she'd killed him, or shocked she'd found him dead?" Ramsay continued.

"How should I know?" Doreen said. "Thinking about it again, I don't think she killed him. She was frozen. Ellen couldn't get her to stand up. I think she froze when she crouched down and found he was dead."

"Would you swear to that?" Eliza cried, excitedly.

"I would say what I think I saw," Doreen said, slowly.

"But I didn't see it happen, like. I don't reckon the clever folk in court would take much notice of what I thought."

"You have a point there, Doreen," Ramsay said. "However, what you did see and what you thought of it may help the defense."

Eliza suddenly asked, "This may seem an odd question, but did you use the Ladies Powder Room that evening?"

Doreen grinned. "Aye, I did. Only don't tell them at the Manor. They don't like the staff using the guests' facilities."

"Your secret is safe with us," Ramsay replied.

"They won't hang that poor lady, will they?" Doreen asked.

"I'm sure it won't come to that," Ramsay said, hastily glancing at Eliza whose expression was suddenly horror-stricken.

"Did we get anything useful from Doreen?" Eliza asked, as they walked back to the Manor.

"I think Doreen's view that your mother was frozen in her crouched position is something the defense can use to create doubt, so I'd say, yes."

Bracken growled despairingly and, misunderstanding his meaning, Ramsay and Eliza stroked and patted him enthusiastically.

"A hot drink and a hot bath for me before we get ready for tonight's shindig," Ramsay said.

"Seven young people, one frail old man, and one retired policeman can't be described as a 'shindig'," Eliza retorted. "It's more like a wake."

31

NEW YEAR'S EVE, DECEMBER 31

The dining room was still cheerfully decorated and the staff, all returned now the snow had receded, were happy and attentive to the guests. Still, it looked a sad celebration of the start to 1965. Ramsay, Eliza, Bracken—who'd been brought along to make up the numbers, the three couples—who appeared to be firm friends again, and the late arriving Mr. Redhill were the whole company.

"It's almost as if we're having the party for him," Eliza said, as Redhill shuffled into the room.

Ramsay agreed. "It has that feeling about it. As if we were all waiting for him to arrive before we can start."

Confirming his words, Frederick stepped on the dais and welcomed everyone to this last night of 1964 and start of the exciting new year. He asked the band, who were in place and waiting to begin playing, to take a bow and, after that, announced that he, Frederick, would be their Master of Ceremonies and organize games for the evening saying, "I know many of you were enjoying our Hypnotist and Lord of Misrule entertainers but after what happened, we feel to continue with our full program wouldn't be appropriate."

He paused to allow an opportunity for comments but there were none.

Frederick continued, "We will have everything planned for the evening that can be sensibly done with our reduced numbers. Meanwhile, please enjoy the band playing during dinner and I'll return to begin the festivities when the coffee and brandy are on the table.

After Frederick finished speaking, Ramsay crossed the room and asked Redhill to join them. He accepted, and they returned to the table where Eliza and Bracken were waiting eagerly for their first course.

As the courses arrived and the wine drunk, people began to forget the darkness outside and around them. The young people grew noisier the more they drank and danced. Eliza once again left Ramsay to join the younger people, leaving Ramsay and Redhill alone. Even Bracken had taken himself onto the dance floor and frisked about the legs of any dancer who'd take notice of him.

As the music and noise grew louder, Ramsay leaned across the table to ask Redhill if they might talk privately for a few minutes.

Redhill didn't appear surprised. He said, "We're private enough here, I think."

"I want to tell you a story of long ago and it also brings us up to the present time," Ramsay began. "It's just a story I made up, but I think you'll recognize some of it. Will you let me?"

Redhill hesitated and then said, "Yes."

"My story starts long ago, in a country far from here and during a revolution," Ramsay began. "Like all civil wars, this one was brutal. Families were torn apart by the different factions the family members chose. There were no prisoners of war, losers were executed on the spot. Political allies murdered each other for gain, power or wealth." Ramsay stopped and looked searchingly at Redhill.

Redhill stared back without showing any emotion. He sipped his brandy in silence, understanding a response wasn't yet required.

As the band began a vigorous Bossa Nova, Ramsay continued, "One day, a group of communists captured a village and here's where my story may be vague. For some reason, a young man is away from his family, who are among the wealthier people in the village. Maybe he watched from a distance or maybe when he returns, he finds his parents, brothers, and sisters dead. Their house has been looted and what the looters couldn't carry they destroyed. Maybe the young man stays anonymous as he helps people bury the dead and maybe he didn't witness the massacre but somehow, he learns the name of the man responsible for this atrocity."

Redhill continued watching as Ramsay took a sip of his coffee, preparing to continue his tale.

"The young man recovered some part of his family's money," Ramsay continued. "Maybe it was hidden in a secret place. He took that and made his way to the coast where he got on a ship and left. One more refugee in a continent full of them. Did I say this happened at the end of the Great War and millions were on the move?"

Redhill smiled. "You didn't but I inferred it."

A brief moment of silence occurred when the band stopped playing and before the dancers applauded. After the applause, the band began again, something too modern for Ramsay to recognize but thankfully loud enough for him to continue his story. "The young man, hardly more than a boy really, ended up in England, and began making a new life for himself using those savings to buy or start a business.

Perhaps, because he had no one to lean on, or perhaps just his nature, he spent his whole life working and his business prospered."

Ramsay paused and asked, "Does this sound like many people you know?"

Redhill nodded.

"One day, decades after he arrived here, he somehow met or saw a man he thought he recognized. The memory he had was of a younger man and yet something, the voice maybe, the way the man walked, or stood, told our hero he knew this man. Instead of shrugging it off as most of us do when this happens, the hero of my story finds the experience upsetting and begins investigating or maybe the truth comes to him in a dream. The truth often does, I find."

Redhill nodded. "Yes," he said. "Dreams can do that."

"Our hero learns more about the man he's recognized and discovers he's as nasty today as he was all those years ago. Of course, the man isn't allowed to openly kill people now and can only take pleasure in ruining them, belittling them, perhaps making some of them disappear."

"Character doesn't change much with the years, I find," Redhill said, conversationally. "Have you found that?"

Ramsay shrugged. "Sometimes they soften, sometimes they grow worse, but it's true. In my experience, they stay much the same. Perhaps you might finish my story. Now it's approaching the present, I find it hard to piece together."

"I will," Redhill replied, "after I've helped with some of the earlier details. I was fifteen and helping neighbors for pocket money, as people say here. One day, while working with an elderly neighbor, a family friend, on his woodlot, the communists arrived. The neighbor prevented me from going to my family's aid. He knew I couldn't help, and he kept me hidden for several days. The neighbor was a member of the same communist faction as the group who arrived in the village. I suspect he may have made the attack possible but didn't anticipate the results; people were often naïve that way. It doesn't matter. I learned, years after, that faction lost out in a power struggle only weeks later and they were all executed."

"A kind of justice," Ramsay said, though the whole episode sickened him.

"Perhaps," Redhill said, before continuing, "My family had been quite prominent in our district over the years. Father had even been presented some small gifts from the Imperial authorities. One of which was a brooch Mother wore to clip her shawl. I remember how proud they both were of it. So much so, I remember that brooch better than I remember their faces." He shook his head sadly, the first sign of the feelings behind his tale.

"I didn't know that the commissar who murdered my family had stolen my family's name and fortune to escape from those who'd been his partners in murder and were now his enemies. He too came to Britain," Redhill continued. "If I'd thought about him at all I would have assumed him to have been executed with the others. I think, as he murdered my family and friends, he must have heard whisperings about the political infighting at the top of their organization and made his plans accordingly. He escaped the fall of Crimea and the purge of his comrades by becoming a White Russian émigré, with my family's papers to prove it."

Ramsay asked, "Are you sure it was him? It was a long time ago, after all."

Nodding, Redhill said, "I wasn't certain at first. He'd changed his name, as I did, but his voice, bearing, and his features were essentially the same. When I saw Mother's brooch being used as his tiepin, I knew I wasn't wrong."

"You didn't really change your name, though. Did you," Ramsay suggested.

Redhill looked puzzled. "Why do you say that?"

"Mrs. Danesdale told us that Chambers whispered 'rosebud' as he died," Ramsay replied. "She thought he was thinking of the ending to the movie *Citizen Kane*. Maybe you know it? A business tycoon whispers 'rosebud' as he's dying, and no one knows why. I thought that might be the answer too, at first."

Redhill nodded. "I understand. How did you know?"

"A man named Pugachev told me, though he didn't know it," Ramsay replied. "Please go on with the story."

Redhill laughed bitterly. "It doesn't have a happy ending, I'm afraid."

"Many, if not most, stories don't," Ramsay said. "I think it was Oscar Wilde who said a happy ending is what we mean by fiction, or something like that."

"When I finally knew he was who I believed him to be," Redhill continued, "I became determined to unmask him. I told the local Russian community and expected that to be enough. However, the fire has gone out of them. They're old. They did shun him, but most were already avoiding him anyway because he didn't do the community any credit."

"So, you decided on direct action?"

Wearily, Redhill said, "Not then. This was five years or more ago, and I still enjoyed living my admittedly sheltered life and my business. I decided to let the man live in peace. In a way I felt better deciding that; forty years later is too long a time for revenge."

"Then you learned you were ill," Ramsay guessed.

Redhill nodded. "Then I learned I was dying. The cancer had gone too far for treatment. It took some time for this to sink in because I didn't feel ill. I didn't look ill. After the first diagnosis, I just got on with things, but at a follow-up appointment they told me I had six months at most. Even then, revenge still wasn't on my mind. I sold my business and retired to France."

"You still felt well?"

Redhill nodded. "Exactly, during those months in France I thought I might live forever. When I returned, I had more x-rays, and they changed my mind. Things were worse, yet according to the doctors I still had six months to live. I went to Spain and all through my time there I thought of him going on in the world after all of us, my family and me, were gone. In my mind, it became a wrong that had to be righted. Particularly as my strength was now noticeably failing."

"You realized how little time you had to act; I imagine." Ramsay wasn't a violent man but listening to Redhill's account he could certainly sympathize with him.

"As you see, Mr. Ramsay," Redhill said, gesturing to his legs and his stick, "I'm not far from being unable to carry out any independent act. Then, a month or so ago, quite by accident, I heard Chambers intended to spend Christmas here with his wife and estranged son. I felt God had told me what I must do. I booked a room, and you know the rest."

"Not quite," Ramsay replied. "Tell me about the actual meeting with Chambers."

Redhill sighed. "It wasn't pleasant. I kept my steak knife from dinner the night before because I knew Chambers would get his way about the games to be played. If you remember, he wanted Sardines so he could squash in with any young women he found hiding. Instead, he got Hide and Seek, which I'm sure he thought that would do as well. He left the room right after the young people, and I told Wright I would retire for the night. Mr. Wright said he would too, which was a nuisance. I'd hoped to be alone when I left. In the end, it didn't matter. Wright wanted to go to the toilet, and I pretended to rest against the doorframe. When he entered the Gents, I hurried down the corridor to find Chambers."

"How hurried?" Ramsay asked, genuinely puzzled.

"I am frail now, it's true," Redhill replied, "but at that moment all the adrenaline I had left in me drove me forward. I planned to find him, and fortune smiled on me. Chambers was standing right there in the corridor. He looked surprised at seeing me. I said, 'Rosenberg' and stabbed him. The knife hit the very brooch my mother wore so proudly and slipped but I pressed harder, and it went in." Redhill shuddered. "A horrible feeling. For a moment, we stared into each other's eyes. He knew why I was doing this, I'm sure. Then his eyes closed, and he slid down the wall I'd pushed him against."

When Redhill paused, Ramsay said, "You took the tiepin?"

"It was mine, not his," Redhill snapped, before continuing, "I pushed it in my pocket and went quickly farther down the corridor. I thought Wright may come looking for me, so I hid where the corridor turns sharply to go to the outside rooms."

"He did come looking," Ramsay said. "He found the tiepin."

"Ah! The police found it on him? That's why they took him for questioning?"

Ramsay nodded.

"I wondered if that's what happened," Redhill mused. "Was that your doing?"

Ramsay nodded.

"Good," Redhill paused, smiling sadly. "Wright wanted

money. He'd seen me hurrying away. With Chambers dead, my feet weren't quite so fast."

"Did he approach you?"

Redhill nodded, before saying, "He spoke to me briefly, telling me what he'd seen. Fortunately, the police took him into custody before he'd decided how much he wanted."

"Fortunately for him. Not for the police who would have liked to charge him with blackmail. What happened after you hid?" Ramsay asked.

"Nothing exciting," Redhill replied. "The corridor stayed empty long enough for me to go back to the lobby and return to my room. That's when I discovered the tiepin wasn't in my pocket."

"Did you wear gloves for all this?"

"Of course," Redhill replied, scornfully. "I'm not a fool. I brought with me those thin rubber gloves that surgeons use."

"The police didn't find them when they searched?"

"The beauty of deep snow is that you can hide things well out of sight without scratching the surface," Redhill replied, "and I'd plenty of time the next day before they began to search."

"How?"

Redhill shrugged. "Think about it. Anywhere the snow has been cut through, such as the drive, push whatever it is you're hiding as far as you can into the snow piled up at the side. Then block the hole you made and smooth it over. The surface of the snow where the object is lying remains untouched and the place you disturbed was already disturbed, so it's effectively invisible. I reasoned it out overnight, did it next morning and it worked for me."

"Probably you weren't the only one to think of that," Ramsay suggested.

Dark Deeds on a White Christmas

"Wright did the same, you think?" Redhill asked.

Ramsay nodded, then said, "I understand your desire to escape justice. Only, you've put Doris Danesdale in great danger."

"She's in no danger," Redhill said, shaking his head. "I fully intend to leave a confession behind when I die. I hope to die quietly, without all the unpleasantness of prison and trials. My confession will clear everyone's name."

Suddenly incensed, Ramsay cried, "She's living a nightmare! You must come forward now."

Redhill laughed, savagely. "A nightmare? She's had a bad dream, that's all. What I've lived through has been a nightmare. I watched my parents and brothers and sisters being slaughtered and, because I wasn't with them at the time, I survived only to spend my whole life ashamed I did nothing to save them or die with them. That's a nightmare."

"You have my sympathy," Ramsay said, "but I must tell the police, and it's better you be with me when I tell them."

Redhill agreed, saying, "I will after this New Year party is over. I want to be a free man as 1965 begins. You see, January the first is my birthday. I will be sixty years old, and that's more than anyone else in my family did. It will sound foolish to you, but my grandfather, who was murdered that day, only reached fifty-nine."

"Very well," Ramsay agreed. With minutes to go before midnight, it was already too late to phone Baldock. "But I'm going to watch your every move until I see you safely to your room—and after."

By one o'clock on January first, Redhill wished Ramsay a good night and returned to his room, amused that Ramsay escorted him all the way.

"I can't run away, you know," Redhill teased Ramsay as he said goodnight.

"You moved quick enough to kill Chambers," Ramsay muttered under his breath as he settled down to watch Redhill's room door. After an hour, with only the sound of Redhill snoring for company, Ramsay left to go to his own room, reasoning that Redhill was on the second floor and unlikely to abscond. He had nowhere to get out except through the fire escape exit.

Ramsay lay on his bed, fully clothed, occasionally venturing to the end of the corridor to be sure there were no fresh footprints in the snow. He dozed until the sounds of the hotel awakening and the faintest scent of breakfast cooking drew him from his bed. Ramsay washed, changed, and went to find a cup of tea with which to celebrate bringing another criminal to justice.

32

NEW YEAR'S DAY, 1 JANUARY 1965

Ramsay had drunk almost a pot of tea before Eliza came to join him. She looked awful.

"Good morning," Ramsay said. "You obviously had a good night."

Eliza sat opposite and poured the last few drops from the pot into a cup and drank it. "Ugh! This is stewed."

"It was fresh only an hour ago," Ramsay replied, sadistically enjoying the moment.

Ellen came with fresh tea and a cup for Eliza, who poured it gratefully and drank it in one swallow. "I blame you for this," she told Ramsay, as she poured another cup. "You set me onto infiltrating those people, and I'm too young for this kind of life."

"Then I've good news," Ramsay said, soothingly. "The case is over. The mystery is solved."

"What? When?"

"I had a long talk with Mr. Redhill, and he confirmed he killed Chambers. He will join us on our call to Baldock today and explain it to him as well."

Eliza took exception to this. "What do you mean 'confirmed'? We never thought he was responsible."

"I have for some days now," Ramsay continued.

"You never mentioned it to me!"

Ramsay's expression became stern. "You told the Hooray Henrys about the tiepin. I couldn't let you give away anything else."

Eliza blushed furiously. "I-I..." She stopped, before nodding guiltily and saying, "I did. I'm sorry. It just slipped out when I'd had too much to drink the other night."

"You were supposed to be learning their secrets, not giving them ours."

"I know, I know," Eliza cried. "Sorry. What can I say. I've been more careful since, believe me."

Ramsay grinned. "I do believe you, as it happens. But you must see why I didn't take you into my confidence at the time."

Eliza nodded unhappily. "Maybe I'm too young for detective life."

"We all make mistakes," Ramsay said, torn between continuing with the doom-laden accusations or sweeping the matter aside. One would end the 'detective agency' Eliza wanted so much and, also, save her from, in his opinion, a disastrous marriage. The other would make both of those futures even more likely.

"What made you think it was Redhill?" Eliza asked, unaware of the thoughts swirling around in Ramsay's head.

"Rosebud," Ramsay replied. "Your mother had seen *Citizen Kane* and the memory stuck, as it does for so many who've seen the movie. But I realized what Chambers tried to say was 'Rosenberg'. It took me a while to realize Redhill is an English translation of the German name Rosenberg."

"But what had Chambers to do with Germans?" Eliza asked, puzzled.

"Many of those who fled the communists in Russia were people of German background," Ramsay replied. "They'd been brought into Russia for centuries by the Czars to farm, manufacture, finance, and pass on all the other skills of a modern western economy. There were many other people too, of course, but they were a large part of the émigré movement, I remember."

"Then why did Redhill kill his fellow White Russian?" Eliza asked. "I still don't get it."

"Chambers wasn't a White Russian, quite the opposite in fact—a Red," Ramsay replied. "A Commissar, no less. He fled, pretending to be one of the Czar's people, with the money he'd murdered to get. Redhill's family were only one of his many victims, but I'm sure he murdered many such families in his time as a Soviet Commissar. Redhill's family, however, set Chambers up with the documents he needed for a new life in the West."

Eliza shuddered. "All this is a bit much on a queasy tummy. The tiepin was what gave Chambers away, I guess?"

Ramsay nodded. "It clinched it in Redhill's mind. That brooch had been his mother's pride and joy in happier times."

They ordered breakfast, Ramsay his porridge and Eliza toast. In companionable silence they slowly nibbled their food, dragging out the meal in the hope Sam Redhill would appear.

"You don't think he's made an attempt to escape, do you?" Eliza asked, when her toast was gone, and he still hadn't appeared.

"He couldn't, even if he wanted to," Ramsay replied. "The snow is still too deep for a fit man to walk far, never mind a man as frail as he is. And he came by taxi. He doesn't have a car."

"He may have decided freezing to death was better than being hanged," Eliza retorted.

Ramsay sighed. Yet he could understand Eliza's impatience. Redhill's confession would finally remove all suspicion of her mother and for that, Ramsay too was relieved. It meant none of Doris's unhappy past need ever come to light.

"I'll finish my tea and we'll ask Joyce or Frederick to accompany us to his room," Ramsay told her. "He's probably enjoying a last morning of feeling free, that's all."

At the reception desk, Frederick, when asked, agreed to escort them to Redhill's room and open the door, if there was no response when they knocked.

Redhill's room wasn't just quiet. It was silent. Ramsay and Frederick exchanged glances before Frederick turned the master key in the lock.

Redhill lay fully dressed on his bed. He looked asleep. Ramsay wasn't deceived. The pallor of the man's face and clasped hands told him everything he needed to know. An open, empty pill bottle on the bedside table only confirmed it. Ramsay felt for a pulse. Redhill's skin was icy cold. Life had left many hours before.

Beside the empty pill bottle were two envelopes. One addressed to Inspector Baldock and the other to Mr. Ramsay. Ramsay opened his and read the sheets of closely written explanation inside.

"He repeats what he told you?" Eliza asked, when she saw Ramsay finish reading. He handed her the pages. Eliza read quickly, stumbling occasionally on the small scribble. She looked up and said, "Wright *was* threatening him with blackmail. Did he tell you that last night?"

Ramsay nodded. He'd hoped to keep that from Eliza, knowing it would only anger her. "You and I guessed the wrong Russian," Ramsay added. "It was Redhill, or Rosenberg, not Pugachev that Wright planned to blackmail."

"I don't suppose Baldock can charge Wright with it though," Eliza said, disappointed. "What a horrible man. All that mother has suffered so he could get rich."

"I fear you're right," Ramsay replied. "He meant to get rich but because Mr. Redhill has taken his own life before parting with money, Wright is free to go."

"On balance," Eliza said, "I think Wright the worse of the two. Redhill enacted justice, long delayed but well deserved, on a man who murdered his family and lived off the wealth he stole. Wright had a case against Chambers, but none against Redhill. Yet he planned to leech off him for the rest of his life."

"I long ago stopped trying to assign judgment on people," Ramsay replied. "If there's a god, he'll know best. If not, our courts do the best they can." He paused before saying, "We need to phone Inspector Baldock. He'll enjoy having another result handed to him on a plate."

Ramsay spoke ironically, imagining Baldock being resentful at Ramsay's continued success. However, Ramsay missed the mark. Inspector Baldock was pleased at the news and said he and his team would be at the Manor in less than an hour.

* * *

AFTER READING the letter Redhill left him, and the one addressed to Ramsay, Baldock nodded, saying, "It's nice when a case is closed without any lingering doubts."

"I didn't see you as a man with lingering doubts,"

Ramsay remarked, surprised once again at Baldock's response.

Baldock shrugged. "You know we can only be as sure as the evidence and often that isn't perfect. All we can do is have confidence in the process and hope for the best."

Feeling he may have wronged the inspector in his mind, Ramsay agreed. "Will you tell Mrs. Danesdale she's no longer a suspect, or should we?"

"It should be done officially," Baldock said. "I'll pop along to the cells the moment we're back at the station and tell her."

When the police and ambulance were gone, Ramsay and Eliza were left feeling bereft. The excitement and the anxiety were over and their companions, good or bad, had gone too. The three couples left while the police were wrapping up.

"They did invite me to Celina's birthday party next week," Eliza told Ramsay, when they discussed their situation. "But it's over near Leeds, and I don't have an easy way of getting there and back."

"Sadly, you won't be able to continue with that crowd," Ramsay replied. "Unless you win a fortune on the Irish Sweepstakes Lottery."

"Should we cut short our stay?" Eliza asked. "Mam might like it if we were there while she recovers."

Ramsay nodded. "I think we should. I'll be sorry to leave because the Price-Ridleys have been good to us, and Bracken loves his new friends. However, we're the only remaining guests and the hotel probably would welcome time to recover before the next guests arrive."

They made their way to reception where Joyce was manning the desk as always. They explained their decision to return to Eliza's home for Mrs. Danesdale's sake.

"We're sorry to lose you," Joyce said. "The hotel will be empty and that always feels sad. We can refund your missing day as part of your fee, if that works for you?"

"I'll send our bill as we discussed," Eliza said. "We can talk about payment then."

Ramsay, thoroughly embarrassed at this talk of money on what to him should have been a solemn occasion, interjected, "We must pack, Eliza, or we'll be traveling home in the dark."

Away from Joyce, he whispered, "Did you have to bring up money? We were talking about helping your mother recover!"

"I thought we agreed, I'm the money manager of this agency," Eliza responded, "and it's *my* mother."

Ramsay gave up. He had little to pack, so he was soon done and went in search of Bracken who he found resting in the straw with Larry, Harry, and Barry. They were all panting, clearly just back from chasing rabbits.

Seeing his friend, Bracken jumped up and came to the gate to greet Ramsay. "We're going to Eliza's house, Bracken," Ramsay told him, opening the gate to let him out.

Bracken liked the sound of 'Eliza' but appeared unsure of the rest.

The Labs had come to the gate to greet Ramsay, and he stroked each one. He felt like a kidnapper, stealing their new friend away without warning. "Bye everyone," he told them, patting each for the last time.

When Bracken and Ramsay reached the bottom of the stairs, Eliza stood there waiting with her cases. "Ready?" she asked.

"Ready," Ramsay nodded. They handed their room keys to Joyce and set off for the garage. "Where's Alfred when you need him," Ramsay grumbled.

"New Year's Day is a holiday in these parts as well," Eliza reminded him. "Not just in Scotland."

"Then it shouldn't be," Ramsay replied, lifting the heavy cases into the car. "I don't understand how your case can be so heavy when your dresses are made of nothing."

"My dresses, as you call them, are in the case I'm carrying," Eliza said. "They wouldn't be safe in your unfeeling hands."

The road out of the dale was wet, its slickness shone in the pale wintry sun. "I love its stark blackness among this sparkling snow," Eliza said. The trees either side of the road were heavy with snow, which glinted in the light as a breeze rocked the branches. "I've never been isolated like that," Eliza continued. "I found it exciting, didn't you?"

Ramsay laughed. "We were in a warm hotel, with lots of food and drink, so yes it was exciting for us. Think of the same thing happening to the farms and cottages out here who might not have been so fortunate."

"It was only a few days," Eliza protested. "And they're probably prepared for it."

"Probably," Ramsay agreed. "Now, what can we do to raise your mother's spirits?" They were still discussing impossible ideas for this when, nearly two hours later, they reached Robin Hood's Bay. The snow here was already melting in the salt sea air and the village merely looked postcard wintry, rather than menacing.

After unloading Eliza's bags from the car, Ramsay went on to find a room for the night before re-joining the family around the hearth.

"Is it really over?" Doris asked Ramsay, when they were settled.

He nodded. "Yes. There can be no doubt about what happened. It won't be revived."

"Poor Mr. Redhill," Doris said, sadly. "Living with that knowledge all your life and then seeing the monster who did it enjoying his life without a care in the world."

"Inspector Baldock told us the story, Tom, but he didn't say how you discovered the truth," Colin commented.

Ramsay considered his reply carefully, explaining Chambers' last word 'rosebud' and what that meant.

"It sounded like 'rosebud' to me," Doris said.

"You heard something, and your mind made a connection that wasn't quite correct, Mam," Eliza said, grasping her mother's hands. "Not your fault. You were in a total state of shock."

"If I'd heard it properly..." Doris began.

"No harm has been done," Ramsay reminded her. "You had an uncomfortable experience, which you didn't deserve, and so did Mr. Wright, who did deserve it. Mr. Redhill died some days earlier than he should have but avoided the unpleasantness of being arrested and all that comes with that. All in all, it was only a few unhappy days that we can all soon forget."

"It's the Price-Ridleys I feel sorry for," Colin said. "It's rotten luck on any business when something like this happens. They may never recover."

"Dad," Eliza cried. "They'll be booked solid for months because of how the story ended. We brought a bit of world history into Yorkshire, and it happened at their hotel. I told Joyce, read *Dr. Zhivago* and use that to advertise the hotel."

"Who is Dr. Zhivago?" Doris asked, trying to make sense of Eliza's excitement.

"It's a book about the Russian Revolution and the people caught up in its horrors," Eliza replied, enthusiastically. "It's dead romantic with love affairs and families and executions and refugees fleeing through the snow to escape. It's Mr.

Redhill's story and, I suppose, in a twisted way, Paul Chambers' story as well. Anyone who reads the book will want to stay at the Manor."

"Has *anyone* read the book?" her father asked.

"Young people have, Dad," Eliza replied, giggling. "And you can be sure everyone in England's White Russian communities have. They'll know."

Her father smiled and said, "Then I'll read it too. I do hope you're right, Eliza, and it turns out that many people want to stay at the Manor. The Price-Ridleys are nice people, they deserve to do well."

"I'd like a cup of tea," Doris said, suddenly brightening with what sounded like one piece of good news out of the affair. "Does anyone else?" She rose and walked into the kitchen without waiting for an answer, almost herself again.

Colin spoke quietly, not wanting Doris to hear, "You know, every year we wish for a white Christmas and this year we got one. We also got murder, attempted blackmail, and a suicide. Such dark deeds on a white Christmas. I'm not sure I'll ever wish for snow again."

33

HOME TO A COLD WELCOME, JANUARY 3, 1965

Ramsay and Bracken arrived home, cold—*the car heater must be repaired*, he'd decided when they were on the high ground of the Yorkshire moors—tired, and in Ramsay's case saddened. His own unhappiness with the horrors of war, it seems, were matched if not exceeded by others all over the world. He could easily understand Redhill's feelings about people who behaved badly toward each other, and particularly those who reveled in the horror.

It was raining in Newcastle when he arrived back in the city. The streets looked grim in the darkness, even though light from the brightly shining streetlamps reflected, flashed, and flickered on the watery road making it look like Christmas decorations. Carrying his cases indoors, he almost fell over the letters piled behind the door. His neighbor had clearly given up on him. The house smelled damp, musty.

Bracken wandered around the rooms looking lost. He too was sad to be home. He sniffed at his basket and cushion before turning away in disgust.

Ramsay turned on the electric fire, its four bars giving off the faintest of heat. "They won't dry the house," he told Bracken. "We need a real fire lit."

Rummaging through the coal shed at the back of the house; while trying to keep the rain off with an umbrella, he finally found enough paper and sticks to start a fire. He carried the meager hoard back into the house, arranged them in the grate, placed coal on and around them, and set the paper alight. At first, the chimney was too cold for the smoke to rise, and he had to cover the hearth to encourage more draft and force the smoke upward. Finally, with the coals beginning to glow, he removed the cover.

"We'll soon have the house warm now, Bracken," he told his friend who sat staring disconsolately at the fireplace and the nearby electric fire. "By bedtime we'll be as snug as bugs in a rug," he continued. Bracken didn't look convinced.

"It can't be colder than the straw at the Manor," Ramsay added, when his friend didn't respond.

Bracken's expression grew sadder at the mention of the Manor.

"We'll feel better with a hot drink for me and a warm one for you," Ramsay said, leaving the living room and entering the kitchen. He was right about the heat. In those short minutes the living room had warmed, while the kitchen remained icy cold. "And some warm food too," Ramsay continued, hoping his forced cheerfulness would raise Bracken's spirit.

He gently warmed some oxo beef stock for Bracken and then put dog food in a pan. For himself, a can of Scotch Broth, heated piping hot, would, he felt, fill the emptiness inside. He'd bought bread and milk on his return journey. The kettle took a minute to fill and be plugged in for hot tea, which he thought might need a dash of Drambuie in it for extra warming. He rarely drank Drambuie; it was too sweet for everyday use, but he'd been given it as an appropriately Scottish gift and now he had a real use for it.

As they ate, and the house slowly warmed, Ramsay said, "What shall we do tomorrow, Bracken? We can't hike any hills in this weather, and walking the streets would be just miserable."

Bracken sat gazing at him. His body language said, 'We should return to the Manor.'

"We can't," Ramsay replied. "I'm not rich enough to live there." He idly wondered if the hotel needed another handyman. Unfortunately, Alfred was more than capable of doing everything required.

They retired from the table to huddle around the fires, Ramsay with his hot tea and Bracken, with a fresh blanket from a cupboard. The radio was no more cheerful than they were. Gales were forecast out at sea, and they were arriving on land now and would last until afternoon tomorrow. Ramsay flicked the dial and found the light music station, hoping for cheerfulness. Sadly, the low time after the holiday season had captured their mood too and the selection of light music didn't have enough lift to raise Ramsay's or Bracken's spirits.

Bracken rose to his feet and padded across the floor to gaze at the photo of Eliza standing on a side table.

"You miss her too, don't you," Ramsay said. "But it would be all wrong. I could be her grandfather. She should have someone her own age, not someone she'll be wheeling about in a chair in another ten years."

Bracken returned to his blanket and lay down with his head on his front paws. A picture of misery.

"I know she's infatuated with me now," Ramsay continued, "but that's how it is with young people. You're still young and think all this lasts forever. It doesn't. She'll be in love with some popstar by next week. Which one was she so excited about when we were there?" He didn't mention the Manor, it upset Bracken. Racking his brain, Ramsay mused, "Mick Jagger or Paul McCartney? Maybe both, I wasn't always listening."

Bracken looked up at Ramsay, barely moving his head, refusing to be drawn into anything that might cheer him up.

"And she wants to advertise now," Ramsay continued, sipping at his Drambuie-imbued tea. "I admit, she did get us paid for our work over the holidays, but it's unlikely to happen again. People who get into trouble aren't usually the sort of people who can pay for expensive sleuthing services." He paused, hoping his argument might actually convince him. "My retirement plan is climbing all the highest peaks of England, Scotland, and Wales. How can I do that if I'm always solving mysteries?"

Bracken's expression didn't change. Ramsay sighed. He'd hoped some of this would sound sensible to one of them. He rose from his chair, took his empty cup to the kitchen sink and returned with a coal scuttle filled with coal.

"It's become nicely warm in here now, Bracken," he said. "We'll move the electric fire up to our bedroom. After the drive, I'm fancying an early night." He switched off the electric fire and carried it up the narrow stairs. He and Bracken were both shivering by the time he arrived in his bedroom.

"We'll soon have this room warm too," Ramsay said, plugging the fire into the wall, switching it on, leaving the room, and closing the door behind him. "I think a quick walk into the garden, followed by a Glenfiddich nightcap, and then to bed. It's no night for dallying outside."

They returned downstairs, Ramsay put on his waterproof Barbour coat, wrapped Bracken in his yellow waterproof coat and, taking an umbrella from the hallstand, they both reluctantly stepped outside. Maybe it was the sound of all the running water, but Bracken quickly finished, and they were back in the house drying themselves.

The warm living room felt heavenly after the January sleet outdoors, and they settled down again, Ramsay sipping his 'wee dram' of whisky.

"While we were enjoying the evening outside," Ramsay said quietly, "I asked myself if I really want to climb all the highest peaks in the land. Or would I prefer to accept commissions for solving people's mysteries. And I came to think, maybe it's the latter." He paused and looked Bracken squarely in the eye, man to man, so to speak, and asked, "What say you, Bracken? Do we dissolve this partnership with Eliza -- or do we let it grow into something more serious?"

On hearing the name Eliza, Bracken's face brightened immediately. His expression said, 'Don't be a fool. Grab it. No one else is interested in us.'

"I think you're right, my friend. I also think we should move to Robin Hood's Bay and start a new life." Ramsay felt better already.

* * *

WITH THE WIND and rain buffeting the windows of their cottage and howling down the chimney, Eliza, Doris, and Colin were enjoying the warmth of their fireplace at home. Colin dozed fitfully while the storm raging out at sea was making landfall, announcing its considerable presence.

Doris stopped counting the rows of her knitting a moment to ask Eliza, "Are you sure being a detective is what you want to do, Elizabeth?"

Eliza frowned. "Yes, Mam, it is. I don't know why you all won't believe me."

"And Tom?"

"What about, Tom?" Eliza replied.

"He's a lovely man, of course, but he's old. You can't still want to marry him, surely?" Doris asked, nervously. She'd asked before and always had the same reply.

Eliza rose to her feet, placed her fists on her hips and said, "For the last time, listen. Tom and I are going to be a detective agency, and I *am* going to marry him. He's being silly about it, as you are, but my mind is made up and that's final. I'm not going to discuss it again – ever!" She sat down with a thump that woke Colin, who stared at them dozily.

"Go back to sleep, Dad. You're not missing anything."

"I wasn't sleeping," Colin protested, "just resting my eyes."

"Then you'll know that I've finished writing the advertisement, and I'm going to use some of my money from the Price-Ridleys to put it in all the local and northern newspapers tomorrow. I expect we'll have a new case by the weekend."

Her mother sighed. "Well, I only hope your new case helps someone like me. You can't really know how grateful I am, we are, to you both."

"It's true, Eliza," Colin agreed. "Things looked so bad and now here we are safe at home."

"Which is why I'm doing it. Harry's death may never have been avenged, and this time you may have spent years in jail, Mam," Eliza said. "Tom and I will save countless lives over the years."

Colin looked puzzled. "Does Tom know this? He was adamant he wasn't doing any more sleuthing when he left here today."

"He'll have thought it through by now and come to his senses," Eliza said, loftily. "Old people, even nice ones, are slow thinkers. It can be frustrating at times, but it makes them more interesting, for me anyway."

"I'm sure you know best, dear," Doris said and returned her attention to her knitting.

* * *

IF YOU'VE ENJOYED READING this book, please help other readers to enjoy it too by leaving a review here: https://www.amazon.com/review/create-review/?ie=UTF8&channel=glance-detail&asin=B0D1ZWTZGK

* * *

AND BUY the next in the series: A Missing Manuscript and Murder:

* * *

MORE BOOKS BY THE AUTHOR

On Amazon, my books can be found at the

One Man and His Dog Cozy Mysteries page

And

Miss Riddell Cozy Mysteries series page.

And for someone who likes listening to books, ***In the Beginning, There Was a Murder*** is now available as an audiobook on Amazon and here on Audible and many others, including:

Kobo, Chirp, Audiobooks, Scribd, Bingebooks, Apple, StoryTel

You can find even more books here:

P.C. James Author Page: https://www.amazon.com/P.-C.-James/e/B08VTN7Z8Y

P.C. James & Kathryn Mykel: Duchess Series

P.C. James & Kathryn Mykel: Sassy Senior Sleuths Series.

Paul James Author Page: https://www.amazon.com/-/e/B01DFGG2U2

GoodReads: https://www.amazon.com/P.-C.-James/e/B08VTN7Z8Y

And for something completely different, my books by Paul James at: https://www.amazon.com/-/e/B01DFGG2U2

ABOUT THE AUTHOR

P.C. James is the author of the quietly humorous Miss Riddell Cozy Mysteries, the One Man and His Dog Cozy Mysteries, and co-author of the Royal Duchess and Sassy Senior Sleuths cozy mysteries.

He lives in Canada near Toronto with his wife.

He loves photographing wildlife in the outdoors yet chooses to spend hours every day indoors writing stories, which he also loves. One day, he'll find a way to do them both together.

Printed in Great Britain
by Amazon